Forever Delighted

SPRING OF LOVE
BOOK ONE

VIRGINIA TAYLOR

Serenade Publishing

www.serenadepublishing.com

A New Page

by Aimee MacRae

It Happened in Paris

By Michelle Beesley

Middle Women

By Jack Garrety

Mim and Wiggy's Grand Adventure

By Jay McKenzie

A Dying Second Sun

by Peter A. Dowse

Winner Winner Chicken Dinner

by Sarah Jackson

Resurrection

M H Austin

For more information visit:

www.serenadepublishing.com

Chapter One

1818, ESSEX, ENGLAND.

The rain drizzled down the back of Anna Winter's neck as she squelched through the mud, collecting more clumps on her old boots. Blinking away the drips from the sodden brim of her bonnet, she left her basket of kitchen herbs on the stone path, meaning to rinse off her boots before she went back into the house. Heaving a sigh, she stepped through the prickly gorse and under the withy branches, making her way to the waist-deep stream that rushed through the vicarage's back garden.

Although she would miss this place of solitude when she left for London, being in the city would not change her life. She would still be the unwed older sister, trying to remain unconcerned while society judged her by her father's misdeeds.

Stepping out onto the old, twisted log, she grabbed an overhanging branch for balance as she dipped her first boot into the stream. The clay soil on the leather dissolved instantly. She changed feet, cleansing the second. Time drifted by while her weary gaze followed the current. She could have stayed watching the water forever, but the cook wanted the herbs for this evening's dishes, not the next.

As she reluctantly turned, a fishing line flickered past her face. She flinched and discovered that her skirts had been caught by a hook. Needing to use two hands to untangle herself, she let go of the branch. Her feet slipped. She overcompensated and landed with a long shriek and a splash that drenched her face.

The icy water dragged her skirts against her legs. While her skin began to numb with cold, she pulled the line to find the hook, but a tug forced her to step closer to the middle of the stream. "Who's there?" she called in a cross voice. "Jeremy? Is that you? Oh, you dratted fiend. Come and set me loose. You have caught me on your hook."

A momentary silence, and then she heard a deep, considered voice. "Forgive me, please. It's the first time I have caught a talking fish."

"Idiot. Come and help me. I'm freezing to death." She dragged up her hem to inspect the hook, but her numb fingers wouldn't cooperate. Hoping not to freeze to death while awaiting him, she squinted her eyes to follow the fishing line, which shimmied up into a group of three trees. The canopy hid the top half of the Honorable Jeremy Hastings, the Earl of Delmore's younger brother. Finally, she spotted his old leather boots, scruffy and loose at the top, crunching out of the overgrowth.

Then Calder John, the Earl of Delmore, moved out of the thicket. Her eyes widened. The man she had always called my lord to his face, or the earl when speaking of him to others, stood staring at her. She thought she had been speaking to Jeremy, his brother. Her face loosened, and she quickly closed her mouth. The dastardly rake whose normal habitat ranged from the gambling dens in London to the establishments respectable citizens mentioned in whispers not meant for maidens' ears, despite said maidens straining to hear, was the last man she imagined would be fishing in this ghastly weather.

"Now, let me see whom have I caught here?" Lord Delmore's tone was the usual—disinterested. His face was the same—undeniably attractive.

The breath she'd been holding whooshed out of her lungs. She had never been more embarrassed in her life, and never more determined not to let her feelings show. Her gaze flickered to the front of his perfectly starched shirt. "One of the poor, sad, untitled I fear."

He stared from his rod to her. "And a pretty one at that."

She heaved a breath. "Oh, for heaven's sake. Here I am above the knees in freezing water, and you want to start a flirtation."

For a moment he appeared puzzled. "Surely there is no better time than when you are at my mercy?" he answered in an affronted voice.

After shooting him an exasperated glare, she lifted her soggy skirts higher than she should to show the hook of his line. Her under-petticoat clung to her legs. Although she tried again to remove the hook, her fingers had grown too stiff with cold to cooperate.

"You'll never remove it that way." To give him credit, he did sound mildly interested in her plight.

"If you imagine I'm about to rip my skirt for your entertainment, you are very much mistaken."

His eyebrows lifted.

She offered him a ferocious glare, understandably annoyed, her mood exacerbated by seeing the amusement on his strikingly handsome face. The Earl had always been too physically blessed for his own good, or so had muttered the ladies in the village of Danbury when they heard about his latest exploits. For the past seven years, since he had inherited his title, he had been fodder for gossip.

Anna herself hadn't been above gazing at his attractive person during the few times she had been inside Delmore House, on the rare occasion he had also been there. He seemed to have spent his most recent years anywhere other than gracing his country estate. "You, my lord, are a monster. No gentleman worth his sable-lined cloak would stand by while a lady stood in a freezing stream trying unsuccessfully to free herself from his lure."

"After digesting your impressions of my character, I find your words mildly astonishing. The ladies I know rarely try to free themselves from my lure." Nevertheless, he hunkered down on the bank and began trying to toe off a boot.

"Though why you would bother removing those old boots is a mystery to me," she said, trying to copy his aplomb. At this stage, she didn't dare drop her gaze, for fear of him assuming he had her measure. Merely standing so close to him had made her breath hard to catch, but keeping her eyes steady on his caused a certain amount of tension in her neck. Finally, she blinked, desperate not to lose her self possession. "Those boots saw better days twenty years ago."

"I'm sure my brother wouldn't keep his boots for more than five years. I think you must be prone to exaggeration." His tone remained cool, but his beautiful bright blue eyes taking in her every facial feature was almost more than any well-brought up lady could bear without blushing or stuttering.

She doubted he had glanced at her for as long in her entire life. Usually, he inclined his head to her or forgot her name. "You need to cut the line to free me from this hook."

"Do you own a penknife?" His suspiciously appealing gaze caught and held hers. He breathed out audibly. Finally giving up the attempt to remove his boots, he took a long step down into the stream.

She was pleased to see the water flood into the top of his first boot. He watched, offering the second with an air of great suffering. "I realized that if I took off Jeremy's boots, I would have to stand on the stones," he said in an unapologetic voice, dragging himself through the water as he moved toward her. "Bearing in mind, I doubt the discomfort would be worth the effort."

"How you have managed to take your place in polite society is a mystery to me." She raised her chin.

"Society isn't as polite as you might imagine." Standing too close to her, he examined the place where his hook had snagged her gown. "As I thought. I'll have to sacrifice the best line I've used in years." Pushing his hand into the pocket of his buckskins, he heaved a groan. "Only the best fishermen come armed with pocketknives."

She noted his dark fringe of thick eyelashes, her belly in

a knot of reluctant envy. "And you are saying you don't have one?"

"Unfortunately, I am an exceptional angler. I have a pocketknife, the unfortunate part being I will now have to sacrifice my line for your gown."

That he now wore a deliberately arrogant expression almost undid her. He was playing with her, and she didn't mind a bit. The tickle of amusement she'd been repressing threatened to burst into a smile. Holding herself together for one last effort, she managed to shrug. "Oh, never mind. I'll haul myself out of the stream and I'll trail your fishing line behind me to the house, where I will find my sewing scissors and cut a hole in my second-best day gown. Then, bearing in mind your noble offer to make a sacrifice, I shall also make one and return your fishing pole and your line to you, intact. Would you mind waiting here for half an hour while I do so?" She held her breath.

He offered her a reproving gaze. "That task, miss, should take you no longer than five minutes."

"I'm very much afraid I shall need to change out of my wet clothes before I return." Laughter bubbling up inside her, she offered him a limpid smile. Her legs had turned to frozen batons, yet his ridiculous badinage held her spellbound.

He cut the line and pushed the end of his fishing hook through. "You know, if your bonnet didn't droop over your face, a man might see who you are."

Her face stilled. Naturally, she had expected him to know who she was, or she wouldn't have spoken familiarly to him. Trying to hide her utter embarrassment, she said, "When wet, my bonnet has a mind of its own."

"Your bonnet needs to be disciplined. Will you allow me?"

"No." She twisted to the side.

"In that case, I must guess who you are. Since you cannot walk to Danbury and back in half an hour, therefore you came from the vicarage. You are either a very nosy parishioner or a relative of the vicar."

Her gaze dropped. She should have remembered that Anna Winters had always been invisible to his family. "Thank you, my lord, for freeing me from your hook at the great expense of your line. I won't need any further help."

"Are you planning to drag yourself out of the stream?" He sounded as if he would happily watch.

"I wish you would go away." She turned into the current.

"My upbringing compels me to get you to dry land. When I have, I'll leave."

She imagined him behind her, pushing while she scrambled gracelessly onto the bank, and she couldn't think of anything less dignified. She faced him, using one numb wrist to move back her bonnet, hoping that when he saw her entire face, the recognition of the vicar's stepdaughter would encourage him to act like a gentleman.

He examined her features until she had to put her whole mind into an effort not to blush.

"How are you normally described? Beautiful? Elegant? I'm sure I don't know, but that lovely mouth of yours needs my expert attention." He stepped into her, resting his palms on her hips. This brought her up against a male body. His heart pounded against hers, causing her breath to catch. Although she suspected he was inebriated, he smelled like a rain drenched forest, fresh and clean. His warm breath tickled her cheek.

She watched his thick eyelashes lower, fascinated while his mouth slowly descended. He lifted his head and glanced at her face. Apparently, he read her expression as hopeful as she felt. Angling his head, he gently took her mouth. She tried to remember that she was a lady and mustn't respond, but with his soft lips covering hers, the last thing she wanted to do was to discourage him. To have someone hold her in his arms was a treat she wouldn't instantly forgo.

When he raised his head, she couldn't think of a word to say. She meant to push him away but needy wretch that she was, she buried her hands beneath the collar of his wool coat instead, raising her face again to his, inviting him to toy with her emotions as long as he wished. His mouth began to play with hers, somehow encouraging her to part her lips. His tongue tasted her top and then her bottom lip while her skin heated like a furnace. The whole time she knew she shouldn't do this with him, but she might never have another opportunity to be carefully kissed by an experienced rake. Every woman should have this chance at least once in her life.

She reached up and brushed his chin. The slight rasp against the freezing pad of her fingertip brought her to her senses. This man, attractively disreputable as he was, shouldn't be tempting her this way. She shouldn't be colluding. While she thought about shifting her palms to his muscular chest and pushing her needy body away, he lifted his mouth. "You're the Winter's girl." He had the grace to sound a little husky. Apparently, he didn't notice her inexperience.

"I am indeed. And now I'm another lady of your acquaintance who has made no attempt to free myself from your lure." Her voice came out with a slight waver.

His gaze caught and held hers. He offered a cynical smile. "I'm an earl, you see. My lures have worth." After neatly stepping back and around her, he scooped his body one-handed up onto the bank on the Beeby side. "Give me your hand and I'll help you out. It's the least I can do now you've paid my toll."

She waded over to him, probably the least attractive woman he had spoken to in years, and held out her hand, blessing him for leaving her with a spark of dignity. If he hadn't recognized her and stopped the kiss, she could have made a fool of herself over a cad she had been warned about. Then again, while she always smiled and nodded, she rarely took advice.

His hand balanced her while she hiked gracelessly out of the stream. Water flowed off the hem of her gown, which clung to her ankles. Her boots squelched as she landed on both feet beside him. "Thank you, my lord. That was a very nice kiss."

"I see I can't impress you, Miss Winters. You've had better, I presume." He gazed at her long enough to make her swallow.

She lifted an uncaring shoulder. "None quite as wet."

"I should apologize for treating you like a kitchen maid but I'm very much afraid the kiss was worth the ruin of Jeremy's boots." The intense green of his eyes glinted.

"False flattery will get you nowhere, my lord. Even a kitchen maid would expect to be compared favorably with Jeremy's old boots."

Finally, his lips twitched with humor. "Why have we never spoken before?"

She smiled politely, knowing she couldn't stand here dripping wet with a foolish lightness in her heart. Without answering, she turned and left, keeping her posture while she dripped half the river to the back door of the vicarage.

Delmore squelched back to the manor house with two good-sized fish in his basket and a frown on his face. Had he recognized the person in the stream as his brother's friend, he would have helped her out and gone on his way. He had promised himself not to become involved with another woman during his rustication. However, apparently he couldn't resist females with willful tongues who spoke with impatient familiarity.

Few women conversed with him without simpering or fluttering. If he had realized who she was before he had been tempted to take a reprehensible but somehow imperative kiss, he might be a little more at ease with himself now. He entered the house by the study door, mulling about the interesting Miss Winters who had, despite his mother's disapproval, befriended his brother many years ago.

His long-suffering valet had clearly been watching him from the upstairs window, for he stood awaiting him with a towel in his hands. He ran his critical gaze over Delmore's boots. "Did my lord enjoy his swim?"

"I could have done without the dousing but as you see, I chose the right boots to ruin."

"My lord's judgment is impeccable, as always." Pickering, as dour as he was meticulous, inclined his head and offered the towel. Delmore wiped down his buckskins, back and front, and moved to the desk chair, where he sat while Pickering removed the sodden boots.

"I can't guarantee the resurrection of these, my lord." Pickering disdainfully held the left boot between his thumb and his forefinger.

"Do your best. I don't want to be forced to buy Jeremy new boots in exchange for the use of his old ones." Delmore accepted the embroidered slippers placed on his feet, and followed Pickering to his dressing room upstairs, where he changed into fresh breeches, a clean shirt, and a waistcoat. Concentrating on his reflection in the mirror, he tied the simplest knot in the Corinthian's handbook, the trone d'amour, and pulled on a pair of his own shining boots.

Pickering nodded his approval. "Lady Hastings said to tell you we eat early during winter."

"A subtle reminder from my esteemed parent for me not to expect dissolute city ways. Or an even more subtle message about the length of time since I was last here."

"As to that, my lord, I don't know. Presumably, you will dress for dinner?" Pickering's haughty eyebrows lifted in query. A former footman, he enjoyed his elevated position, which he had held since Delmore had settled in London six years previously at the age of twenty-three.

"Not formally until our guests arrive, Pickering. I prefer our comfortable country ways while we are here."

Accepting the change to his usual routine with a dissatisfied blink, Pickering took Delmore's discarded jacket and his soaked buckskins over one arm and left the room. The valet's posture showed Delmore that, yet again, he had lowered himself in his servant's esteem.

Pickering had barely tolerated Delmore's last mistress who, merely a week ago, had stormed into Delmore's town-house and grabbed armloads of his clothes to toss out onto the streets. Having caught her out with another man, Delmore had earned her undying fury by dismissing her before she could leave him. Pickering had clicked his tongue, but his expression had lightened. He had been less pleased when he heard Delmore planned to rusticate, but Delmore didn't care to see his newest green jacket currently being worn by a chimney sweep. Pickering had disdained that jacket from the start, being made, he said, of inferior cloth.

Now suitably attired, in Pickering's opinion, in a blue superfine merino jacket, Delmore wandered down to the library. This morning, he had asked his agent to present the running costs of Hastings' House to him. Reading through the list had caused his head to ache. Although he let the gossips assume he had left town because of his ex-mistress's tantrums, the truth was he needed to adjust his expenses. For reasons unknown, his income had gradually been diminishing.

During the time he had diverted his mind by watching the bobbing of his fishing line in the stream, he had reconciled himself to looking into the management of his estates. His late father's system apparently worked no longer. A holding as large as his ought to be hauling in money. Delmore never had cause to question the decisions of his steward and likely wouldn't, but if he couldn't find the money to live the lifestyle he expected, he would need to sell off land, or so his man of business had suggested.

"There you are." His brother, Jeremy, stood in the doorway, his tall hat in his hands, his light chestnut hair neatly brushed. The lad had the Hastings' height and muscled build, and their mother's careful smile.

Delmore shut his folder. "I would be flattered to think you may have been searching for me, but you have neatly put me in my place. I have been here in full sight for at least an hour. Have you spent a pleasant day?"

"I'll say." Jeremy grinned, stripping off his gloves, which he dropped into his hat. "I won ten guineas. Temple said I couldn't vault onto his horse three times in a row without being bucked off. The nag is as docile as a cow. The only person the horse dispenses with is Temple."

"I'm pleased to see you don't waste your days in trivialities," Delmore said drily. "I met your friend, Miss Winters, down by the stream."

"The border?"

"If that's what you call the place where the vicar's boundary ends."

"We do, but we don't meet there anymore. After she made her debut, she expected me to call on her."

"She has a sister, does she not?"

"Jonquil Beeby. A stepsister. She's grown into a pretty little thing. You wouldn't recognize her."

Delmore shrugged. "I've never seen her other than in church, hidden under a hat."

"My friends are making knuckleheads of themselves over her. Fools. It's not as if she has been reborn."

"I rather think that happens to young ladies at a certain

age. Do your friends make knuckleheads of themselves about Miss Winters?"

"She doesn't encourage them, though she said she likes to keep them onside because she needs dancing partners now and then."

Delmore repressed a smile. Miss Winters would say that. "Apparently the social life here is rather more interesting than I recall as a youngster."

"You're no more than four years older than I. Stop trying to make yourself out as a wise old elder. I imagine even you would enjoy yourself at the local assemblies."

Delmore cast his gaze back onto his accounts. "I rarely attend society functions."

"Everyone here goes. If you don't, you'll be deemed snobbish. Mother attends to gossip with her acquaintances. She will expect you to be there, too. So will our aunt when she arrives tomorrow."

"Ah. The Carringtons. I almost forgot. I shall attend to keep Sir Walter company around the punch bowl."

"Ha. You are imagining brandy punch, are you? I can tell you now that at best you will be standing around a fruit bowl. Not your taste at all." After this timely reminder and a grin, Jeremy left.

Delmore rubbed his hand over the back of his neck, wondering if Miss Anna Winters attended the assemblies. Meeting her again could be rather interesting.

"You'll never believe what Papa just told me."

"What did he tell you, Jonquil?" After changing into a

dry gown, Anna had made her way to the morning room to catch up with her mending. She patiently rested the old pillowcase on her lap as Jonquil Beeby, her nineteen-year-old stepsister, the vicar's daughter, her blue eyes wide and her cheeks dimpled with an expectant smile, sat beside her on the faded sofa.

As a child, Jonquil had been a plump and fearless tattle-tale. During the past two years, she had grown quite tolerable. "I'm to make my debut in town after Christmas. Your mama wrote to her sister, Lady Prescott, who said I could stay with her."

Anna nodded. "Lady Prescott is a dear. She sent me the orange beaded reticule when I came out." The reticule was still the prettiest thing she owned, but living in a country vicarage didn't call for extravagant frivolities.

"And that's not all." Jonquil's expression resembled the kitchen cats when she spotted a spilled puddle of milk. "You are to be my companion."

Anna clicked her tongue with faked disapproval. "I don't know how I will spare the time."

Jonquil looked aghast. "Anna, you must. I won't be able to manage without you."

Anna patted Jonquil's hand. "Although I know you would, I would be delighted to be your companion." These were not exactly the words she had used when the matter had been put tentatively to her a week ago, but she had now resigned herself to watching society from the sidelines. Fortunately, Mama had been hiding scraps of material away for years. She and Anna would manage to put together a respectable wardrobe for her. The vicar's money had to be spent on Jonquil, whose beautiful face should help find her a well-to-do suitor. She might attract a purse larger than any held by a local lad, most of whom had joined her merry band of swains. Her birth was certainly respectable, unlike Anna's, which was the bane of her existence. "A come-out is a wonderful opportunity for you, Jonquil."

Jonquil's pretty blue eyes sparkled. Today she wore a gown of heavy cotton in a mid shade of brown, and a cream woolen shawl wrapped tightly around her shoulders. The ringlets she had ragged last night drooped from a floral tie at the back of her head. "Lord Delmore is expected home soon. I think your mama wants to hide me out of the way while he is here. If she packs me off, she assumes he will avoid him spotting me and throwing out his lures."

Anna's cheeks warmed. "Fortunately, the dastardly man is otherwise engaged, by all accounts." Although she had always enjoyed a good gossip about the man who had scandalized London since he had inherited his father's estates seven years ago, now that he had kissed her, she could hardly prose on about the type of women with whom he normally consorted.

"Jeremy Hastings tells you all the town gossip. He never says anything shocking to me." The corners of her mouth expressing her dissatisfaction, Jonquil picked through Anna's embroidery silks and left them even more tangled.

"You must remember that he sees you as my little sister. I doubt he has noticed that you have grown up." Though, as Anna recalled, only the other day Jeremy had mentioned how Jonquil had blossomed, but pretty little buds interested him no more than they interested his disreputable brother. "I wonder why the earl has decided to rusticate here at this time of the year?"

"He's probably under the hatches."

Anna laughed. "Where do you pick up this disgraceful language?"

"You forget. I have suitors who say all manner of things while they are competing to hold my cloak or trying to kiss me." Jonquil elevated her nose, a smug smile on her face.

No one had ever competed for Anna, and the only man who had tried to kiss her had succeeded. "It will do you the world of good to meet other young men. I find I am in perfect accord with your papa."

Jonquil picked at her fingernails. "Do you suppose Jeremy will go up to town too?"

"He usually leaves for the season," Anna said placidly. "And he'll have the added pleasure of being able to introduce you to better connected young men than you meet here."

"Do you think he will?"

"Of course. He is the most obliging gentleman of my acquaintance."

"And he is also very handsome." Jonquil glanced at her entwined fingers. "I expect we will be choosing new gowns very soon. You will help me, won't you? You always dress so smartly yourself."

Smiling wryly, Anna accepted the compliment, rolling the new hem for the worn pillowcase. Anyone who didn't have an allowance for gowns but had to suffice on whatever her mother could scrape together from her father's deceased estate needed taste, and skill with the needle. Jonquil's father, Horace Beeby, not a wealthy man, had a great objection to supporting his stepdaughter. He thought Anna's own father should, but her own father had most inconsiderately died without knowing her mother would be delivered a child not more than seven months after his funeral. In any case, the waster hadn't put away a penny. According to mama, they had lived on her tiny income, which these days she shared with her second husband.

However, making a new wardrobe out of nothing would be a reasonable way to pass her time in the winter months. No one knew better than Anna how far a pound could be stretched. She slipped her needle in and out, already planning how to resurrect an old ball gown of her mothers for herself.

"Papa wasn't quite certain your aunt would be able to manage us." Jonquil giggled. "As if either of us doesn't know how to behave."

Fortunately, she didn't glance at Anna, who would not have been able to meet her gaze. In theory, she knew how to behave. She simply hadn't put her knowledge into practice today.

Chapter Two

Delmore had barely finished his shave in the morning when the grating of wheels on the loose stones of the carriage-sweep caused him to pause and turn his head.

In response, Pickering glanced out the dressing-room window as he wiped Delmore's blade clean. "Sir Walter and Lady Carrington have arrived in a very fine coach and four." When the valet spoke about the aristocracy, his nostrils had a tendency to pinch. "Shall your lordship wear the black jacket today?"

"Indeed." Delmore used his fingers to comb back the annoying lock of hair that invariably fell onto his forehead. "My Aunt Carrington must have arisen before dawn to be here at this hour."

"No doubt she and Sir Walter stayed overnight at a nearby inn." The valet folded the razor, which he placed into the leather case. He handed a white cravat to Delmore and held the mirror, angling the reflection toward Delmore's face.

Delmore tied his cravat and progressively lowered his chin until the folds sat in place. With the help of Pickering, he donned his jacket.

Pickering stood back and ran his gaze up and down Delmore. "You do me credit; indeed you do." Lips pursing, he carefully replaced the shaving kit into the top drawer of the rosewood chest that sat at the end of Delmore's four-poster bed.

"I'm flattered, Pickering," Delmore said, gently. "But I would prefer to be complimented about my deeds rather than the fit of my jacket. You must admire the fact that I am able to walk upright when drunk and I never insult anyone who shoots better than I."

Pickering heaved a long-suffering sigh. "If you don't mind me saying so, my lord, you handle your drink like a gentleman, and I have never seen you as much as fumble with a pistol even while you are cleaning them. And the whole world knows about your prowess in the boxing ring."

The whole world, in Pickering's mind, being the precincts of London. Delmore took the compliment with his usual cynical smile. Clearly, country living bored Pickering, and he thought he could flatter his way back to the city. Delmore buttoned his coat. "Now that you have set me up with your compliments, I'll wander down and welcome my aunt, a task that could well give me quite an amount of pleasure."

Having suffered the past two nights of early dinners, each course served with watery sauce, barely three or four removes, and a poor selection of wine, Delmore proceeded down the main stairs to the wide hallway where he saw his aunt being kissed by his mother. He offered his hand to Sir

Walter, a tall man with an imposing belly and graying hair combed across his head to hide his bald patch. To compensate, his gray side-whiskers grew past his jaw.

"I must apologize for the unseemly hour of our arrival." Sir Walter wrung Delmore's hand. "We stayed the night at the Smugglers' Retreat, aptly named, my boy, for we found a very smooth little port."

Lady Carrington grabbed Delmore's shoulders and kissed him soundly on each cheek. "He insisted on bringing along a dozen for you, too. Coals to Newport, I would say. Country life suits you, my dear nephew. Or is it leaving the other matter in town?" She examined his expression.

"We don't discuss the other matter in my mother's presence." He glanced sideways at his unreadable mother, who never mentioned his dalliances, and still refused to acknowledge the existence of his father's mistresses, two of who had bourn him a child.

"I expect he has already forgotten the other matter," his mother said, raising her eyebrows at her taller sister, whose mid-brown hair color she shared. Both had bluish eyes, and both dressed a la mode. Each lady had expensive tastes and wore long-sleeved gowns, the dowager Lady Delmore in stripes of blue and red embellished with two flounces on the hem. A warm cashmere shawl covered her shoulders. Lady Carrington wore dark burgundy. Both had been renowned beauties and had married well, despite being the daughters of a mere baron. "Have you not, Delmore?"

"Forgotten what?"

"That's the way." Sir Walter gave him an encouraging clap on the shoulder that would send the average male staggering across a room.

Delmore barely moved, having braced himself to Sir Walter's hearty tap. As it happened, the other matter, that of his tempestuous mistress, had barely crossed his mind in the two days he had been in the country. Money matters absorbed him, and he mulled about Miss Winters more than he would have liked. He should not have taken liberties with a woman who spoke like an educated lady. He blamed the heavy ale he had consumed instead of breakfast for a misbehavior he certainly didn't intend to repeat.

"Are you planning on raiding my library again?" he asked the older man. Delmore's father had gathered together a fine collection of eastern erotica, which had caused Delmore many sweaty nights at the age of sixteen. These days, his jaded tastes leaned more toward one woman for a single night, to which his former mistress had objected, his latest woman being unknown to her. Since Delmore had been drunk, the woman had also been unknown to him too, until he had tupped her. Afterward, he discovered she was married to an acquaintance.

"Perhaps." Sir Walter tapped the side of his nose and grinned, managing to look mischievous and knowing at the same time.

The housekeeper and two maids entered the hall and grabbed up various small leather-strapped bags. His mother escorted her sister upstairs while Sir Walter pondered over the placement of the rattling crate of bottles, currently held by a waiting footman wearing yellowing cravat lace. "Do you have entertainments planned for our stay?" he asked Delmore.

"I'm sure my mother has. We'll find out soon enough.

I'll have these bottles cellared," Delmore said to the footman.

Jeremy wandered into the hall, dressed in buckskins and tall boots. His shirt points reached to his chin and his hair had been neatly brushed back. Perhaps his starching was less than perfect, but he hadn't adopted a particularly careless style today. "Uncle. Good to see you. You and my aunt will keep Mother busy."

"And then she won't notice what you're up to?" Sir Walter's hearty face creased with amusement.

Jeremy gave a short laugh. "It's dashed boring here. Nothing to do, other than a few functions with the local beauties."

"You have beauties here?" Sir Walter's eyebrows lifted.

"I suspect you would see more in London," Jeremy said with a conscious smile, "but no one could discount Miss Winters and Miss Beeby. Miss Winters was the daughter of Richard Winters. Her mother married our vicar, Mr. Beeby."

"Ah, yes. Richard Winters. Bad luck, him dying that way. His wife was a beauty, as I recall. He snapped her up during her first season. Is Miss Winters as lovely as her mother?"

Jeremy's sudden blink expressed his feelings about being asked to assess the looks of Mrs. Beeby. He glanced at Delmore for help before accepting he would be offered nothing but a shrug. "Her mother is in her forties. I can't say I have ever noticed, but Anna is a good sort of woman, the type a chap can share a joke with. Her stepsister Jonquil is all the go at the moment."

"Perhaps we will have the pleasure of seeing them both this visit."

Jeremy expressed his doubt by clamping his lips. "As a rule, my mother doesn't socialize with the family. She is no more than polite to Mrs. Beeby, and Beeby himself is a bore of a man. Always wanting to improve people with some sort of biblical text or other."

"You sound as if you spend hours by the man's side." Delmore's gaze followed the crate of port down the passage, wondering if he should have grabbed a bottle for his study where he had resigned himself to spending the next couple of dreary hours.

"Not if I can avoid him. I'm off to call on them with a bundle of magazines my mother has finished with. The ladies like to keep up to date with the latest fashions, you know. You are welcome to come with me, Delmore, if you like."

"Perhaps not." Delmore glanced at Sir Walter. "My uncle would see me as a very poor host if I toddled off to visit a couple of beauties before he was settled in as our guest."

"Quite right too." Jeremy ignored the subtle hint about him staying at home. Apparently, he considered both young ladies to be more attractive than Sir Walter. "As for that, I wouldn't want you cutting me out, though there's probably no likelihood of that—they're too respectable for you." Placing his hat carefully on his head, he nodded at the waiting footman who held the front door open for him.

"Is that my reputation? Do I only mix with disreputable people?" Delmore widened his eyes and offered a faint smile to his amused uncle.

Sir Walter scratched behind his ear. "I've heard you dropped five thousand on the card tables last month. Can you afford that?"

"I thought I could, but it seems I was misinformed. I may have to sell my grays to make up for the shortfall."

"Word got out. Not a good thing. Before you know, everyone will be dunning you."

At this stage, few were calling in Delmore's debts and he still had the money to keep afloat. Barely. Some of the smaller tradesmen had been paid, but he knew he had to cut down on his spending. A month in the country would keep him out of trouble until he could regroup. He changed the subject. "Damn you for arriving so early. The very idea that my brother is visiting two beauties while I am forced to entertain two people I like very much is lowering." He managed a dour smile.

Sir Walter gave him another of his encouraging taps. "Though, I doubt that a couple of provincial beauties would turn your head. La Gloriosa, though. Shame, that. I heard your red brocade waistcoat was last seen on a pig."

Delmore shook his head. "According to La Gloriosa, the pig looked more dashing in it than I did."

Sir Walter slapped a thigh. "You have to admit…"

"I do." Delmore finally laughed. "It's the sort of show she likes, and in the end I'm well rid of the dramatics and the expense. Now, I wonder if you have any advice for me about investing in the funds."

Anna used a roll of string to tie the edges of the muslin scrap around the last of the Christmas pudding mixture. She and Cook had prepared twenty that morning, using the dried fruits that various parishioners had been donating all year. The very poorest families would receive at least one luxury during the coming week.

"Done," she said, satisfied. This year, the mix seemed tastier than usual. She nibbled at a scrap of raw dough drying on her thumb. The spices smelled delicious, making her nose twitch. Cook had packed the others in the bottom of her biggest pan. She added steaming water as Anna watched, rubbing her hands to remove the last of the hardening mixture.

"Miss Anna?" Her mother's maid, Morag, who had been with her since her first marriage to Anna's father, stood in the doorway. Her thick grey eyebrows sat in a severe line, and over the years the sides of her mouth had turned down to show her pessimism. A word of praise from her was akin to winning the silver spoon at the Danbury picnic races. "Mr. Hastings has come to call. He is awaiting you in the morning room."

"Thank you, Morag." Anna wiped her hands on her apron, which she subsequently removed. Jeremy wouldn't care if she had flour on her face. Nonetheless, she had the idea that attention to detail might compensate for her lack of fashionable gowns and inspected her reflection in the window. After brushing down her skirts and running a hand over her hair, she hurried to the morning room. The small fire in the grate heated only half the area.

Jeremy, looking dashing in a high cravat and a dark blue

coat, stood as she entered. "I brought these magazines over from my mother."

"How kind. Please thank Lady Delmore for us." She put the pile on a table beneath the window, pushing aside a vase painted with daisies.

"Delmore arrived unexpectedly yesterday. Rot his black soul. Now Toddie and Temple will do the race from the town square to the main road without me."

"Oh, no. How devastating for you."

"Well, it is." He frowned in reproof. "I was bound to win and now one of those numbskulls will have a chance. Naturally, you wouldn't understand. You don't have a curricle, but what are we fellows supposed to do to pass the time in the country?"

"May I suggest smuggling? We are quite close to the sea. No? Perhaps you could take up highway robbery."

He grinned. "That was Temple's suggestion. Toddie thought we could have a shooting competition but there's nothing to shoot at this time of year."

"I might suggest that telling a woman who never has a spare moment that you are bored is a trifle tactless. You are at this moment keeping me from packing lemons into a box with bay leaves."

"In that case, you ought to be grateful to me." He nodded at her, unrepentant, which was his most attractive trait. Nothing bothered him. His steadiness had been her salvation, keeping her frivolous nature at bay.

"I am. So, Lord Delmore's here?" She couldn't meet his gaze. To hide what may appear to be a guilty expression, she sat on the sofa, patting the space beside her for him. "Does he have anything of a debauched nature planned?"

Jeremy screwed up his face. "If so, he hasn't enlightened me. My aunt and uncle arrived this morning too. That ought to keep Mother busy, at least." During his fidgeting, he moved her sewing box. Her thimble wobbled from the top and bounced onto the floor. "Damn," he said as he moved down onto one knee to stop the thing from rolling too far away.

The door opened, and Jonquil appeared. "Anna, did you ... oh ..." She stared from Anna to Jeremy. Her mouth loosened. Although Jeremy, on his knees before her, could have been misconstrued, she set her face firmly and moved into the room as upright as a dowager. "Mr. Hastings. I did not know you were here."

He rose to his feet. "If you mean to call me Mr. Hastings, I'll have you know that I don't plan to call a chit I have known since she couldn't blow her own nose Miss Beeby."

"Do please continue to call me Jonquil." With the air of a martyr, she sat on the edge of the old red armchair, careful not to move back too far in case of being swallowed up in the sag caused by the lax webbing. "Anna, I wish you would walk down to Danbury with me. Mama says she would, only Papa needs her for his sermon on Sunday. He likes to practice his sermon on her," she explained to Jeremy who already knew that from Anna's mutterings. "And I need to choose fabrics for my come-out in London." Having so unsubtly declared her news to him, she clasped her hands and hid the triumph in her eyes by lowering her lashes.

"You are making your debut in London?" Jeremy leaned forward, clearly astonished. "What about Anna?"

"She is to be my companion, aren't you Anna?"

"So, I've been told."

"You a companion?" He turned to Anna with a surprised expression that turned into a smile. "By all that's wonderful. I'll be able to introduce you about, at last. And perhaps the chit ought to call me Mr. Hastings while we're in London."

"Why?" Jonquil's face looked mutinous. "I've always called you Jeremy."

"You set a precedent just then when you walked into the room." He crossed his arms. "What was that about?"

"Nothing. But you looked so silly kneeling on the floor. I thought I should add some dignity to the occasion." Her eyes glossed over, and she began to blink rapidly, never too proud to shed a tear or two when needed, though why she would need to look put upon at this moment was anyone's guess.

The effect was lost on Jeremy, who had known her too long. "Now see here, chit. A seventeen-year-old will never add to my dignity."

"I'm eighteen." Jonquil's bottom lip trembled.

Jeremy considered. "Well, if you two want to go into Danbury, I have my curricle outside—save you a walk."

Jonquil's face cleared in an instant. "Oh, yes, please. I hate the walk. I always end up with dirty boots and sore feet. But we'll have to ask Mama. You should ask, Anna. She always says yes to you."

"I'll ask, but you'll have to wait, Jeremy. It will take us a minute or two to put on our hats and pelisses."

"I'll wait. I'll read one of these." He picked up one of Lady Delmore's fashion magazines. "Good lord. Skirts are narrower this year. Soon you ladies won't be able to waddle faster than a duck."

Anna ushered Jonquil out the door. "Mama will give her permission and I won't take any time to get ready. I'll meet you back here in ten minutes if you can manage."

"Of course I can. I've never been in Jeremy's curricle. I hope we'll all fit."

"It won't be easy, but we'll be able to squash up somehow. It will give us a chance to arrive in Danbury looking tidy, for a change."

Mama said yes, usually inclined to agree to any of Jeremy's suggestions, and Anna donned her brown pelisse and a brown velvet bonnet. When she arrived back in the morning room, Jeremy was putting the magazine back into the pile. He gave Anna one of his blinding smiles, for a moment looking so like his brother that she needed to blink. She had never seen Jeremy as a handsome man before this. He had always been just Jeremy.

"You'll want to buy an armload of feathers too, while you're about it," he said, straightening. "For your hats." Then he looked like comfortable Jeremy again and not the heartbreaking rake. "Feathers are all the rage this year, says Mrs. Bluebell in the magazine. I wonder if that's her real name?"

She laughed. Jonquil, dressed in her blue pelisse and her matching hat, a pretty contrast to her fair hair, joined them in a few more minutes. In the curricle she and Anna had to hold onto each other to fit, but Jeremy managed his horses well, as she had discovered during former trips from her house to Danbury. His elderly groom occupied the seat at the back of the vehicle, supplying Anna and Jonquil with unneeded chaperonage.

When Jeremy reached the small collection of shops

lining the main road through the town, he tied his reins to help Jonquil and Anna down. "I'll wait for you out here, shall I?"

"We could be quite some time," Anna said while Jonquil said in a tiny voice that she would be most grateful.

"In that case, I'll go to the tavern and come back in half an hour."

Anna doubted Jonquil could make a decision in half an hour. However, the low-ceilinged haberdashery didn't sell a wide range of fabrics or many suitable for evening gowns. Within five minutes, Jonquil found a pastel-green striped muslin that, held under her chin, brought out the blue of her eyes. She decided to take that for a walking gown, which could be started right away, or so she told Anna, who would cut out the pattern.

Anna fingered a length of voile in pale lemon. "If we order a white silk fabric, I could embroider flowers on this. It would make a pretty overskirt for an evening gown."

"Would you?" Jonquil's eyes shone.

"We would need to take the fabric right away so that I would have time."

Both fabrics were carefully cut and packaged while Anna gazed longingly at colorful umbrellas. She would love to own the purple one. Her old black umbrella had a broken rib. Jonquil dithered over hat shapes, trying one and then another, though today they had no hat budget. The doorbell tinkled as another customer entered the shop. "Your parcels are ready, Miss Winter," called the haberdasher, Mrs. Pointer, who had hair colored an unlikely orange, while she stared in the direction of her new customer.

Anna turned.

Jeremy stared at her; his face creased with apology as he indicated his devastatingly handsome older brother. "Delmore drove by the tavern." He eased his high collar from his neck as he glanced at his spectacularly groomed sibling who, beneath his multi-caped greatcoat, wore a perfectly tailored black coat with light breeches and a buff and white striped waistcoat. He held his hat. A rakish lock of dark hair hung over his left eye. "He said he would like to be reacquainted with you and Jonquil."

Jonquil stood, jaw dropped, beholding the magnificent creature, who stood with a politely bored expression on his aristocratic face.

Lord Delmore moved forward and with no other choice, Anna held out her gloved hand, which he took lightly. "Miss Winter. Delighted. And Miss Beeby. I hear from Jeremy you are about to make your debut in London."

Jonquil swallowed, her eyes huge.

While he loomed so close, Lord Delmore's powerful frame seemed to fill the small space. The top of his hat was barely two feet below the ceiling. Anna tried to say a civil, or possibly even an intelligent word, and came out with, "How long are you planning to stay?" Her cheeks a little warm, she took her hand back, not knowing how she came to have kissed this cool, elegant stranger.

"I haven't yet decided. If you are asking how long I need to stay away from London, the answer is probably for a week or so. No one is remembered longer than that." His cynical gaze flickered over her face. Somehow, he managed to caress her with his eyes. For a single moment, her whole body heated with a stark and hopeless longing.

She dragged in a breath. "I suspect we won't find much to interest you here."

"Don't be so sure." His eyes hooded. "I've been perfectly well entertained so far. I had some luck yesterday."

The sardonic curl of his lips worried her. The light in his eyes intensified with an odd sort of calculation. She was sure he would mention their meeting and then Jeremy would wonder why she didn't. Dreading Lord Delmore's next words, she said hurriedly, "We really must be going. We can walk home, Jeremy, while you choose feathers for your hat."

Jeremy grinned. "Not my hat, Anna. Your hat."

Lord Delmore smoothed the back of one elegant calf-skin glove. "And who will carry your parcels?"

"If we had come without Jeremy, we would carry our own parcels." She turned toward the door.

"I can't allow that. Fortunately, I brought my mother's landau. I will take you both back in comfort. You can't have liked swaying in that high curricle of Jeremy's."

"I'm perfectly happy with Jeremy's curricle," Jonquil said quickly, grabbing the sleeve of the younger Jeremy Hastings. "Today is the first time he has driven me, and I was frightfully comfortable."

"Well, then, I shall have to be satisfied with Miss Winters and her parcels." Lord Delmore's mouth curved, and he offered Anna a querying glance from beneath raised eyebrows.

"You put me in an awkward situation, my lord. If I

insist on going with Jeremy too, you would hear that as a major snub."

Again, he glanced at her with a smile lurking behind his eyes. "I mean to visit your mother this morning, Miss Winters, bearing an invitation from my mother, which she asked me to deliver," he said carefully. "It was sheer coincidence that I saw Jeremy's curricle as I passed by the inn. I would be honored to drive you home."

"In that case, I can see I have been outflanked. I would be delighted to accompany you, my lord. Since I have no choice other than to be very rude." She couldn't help glancing up at him.

"I'm delighted to hear you don't mean to be rude, Miss Winters." He slid her parcels from the countertop while she carefully replaced the purple umbrella, she would have given all her pin money to possess, if she had pin money, back into the rack.

Outside, Jeremy handed Jonquil into his curricle, whose sides she clutched while she stared nervously at Anna.

"Jeremy will drive very carefully, and we will be right behind you," Anna told her, making certain Jeremy heard. She wasn't at all sure her mother or her stepfather would approve, but the situation was awkward, and she needed to make the best of it.

In a trice she was handed into Lady Delmore's landau. Lord Delmore seated himself beside her. On the way back to the vicarage, his driver stayed behind Jeremy's curricle, a foresight that kept the former's pace sedate. "I see you have my brother's measure," Lord Delmore said, his tone amused. "Does he drive around with you in that rattlebox?"

"Not without a groom, if you are trying to make me out as a fast woman."

"I'm not sure you aren't. You do, after all, kiss strangers in the stream." He sounded impartial.

"You were no stranger. I knew who you were." She raised her chin and clasped her gloved hands together, staring straight ahead. "Of course, I knew."

"In that case, I'm surprised you didn't fight me off."

She frowned. "I am too, but you are an experienced man. You didn't scare me."

"I'm glad. I must apologize. I'm not in the habit of kissing young maidens in the woods."

"I wouldn't advise it." She glanced at him, repressing the urge to smile. Being called a young maiden tended to melt a woman's heart.

"Will this be another useful hint like not kissing maids?" His gaze settled on her mouth.

"I hope so." She swallowed. "You might kiss someone who takes you seriously. Then you would need to explain to her parents. Luckily, I know you can't help yourself and you don't mean a thing when you kiss maidens in the woods."

"That's where you're wrong. I might start out as a casual marauder, but I take my spoils seriously, especially if they turn out to be more than simply pretty."

Her cheeks tingled. She had never thought of herself as ugly or even unattractive, but to have a hardened flirt call her pretty bolstered her a little. "Do your spoils ever take you seriously?"

"I am vain enough to say always, but wise enough to

know that I have found exceptions. Have you accepted my apology?"

"Of course. We're neighbors and your brother is one of my favorite people. I wouldn't dream of making much of an episode that I have already forgotten."

"Well done," he said with a certain amount of mockery in his tone. "You have very nicely put me in my place. Forgotten already."

She turned away from him to watch the passing scenery, which she knew so well that if a branch fell from one of the bare trees lining the road she would have noticed. A flock of geese swirled in the wind, soaring ever higher among the dark clouds. "You are wise to have taken the landau. I fear Jeremy might be returning home in the rain."

"I would have taken my phaeton had my groom not mentioned a slight misalignment of one of the wheels. I didn't take into account the color of the sky. Let's hope my brother doesn't get Miss Beeby wet."

Anna smiled. "He would be sure to pull out his water-proof if the drops are large. That's what he gave me one day when we were caught in a shower. He himself took a soaking. He had lovely manners, you know."

"Yes. Of all the brothers I could have, I would prefer mine. What do you think of his plan to begin renovating Drake House in the new year?"

Surprised, Anna turned to him. Although Jeremy still lived with his mother in Delmore House, this year he had taken possession of a not inconsiderable inheritance from his great uncle, Mr. Bodger of Drake House in Maldon, not more than an hour's drive from Danbury. "Has he finally decided? That's good to hear. He took me to see the place a few weeks ago. The garden has been left to rack and ruin but the house itself should come up well with a good dusting."

"Are you interested in gardens, Miss Winters?"

"I think you must call me Anna since Jeremy does. And yes, I love gardens. I wish my stepfather had an area he would like me to redesign, for I would dearly like to grow roses."

"You sound like my mother. She takes great pride in her rose garden. Perhaps you can help Jeremy design his garden."

"I think it would be best if I didn't at this stage. That might be seen as taking over. In the fullness of time, he will marry, and the new Mrs. Hastings will want her tastes regarded."

He stared at her. "Are you saying I shouldn't ask for advice from anyone other than the poor nameless innocent I marry? I have no countess, only my mother who first planned the garden for Hastings House."

She frowned. "Why would you marry an innocent?"

"Who else would have me?"

"I imagine any number of women are holding their breath at this very moment."

"You are prone to overstating the case."

"So, I have heard. The only entertainment in my life is exaggerating wildly. I make myself sound so much more important."

He smiled right into her eyes. Her insides warmed. Dratted man. He could charm the sulks out of the village scold.

With the vicarage in sight, the driver began to rein in. In

front, Jeremy had already arrived at the front gate and Jonquil had begun a timorous attempt to climb down without aid. Lord Delmore frowned. "He should have told her to remain patient for a moment longer."

The landau stopped and he sprang out, leaving the door open behind him. From her seated position, Anna watched him dash to the curricle and catch Jonquil, as she made a clumsy leap to the ground. Her bonnet sat askew, and she clung to him for dear life. Anna stepped out of the landau with the parcels. She thanked the driver and proceeded toward the entwined couple. Lord Delmore set Jonquil safely on her own feet, and she stood staring at him, trying to straighten her hat.

"Thank you, Calder," Jeremy said in an irritated voice. "The chit had her foot on the deck instead of the step and she was never going to get to the ground that way."

"I thought that was what you told me to do." Jonquil's bottom lip jutted.

"From the deck to the step, not from the deck to the ground."

"I gather you are not to accustomed to escaping curricles." Lord Delmore untied the ribbon of Jonquil's bonnet, put her hat at a more becoming angle, and retied the bow.

Only an experienced rake would attempt to do this. Jonquil's astonished gaze fastened on his face. "Thank, you my lord," she said in a breathless voice. "That's the first time Jeremy has taken me up. He normally drives Anna."

"Does Anna leap down without assistance?"

"Anna does not." Anna eyed the couple, one of whom blushed. The other had possibly never blushed in his entire life and looked entirely satisfied with himself. "Anna is a managing kind of woman and insists that Jeremy remembers his manners. He might need them someday." Anna lifted her head and eyed Jeremy with severity. "I think he may have forgotten that Jonquil is no longer a child but a young lady about to make her debut."

Jeremy made a chastened face. His two horses, country cousins to high steppers, champed at their bits and shifted restlessly. "Sorry, Jonquil. I did forget and it's badly done of me, but I will forevermore treat you like the lady you will learn to be under Anna's tutelage."

"Oh, tosh Jeremy," Anna said, smiling at her friend. "Thank you for the drive into town. Tell your mother I have made the yearly Christmas puddings and thank her for the flour."

Jeremy tipped his hat with the handle of his whip. Anna didn't watch him drive off. As she opened the squeaky gate, her packages were removed from her hold and somehow Jonquil was propelled forward, leaving Anna and Lord Delmore following. The man was a master maneuver.

Morag opened the front door, her frown fixed on the unexpected visitor.

Anna smiled at the elderly maid. "Morag, here is Lord Delmore come to call on Mama. Perhaps you could find a cup of tea for him?"

"Of course. Miss Anna." Pursing her lips, the woman walked toward to the kitchen at the back of the house. Without a doubt her next stop would be above stairs to warn Mama about her illustrious visitor.

Chapter Three

Delmore rose to his feet as Mrs. Beeby entered her sitting room. Sir Walter had been right about the lady. Slim and graceful like her daughter, she greeted him with a polite greeting, her eyebrows slightly raised in the way she would use to keep her husband's parishioners from wasting her time with gossip. Her eyes, although bluish gray like her daughter's, missed being captivating because of her expression of resignation. She held out a hand, which he bowed over.

He waited for her to seat herself, glad to see that Anna intended to remain. The mother and daughter shared similarities in facial bone-structure, both with perfectly straight, determined noses, and firm mouths and chins. However, Anna's mouth tilted up at the corners and her eyes gleamed with humor. The older woman looked watchful, as if she needed to remain on her guard. Had her first husband, Anna's father not been a rash young fool, her life would have followed much along the same path as Delmore's mother.

However, not one to waste too much time regretting the paths of rash young fools, for he had also been one, Delmore answered the question on the woman's face. "My aunt, Lady Carrington, is visiting. My mother decided we must entertain her. She has invited the squire, his lady, and his son and daughter to an informal dinner tonight. Mrs. Toddington will also attend with her son." Without a blink, he added the invitation from his mother that he had invented while he was in the village shop, watching Anna focus a longing gaze on, of all things, a plain purple umbrella. "She hoped that you and Mr. Beeby, and Anna as well, would join us. With such late notice, my mother hopes she won't earn your censure."

Mrs. Beeby widened her eyes, her surprise unfeigned. "I would be delighted to see your Aunt Alice again. We made our debuts together, you know, a few years after your mother. I haven't ..." She cleared her throat. "Mr. Beeby and I don't normally socialize with your family. If you are sure ..." She glanced at Anna as if seeking her reassurance.

"She thought it was her duty to put the young people of the district together," Delmore said firmly, deciding his mother ought to feel this way. After all, she was the Countess of Delmore and should be Danbury's social leader.

Mrs. Beeby cleared her throat. "I don't know if you heard, but Jonquil is about to make her debut in London ..."

For the slightest of moments, he missed the hint. When he understood her allusion, he ploughed on. He may as well be shot for a goose as a partridge. "And may I take the opportunity to invite Jonquil to the dinner as well? My mother wasn't quite certain if you would approve of her anticipating her debut."

His mother had shuddered last night when Jeremy had pointed out the uneven numbers at the table and suggested inviting Anna. "Really, Jeremy," his mother had said haughtily. "It would be very remiss of us to disrespect your father that way. It would be tantamount to saying he was in the wrong."

Jeremy had shrugged, sending Delmore a heavenward glance. Likely this argument had been played out before. Delmore hadn't been home often enough to know the ins and outs of the local factions. And now he had placed the pigeons among the cats. However, the pretty Jonquil, being all the rage would please the younger members of the party, Jeremy, Toddie, and Temple, and right the fault in the numbers. And Delmore would hold off the tedium of the dinner by idling with Anna.

His mission accomplished, Delmore rose to his feet. He would have shown himself to the door, but the white-haired elderly maid answered the summons to do the honors. She sniffed her disapproval of him to the exit and again as he took the slate step to the path. The landau's driver grabbed up his whip as soon as he spotted Delmore.

He arrived home slightly envious of his younger brother who, not having taken up his inheritance as yet, had time to cut a dash with the local beauties. Delmore hadn't impressed Anna, and Jonquil seemed unable to speak above a whisper in his presence.

All he had done to deserve his poor reputation, which clearly intimidated her, was to make bad choices every year since his majority. A few weeks after that momentous day eight years ago when he had come into his inheritance, he had decided that his father's trustee, William Evans, was a fusty old man. His ponderous advice about gambling, drinking, and a dalliance or two with an experienced woman was something Delmore's father had clearly never heard. Nevertheless, Evans understood the handling of legal matters regarding tenants and rents.

Today, Delmore's earlier inspection of his properties showed his land to be in better condition than he might have expected, given the diminishing income he derived. The discussion he had afterwards with his steward about improvements had called for more funds. The ideas the man put to him would help empty his pockets and go against the spokesman for the tenants who would do no more than add a bitter grunt when asked how more money could be squeezed out of the various holdings.

Evans had tentatively put revising the land boundaries to him and his steward had scoffed at the idea. This left Delmore considering ways to cut costs on building maintenance. Surely even a failed Oxford scholar would be able to fathom how.

He massaged his forehead and rang the bell. His butler, Westerfield, arrived. Delmore told him to bring a bottle of Cabernet from the cellar. After he had filled his glass with a healthy slug, he sat at his study desk. He tapped his pen against the inkwell a number of times, made a blot, cleaned his nib, and leaned back, sighing. His desk looked as untidy as his mind, with a splotched blotter, two broken quills, and estate books that didn't make sense to him.

Clearly the rest of today would not be productive, and tonight he intended to relax with a convivial, well-presented meal, while he discussed anything other than money with a few genial companions. With Miss Winter. Mentally he shook himself. He had barely rid himself of his mistress.

Tomorrow he would again try to put his mind to the more than forty employees whose livelihood depended on him putting his affairs in order. He took his first invigorating gulp from the glass. And another.

Before he went upstairs to change, he finished off his first bottle for the day.

Anna and her family were ushered into the enormous Georgian hall of Hastings House. Cool drafts eddied from the front door, the two side doors, and down the stairwell. She clutched her cloak around her, her fingers freezing beneath her gloves, and stared at the intricate pastel-colored designs on the domed ceiling. The butler indicated the wide staircase that led up to the formal rooms. He preceded them and announced their presence. A maid took the cloaks. Anna draped her shawl across her arms, resigned to appearing unfashionably dowdy rather than blue with cold.

She proceeded into the predominately yellow room. The area had been blessed with enormous logs crackling in the fireplace at the far end. On the walls, columns of dark marble with blue finials supported naked men who had apparently been given the job of holding up the cloud-painted ceiling. Without seeming to be bumptious, she couldn't push closer to the fire.

Only once before had she been invited to sit down to a meal in this gracious house. That was the night of her own debut five years previously when Lady Delmore, determined not to be seen as unbending, had been forced to invite Anna with a few young, more acceptable debutants to a dinner before the town hall presentation. The formal dining room had not been offered that night, but a smaller one nearer to the kitchens.

During the night of her debut, she had amused herself by flirting with Jeremy's friends, most of whom she had known since before they had taken to wearing collar points so high that they could barely turn their heads. Lord Delmore had gone to London the year before, which even then had been a great disappointment to her. The rare glimpses she had of him always made her hold her breath while shivers of pleasure rushed through her, rather like when she spotted a rare and beautiful bird.

The man who had occupied her thoughts for the past two days stepped forward, looking far too handsome in a formal black jacket and black knee breeches, set off by a white waistcoat. His dark hair had been brushed back. Only that single errant lock flopped onto his forehead, giving forewarning of his dissolute habits. He smiled; his eyes so focused on her mouth that she could almost read his dastardly thoughts about kissing women. Unfortunately, the depth of his gaze made her tingle. She quite understood how he had earned his dreadful reputation. Likely he had this effect on all impressionable females, but her heart skipped a beat, regardless. She smiled, her yearning scrupulously masked.

He took her gloved hand and moved her forward. "I believe you haven't yet met my aunt and uncle. Sir Walter and Lady Carrington, meet Miss Winters who plans to go up to town for the season next month with her younger sister, the older as a companion to the younger."

"You hardly look old enough to take on that role, my dear," Lady Carrington said with a smile. "And you resemble your mama enough to break a few hearts yourself." She reached over to mama and kissed her on the cheek. "Elizabeth, you rogue, you haven't aged a scrap."

Mama took the compliment with a defensive smile. "Alice, my dear flatterer, might I also present my husband, Horace, and his daughter Jonquil who will be making her debut."

"Indeed." Lady Carrington smiled brightly at the two and shook Stepfather's hand. "We must see what we can do for her when we get back to town. Sir Walter, we shall have a ball." She rapped her gold painted fan on the shoulder of her husband, who turned.

"Whatever you say, my dear." The tall gentleman, his belly imposing in the requisite evening dress, put up his glass to examine Anna and Jonquil. "I doubt these young ladies will have a problem with dancing partners." He smiled at Anna and nudged Horace Beeby with his elbow. The latter offered a puzzled glance. Any subject not about him was not worth pursuing.

"Not I, Sir Walter." Anna smiled, charmed by his bluff manner. "I'll be sitting with the companions."

"What a waste." Lady Carrington glanced at her sister, the dowager Lady Delmore, who managed to maintain her polite expression. Not a word passed between the two, but Anna knew her father's name had been significantly hinted by the pursing of the dowager's lips. The muscles beneath Anna's chin tightened.

Jeremy joined the group, followed by the squire's son, John Temple, a reckless young gentleman who appeared to be moonstruck by Jonquil. She in turn flapped her fan like a professional fire starter and the party moved into separate conversations all going at once. Then widowed Mrs. Toddington arrived with her son, Rodney, known as Toddie. Shy Rodney, who usually tried, and failed, to be inconspicuous, edged his way to Jonquil's side.

Lord Delmore made himself pleasant to the older folk and then he turned once again to Anna, leading her closer to the fire. "I assume you will be busy until you leave, ordering your new gowns for London."

Letting the warmth of the crackling wood seep into her, Anna considered her answer to his lowering question. A new gown would be delightful, but impossible, considering the state of her mother's finances. "I suppose a person could make herself busy by ordering new clothes, but I am to be a companion, Lord Delmore."

"Do companions not also have extensive wardrobes?" He toyed with his fob watch.

She stared at the logs crackling in the grate. "I won't be on show, my lord. I shall help my mother outfit Jonquil. She is pretty enough to marry well."

"And you are not?"

"My debut passed some five years ago. I am decidedly on the shelf." Even she, the only optimist in a house of pessimists, knew no one would be scrutinizing a companion the way they would a debutante.

"Do you not think of marriage for yourself, Miss Winters?"

She eyed him, her mouth curled into a cynical smile. "Only the bravest of the brave would offer for me."

"Not necessarily. Your assets are not invisible." His glance passed lazily over her bosom.

She squared her shoulders. "For all you know, I am a wicked witch, or a fast woman, or I cook babies for breakfast."

"You are certainly the second." He hooded his gaze.

"That is not a gentlemanly statement to make, not when you have no proof."

"I certainly do have proof. Might I remind you of a certain stream and a certain fisherman?"

"I think the fastness came from the other side, my lord. In that case I was but a village maiden snared by a line – which was accidental but nonetheless diverting to say the least."

"I am rarely called diverting." He leaned back, examining her expression too closely.

"I can hardly describe you as wicked because accidents are accidents, and happen to rakes as often as to maidens, I suspect."

Lady Delmore glided up beside him and tapped him on his shoulder with her fan. "Calder, could you take your aunt into dinner? I think young Temple must take Anna." His mother, cool and self possessed, used her demeaning, ultra-polite expression when glancing at Anna.

Lord Delmore nodded, glancing across the room. Almost instantly, John Temple arrived and escorted her into the enormous dining room. Each wall had been papered in dark pink. A cast brass chandelier hung high above the centre of the long table. Candelabra of silver formed a row from end to end. Anna discovered with amazement that she would be seated on the left of Lord Delmore, who waited for the ladies to arrange themselves before taking his place at the head of the table. After a few polite words to his aunt on his right, he turned to Anna, his expression veiled, and his voice low. "My mother thought I should have the squire's wife on my left, but since that would put your stepfather on hers, she decided we could dispense with a little formality."

Anna laughed. She knew that a vicar's stepdaughter would normally be seated much farther down. Mr. Beeby, willfully crashing bore that he was, sat on the opposite side, between the Squire's wife and mama. The squire's wife had always hung upon his every word, for Mr. Beeby was a breathtakingly handsome man who used his mellifluous voice to make platitudes sound original and important. Perhaps Anna's mother had married him for his looks. She certainly hadn't married him for his money or his sharp wit. "I wondered why I was so honored, my lord."

He raised his eyebrows. "So, now you feel honored by my attention?"

"Your public attention, yes, my lord." She tried to appear blasé.

"Consider me rebuked," he said smoothly. "You see me here tonight, reformed. Rusticating on my estates is enough to keep me from my usual depths of depravity."

"In that case, the depths weren't particularly deep." She couldn't believe her luck to be seated near the most intriguing man she knew. Then again, as an unmarriageable woman, she would hardly been seen by the countess as a snare for the man either side of her, the wolf, Calder John, the Earl of Delmore, or John Temple, the pup.

The first remove arrived, served by two footmen in formal white wigs and wearing green and red jackets. Soon the table filled with delicious food, the like of which she never saw at the vicarage. Lady Carrington, opposite Anna, occupied herself with an animated conversation with the squire. Anna turned to Lord Delmore. "How do you plan to entertain yourself while you are in the country?"

He reached for his wine glass and finished the last half with a few hearty swallows. "No doubt I'll think of something frivolous. My friends are having their gardens redesigned. Apparently sweeping vistas are all the rage. I might consider planting a row of trees down to the lake."

"I scarcely wish to mention this, my lord, but you don't have a lake."

"Not yet, no, but I could widen the stream at that point." His green eyes filled with slow amusement. "In order to trap young maidens."

She dragged in a breath, dropping her gaze. "Trees and a lake would be perfect. And a rustic vision of wildflowers, thousands of wildflowers."

"Wildflowers? Which should I use, do you think?"

"I'm sure your gardener would answer that better than I."

"The gardeners appear to be taking a winter break." Expressionlessly, he carefully placed his glass back onto the table.

"I don't think this is the weather for planting."

"Perhaps that is why I haven't yet spotted a gardener.

Could some have been shifted to Drake House?" He frowned.

"Jeremy's Drake House? I shouldn't think so. He doesn't have plans for his garden as yet."

"You sound well informed. Does he tell you everything?" He stared into her eyes as if he was asking her another question entirely.

She assumed that, like her mother, he had paired her with Jeremy. She wished people could understand that she and Jeremy had no plan whatsoever to end up as man and wife. Aside from the fact that his mother made obvious that Jeremy was meant for an as yet not chosen, well-connected and titled young lady, Anna wouldn't concede to a no-more-than-comfortable marriage to a man she liked so well. Jeremy deserved to marry a woman whose insides thrummed with excitement whenever he neared. He deserved that feeling she had when she was with Lord Delmore, the smile inside that ached to be shared, the glance that had to be dropped for fear of showing too much interest. "He told me he has no plan yet to shift to Maldon."

Lord Delmore shrugged. "He is certainly taking his time. As it is, he seems to think the coming season in town is more important than setting up his own household. He speaks well of you. One might suspect you have some influence over him."

"One should stop suspecting. I have none. Aside from that, I think setting up a household is a huge responsibility for a man his age."

"He has to start at some time, and the sooner he does the better. No one would want him to follow my example."

"He will go his own way."

"I'm pleased he has your confidence."

"We are the best of good friends."

"And will remain so for the rest of your lives," he said in a bored voice, as if he had heard those words many times. "You must try some of this fricasseed rabbit." He offered the dish to her and then signaled to the footman to refill his glass.

She helped herself to a morsel. Lady Carrington, on his other side, claimed his attention and John Temple on Anna's other side muttered and fidgeted by her side. "May I offer fricasseed rabbit to you?" she asked, seeing the hard set of his face.

"He keeps talking to her." With a flick of his head, he indicated Jonquil, who appeared absorbed by Jeremy's conversation.

"Be fair, John. He can't spend the night only talking to his mother. He can do that any day, and I am pleased to see he is taking notice of Jonquil. He has spent so many years avoiding her, that he didn't notice she has grown older."

"Well, he has certainly noticed tonight," John said through gritted teeth. "I've spent months courting her while he laughed at me, and tonight when I am seated beside her, he can do nothing more than try to cut me out."

"Be careful, John, or you will put me in danger of thinking myself a regular bore."

"You know you're not, Anna. You're the greatest female of my acquaintance but you're not ..." His words trailed off and he shrugged.

"Delicate and impressionable?" she suggested. "At a loss in exalted company? Jeremy relaxes her. If you want her attention, offer her the fricasseed rabbit. Then start discussing an interesting subject, like her new gown, anything but your dogs or horses or the way you tie your cravat."

"Very astute advice," Lord Delmore said from her other side. Lady Carrington was again being entertained by Squire Temple who was a good natured and hearty soul, like his son enamored of his dogs and horses and willing to expound on the good points of each to Lady Carrington, who possibly didn't mind at all. "On the whole, ladies rarely show interest in dogs and horses, or the knot of a cravat." He concentrated on his glass.

She noted he barely had a drop of wine left in his new refill. Talking civilly during a meal must be wearing on the man. "At times, I enjoy a good dog story, but I'm sure when I was about to make my debut I would rather have talked about gowns and dancing."

"Do you enjoy both?"

"Of course. Do I seem at my last gasp to you, my lord?" she said, her voice beginning to wane. Having an attractive rake by her side who took more interest in his wine than in flirting with her was an experience sure to lower the spirits of any spinster.

"To me you are a mere fledgling. We were speaking of gardens, and my aunt overheard the mention of Drake House. She would be interested in making up a party to see the place sometime during the week. She hopes to have the pleasure of your company."

Anna blinked. She had no idea why Jeremy's family was suddenly taking her up. From barely tolerated by his mother to having his aunt wanting the pleasure of her company in the space of an hour? She nodded at Lord Delmore. "If Jeremy agrees to open the house, I should be delighted."

As soon as the meal ended, the ladies vacated the room, leaving the gentlemen to enjoy the bottles of port brought in by the footman. Unlike at the squire's heavy dinners, this procedure lasted no more than half an hour, after which the gentlemen joined the ladies who had all refreshed themselves by this time and had settled back to gossip about the Christmas entertainments planned in Danbury.

The gentlemen dispersed themselves between the ladies in no particular order. Jeremy sprawled beside Anna. "Delmore asked if we could take a picnic party to Drake House on Friday, next. Apparently, he thinks it was time I was shuffled out of his house," he added in a disgruntled tone.

"I'm sure he is merely trying to entertain your guests. A picnic party in winter is an unusual idea but rather nice, don't you think?"

"Next he'll be wanting me to make decisions about rooms and furniture." Jeremy crossed his arms.

"I'm sure your mother would be delighted to advise you, and also your aunt."

"You'll come. Do you think Jonquil might like to join us?"

Anna smiled. "I'm sure she would see it as deadly dull, but she needs to learn how to conduct herself in society before she is presented. A little buttering up of your aunt and uncle is a good idea, since your aunt was pondering about inviting us to a ball once we're in town."

"Perhaps it might not be so bad. Your mother seems to be enjoying herself tonight." Jeremy glanced at mama who appeared to be interested in Mrs. Toddington's conversation about finding a suitable wife for Rodney, one not beneath him, for one day he too may inherit a title. Mrs. Toddington hoped for the unlikely event, but at this stage, Toddie was two removed from an Earldom. When he showed interest in marriage, no one would need to find a wife for a good-natured man who had soft brown eyes, framed with thick eyelashes, and dark curly hair. When he controlled his stutter, he became a creditable conversationalist.

"Sometimes she forgets she is the wife of a vicar and lets herself socialize. It's good for her. She wasn't meant be cooped up all day in a vicarage." As she spoke Anna wondered if she voiced her own dislike of her life instead of her mother's. Certainly, living in the vicarage hadn't added greatly to Anna's life. She enjoyed the parishioners and visiting the sick and elderly, but piety and reading sermons didn't suit her one bit.

Had she been a raving beauty like her mother in her heyday, perhaps she could have had a season in London herself. Five years ago, her mother's sister, Lady Prescott, had offered to sponsor Anna, as she had this year offered to sponsor Jonquil. However, the reverend Horace Beeby hadn't been able to find the money five, or even four years ago, for Anna. Were the truth to be told, she was too useful to lose. While she ran the house, her mother had time to devote to him. The man was completely self-absorbed. Anna would much prefer to marry rather than to spend the rest of her life listening to his long-winded platitudes.

"Do you play the piano, Miss Winters?" asked Lady Carrington from a nearby couch, clearly needing respite from the squire and Mr. Beeby, who flanked her either side. She moved a powder blue cushion to the small of her back.

"Indifferently, Lady Carrington." Anna spotted Jonquil sitting beside her mother, her face a thundercloud, apparently in a fret about something. "But if you can persuade Jonquil to sing, she might drown out my mistakes with her beautiful voice."

"You sing, Miss Beeby?" Lady Carrington directed her gaze to the younger woman who remembered her company manners and rearranged her pretty features into a demure smile.

"I would be pleased to do so if Anna accompanied me." She looked a question at mama, who nodded.

Anna rose and picked through the music sheets until she and Jonquil agreed on a tune. Jonquil had a wonderful voice, which soared over the high notes and made intimate details of the lower ones. The guests sat in muted silence until she finished. Anna smiled proudly. At last Jonquil had a chance to shine. Even Lord Delmore appeared to be impressed.

"You'll certainly take the gloss out of the town beauties with that voice," he said as he watched her seat herself again beside mama. "Aunt, you could help make her noticed." Although Lord Delmore didn't bother to hide his boredom with the subject, Anna suspected he did this so that no one could suspect him of being thoughtful.

"I believe Lady Prescott has that honor. Now, have we organized the trip to Drake House? Miss Beeby must come with us as well."

Jonquil looked a question at Anna.

"Do come, Jonquil. I would love your company." Anna

smiled hopefully at her sister. A day with the two Hastings brothers and the Carringtons called for defensive measures. Jonquil would be a good back-up for Anna, who wasn't sure why she, the family drudge, had been so honored.

On Friday morning, driving his phaeton with Jeremy as his passenger, Delmore passed Sir Walter's carriage on the road to Drake House in Maldon. A dull grey sky hovered overhead. "Did you warn your staff to prepare for guests today?" he asked his brother.

His face barely visible above his wool muffler, Jeremy turned. "Mother sent a message this morning. My so-called staff consists of a grounds man and his wife, who act as caretakers."

"You'll need more than a couple of servants to keep your house for you. We have a staff of forty at Hastings House." Delmore didn't add that at least twenty of these appeared to be invisible. The butler had taken almost fifteen minutes last night to find him another bottle of wine.

"I'll employ more when I'm ready to move in. My steward is attending to the grounds using local workers, and most of the land is tenanted. I don't see anything I can do at this stage but keep the place maintained." Jeremy sounded defensive.

Delmore understood his attitude. At Jeremy's age, his had been the same. He had seen no need to look over his lands or make sure of his rents. He trusted Evans to uphold the status quo. Recently, in fact sometime during the past two years, his estate had begun to lose money, though not in any significant way. The quick sale of his racing curricle paid his gambling debts, and his holdings still ran smoothly enough to keep his mother and brother in comfort. However, lately he hadn't been able to splash money around. Disencumbering himself of La Gloriosa had given him a slight respite, since he no longer paid for the cost of her extravagant wardrobe and her ever-growing upkeep. "The pot lecturing the kettle. You may change your mind if you stay there for a week or two."

"And I will after the London season. I see no point in heating up a large place when I don't plan to be there for any length of time."

Delmore shrugged. The lad would also need to hire servants who would be left idle for months. Better he did this later, when he was ready to move in. With the chaise now behind, Delmore had no need to make time, but he gave in to Jeremy's plea to let the horses have their heads along a straight stretch of road. His chestnuts had only a modicum of exercise in the city.

"If Temple could see this, he would turn green," Jeremy said holding his hat as the phaeton paced along a potholed road edged with naked tree trunks. Only a few evergreen gorse and bracken lightened the stark winter landscape. "Let me take the reins."

The groom behind Delmore gave a click of disapproval. "My lord don't let no one take control of them horses but hisself."

"But this is my brother, Wilson, and he deserves a treat."

"Make sure you take back them reins if he springs 'em,"

Wilson said in his reedy voice. The man, an ex-jockey in his early twenties with the requisite small stature, had been with Delmore for the past two years and had proved a wonder with the horses.

"I shall, Wilson, I shall." He handed over his reins.

Jeremy finally slowed the pair at the bend and smiled delightedly at Delmore. "Will you help me choose a new team when I'm in town." The eagerness in his eyes was hard to resist. Light sprinkles of rain began to spot his tall beaver hat.

"I'll let you borrow Wilson, who helped me choose these."

"That's a cracker if I ever 'eard one, my lord. You wouldn't take no notice, not even if I did give you the nod."

"My groom is a tyrant and tries to make me out as someone he wishes I were, rather than the man I am."

Wilson mumbled but Delmore ignored him. His statement was the story of his life. No one saw him as who he was, but as his father, an autocrat with decidedly sensual tastes. Delmore shared the former, but he was damned if he would be touted as a debaucher of innocents any longer.

His first love, the daughter of one of his tenants, swore he was the father of her child and no doubt in his enthusiasm he could have been, which was why he set her up with enough money to support his by-blow, with promises to make sure of a trade for the child some time in the future.

After the birth of the healthy sized, red headed girl two months too soon and the image of the man Maggie married within the month of receiving her stipend, he knew he had been taken on a journey into the fantastical. However, he kept his word, despite knowing the truth. Had the child really been his, he would have wanted to do his best for her, make sure she had a dowry at least. But the lass, now seven years-old, was a sturdy replica of her real father and showed no propensity to concentrate on her sewing, but instead worked with the cattle on the small tenant farm belonging to Delmore.

After that, Delmore went wild, for he had imagined himself in love with the demure maid who had used him to further her fortunes. One mistress followed another, all beauties with cold hearts and hands ever out for money, which he didn't begrudge. All he expected from them was faithfulness. If he supported a woman, she was his for the duration. La Gloriosa had played him false but as his heart had never been captured by any woman, he could move on with a shrug. Only the tragic loss of his red brocade waistcoat to the pig caused him pain.

Freezing rain began to mist his view. He maintained the distance from the chaise, encouraging his horses to trot in order to keep warm. Drake House finally reached in another half hour, he pulled up the phaeton at the front door, which remained closed. Jeremy sprang down and rapped on the knocker himself. Finally, the door creaked open.

A short conversation brought the grounds man/caretaker outside to take the horses. "We had word, my lord, and my missus is warming up the sitting room. She has the stove going in the kitchen and all should be right and tight. I'll take your 'orses to the stable."

"Show Wilson where. After that, Wilson, report to the kitchen for a warm meal, if you please." Delmore followed his brother through the front door. Since no servant waited to take the hats and greatcoats, he and Jeremy left their outerwear on the hall table.

The shabby sitting room had been occupied by an old man until his death, and hadn't been refurbished for many a year, which somewhat eased Delmore's mind. Although he had no reason to suspect his brother of helping himself to the Delmore inheritance, if he had, he certainly hadn't used any on his own property.

"Not too bad, eh?" Hands on his hips, Jeremy glanced around the room. A newly laid fire crackled in the grate. "No dead mice on the carpet, at least, and the dusty cobwebs have been removed."

"That should impress the ladies. They'll enjoy themselves giving you advice on how to make the place more habitable."

"Some of this furniture needs recovering," Jeremy said dismissively. "That dresser looks interesting. The old codger used it as a place to store his books and letters. His study is a treat but needs a scrap of refurbishment. How far behind do you think the chaise might be?"

"Certainly no longer than ten minutes. Shall we see to the arrangements made for dining?" Delmore checked the dining parlor, which he found dusted. A tablecloth had been set but the cutlery had been left on a side table. Knowing the place was irregularly staffed, he let his nose direct him to the kitchen at the back of the house. A cook stood casting spells over a hot stove. "Good morning. I'm Delmore. Would that, perchance, be a warming soup?"

The woman turned, her hand over her heart. "You scared me, m'lord. I have a nice potato and bean soup here and a loaf of bread. I was told Lady Delmore would be bringing picnic supplies, for we have nothing in the house. My Jim brought up the potaters from the cellar just this morning."

"Lady Delmore decided not to come today and, in her place, we have Lady Carrington with a basket of food. We will all welcome a potato soup—" The back lobby door crashed open.

Delmore turned.

"My lord." Travers, the driver of the tardy chaise, his plaid woolen scarf half-covering his white face, pulled up short when he spotted Delmore. "Disaster has struck. We broke a wheel not ten minutes away. Sir Walter sent me to get help. I took one of the carriage 'orses and rode 'im helter skelter here." He leaned over, one hand on the doorjamb, trying to catch his breath.

Delmore narrowed his eyes, turning to the cook. "Where would we find the nearest wainwright?"

She left her stirring spoon in her soup, her forehead creased with worry. "In the village. Do you want me to send my Jim?"

"I'll send Travers here, if he could borrow a saddle."

She wiped her hands on her apron and went through the lobby to the back door from which she yelled for her husband. After a short discussion, Merriweather escorted Travers and Delmore to the stables to pick through a number of old saddles. When Travers had replaced a girth strap on the best, Delmore saw off the groom. He discovered Jeremy in the library trying to find secret drawers in the central desk and explained the chaise problem.

Jeremy ran his hand through his hair. "This was a

dashed silly idea coming here, you know, in this weather. Now what's to do?"

"We remain undisturbed. The wheel will be repaired, and we shall decide how to transport your guests here. I see you have a landau in the stables, but not a horse other than my team."

Jeremy shrugged. "We put Uncle Bodger's horses out to pasture. Jim Merriweather will know where, but any sort of transport left in the stables is bound to be decrepit."

"Then, we will go adventuring." Strangely, Delmore's spirits lifted. Having a smaller problem to solve than that of his disappearing finances would keep his restlessness at bay for a time. His phaeton would hold no more than two extra people. A larger conveyance was needed for three ladies and gentlemen.

With Jim, the outdoorsman, he inspected the cracked seats of the landau and the ancient hood that opened after an oiling. Jim pronounced the equipage sound enough for a short trip and he dusted off the seats. Wilson hitched up Delmore's horses, which used swishing tails to express their outrage about being attached to such a decrepit rig.

"I'll go, my lord," Wilson said with a glance of disdain at the set up.

"Allow me to race to the rescue, Wilson. I rarely have a chance to be the hero. We would all be better off if you helped my brother prepare for four cold and possibly disgruntled guests. We'll want hot drinks, warm blankets and crackling fires. Between the two of you and the cook, that should be possible."

The chestnuts pulled the rig out of the coach house and onto the driveway. Once on the road, Delmore urged them to a fast trot and within ten minutes he spotted the chaise, listing to the front with the outside wheel cracked and lying on the road. Three horses stood, tails bedraggled, and heads lowered against the drizzle. Four worried people, caped with blankets and holding padded hot bricks, stood miserably by the edge of the road.

Sir Walter moved out to hail Delmore but, recognizing him, dropped his arm. "Delmore, well done," he called encouragingly. "You have come to transport us in what appears to be luxurious comfort."

Delmore smiled. "It could well be." He turned the rig a half circle, no mean feat on the narrow road, and stopped. "I presume no one is injured. No? Well, step up and I will take you to hot soup."

Sir Walter unhitched the remaining horses and tied them onto the back of the landau. The now sodden guests proceeded to Drake House.

Chapter Four

The creaking landau pulled up outside Jeremy's house, the front door of which could do with a good scraping. Resembling a large bear in his caped greatcoat, Lord Delmore, described by Sir Walter to Anna in a reverent voice as a renowned whip, had shown perfect control of his horses and the situation. His spirited steeds had snorted with affront during the short trip. To alight, Anna accepted the aid of a slim young groom dressed in a green topcoat with beige knee breeches.

One by one, the chastened party stepped out, Sir Walter clearly taken-aback by the unkempt appearance of the old greystone manor. Knowing from her previous visit that the inside matched the outside, Anna assumed the inspection would be faster than the trip, which had been pleasant until the lurch that anticipated the breaking of the wheel. Waiting by the side of the road, no one could have been more pleased to see Lord Delmore than the countess, who had shivered without the protection of the chaise.

Fortunately, the ancient landau that had scraped to the

rescue held coverlets, which somewhat insulated a person against the moisture laden weather. Anna, however, feared for her hat when she saw how Jonquil's feathers drooped.

Lord Delmore's groom held a big black umbrella over her while he escorted her to the open front door where Jeremy stood, well-sheltered, and wringing his hands with distress for his guests while the groom raced the umbrella back for Lady Carrington and Jonquil.

"Honestly, Jeremy, the situation isn't dire," Anna said to him with her hand caught under the warmth of his arm. "And won't be unless your mother's chaise can't be repaired this afternoon. We've suffered the worst, and now only require a nice warm room with a mirror to restore ourselves to our former glory."

After Lord Delmore climbed down from the driver's seat, the groom took the landau around the back of the house to the stables. Lord Delmore joined those awaiting him under the shelter over the slate step. "Nothing beats an adventure to whet the appetite." His hat sat squarely on his head and his face expressed the sort of cynical amusement she had come to expect from him. She wished the sight of him didn't cause her blood to race.

"I'm sure we will all be quite comfortable after a light repast." Lady Carrington warmed her hands under the fur collar of her pelisse.

As the Delmore household had supplied a basket of food, Anna didn't doubt all sorts of wonderful treats would soon be offered.

"Jeremy's cook has managed a good hearty soup." Lord Delmore's glance encompassed everyone. "If you can make yourselves respectable in half an hour, you can find your way to the main dining room, which I believe is one of two rooms heated today."

Lady Carrington gave Lord Delmore an affronted frown. "To imply that I look less than respectable takes a very brave man. Walter, call him out."

"Not I," said Sir Walter, holding the front door open. "I'm too hungry to aim straight. Perhaps tomorrow."

Lady Carrington glanced heavenward. "Come along, ladies. We'll leave the gentlemen to manage the situation while we make sure we are neat and tidy." She took the lead into the house, where a serving woman stood, pushing stray hairs back under her white cap.

"I'm Mrs. Merriweather, lately Mr. 'asting's 'ouse-keeper. If you would follow me?" The woman gave a quick and wobbly curtsey. "We 'ave the bedroom that used to be occupied by Mr. Bodger's wife ready for the ladies to use as a retiring room." She led the way up a curved flight of stairs into a clean but faded room dominated by a huge tester bed dressed in quilted blue satin. On a walnut dressing table under the window stood a bank of mirrors, each reflecting different parts of the room. In front, brushes had been arranged, and a flower painted dish contained hairpins.

"We shall help each other," Anna said, mainly to Jonquil, but Lady Carrington nodded, untying the ribbons of her tall, crowned hat.

Anna removed the warm shawl that covered her pelisse, noting via her reflection in the mirror that her brown bonnet was slightly more bedraggled than she had hoped. The high peak had flattened on one side. "Lady Carrington, would you accept my skills as a hairdresser?"

Lady Carrington agreed with an inclined head, removed

her pelisse, and sat on the dressing stool. "What a strange day this has been. Imagine Delmore driving that dilapidated old carriage. I swear, I never thought to see him atop a rig that was anything other than immaculate. He has always maintained his standards."

Jonquil placed her pelisse on the bed with the countess's. Her hat followed. "It was good of him to do so, but I don't understand why he didn't leave the driving to his groom," she said, her pretty blue eyes blinking with puzzlement. "I was awfully nervous when I saw he was in charge of those fractious horses."

"No need. The man drives to an inch. He's a top whip." Lady Carrington smiled patronizingly at Jonquil. "He's also a prime athlete. Almost too good to be true, as his mother says. If it weren't for his one failing, the man would be quite perfect."

"He doesn't seem at all disreputable. He's quite good looking for an older man." Jonquil frowned, perhaps pondering his one failing, which, being an innocent, she didn't query.

Nor did Anna, not sure if his one failing was his shocking ability to cause females to hope for second dangerous tempting, or his drinking. "His looks would be the secret of his success," she said with a smile, finally removing her damp brown pelisse and softened hat. The latter could, no doubt, be resurrected when the fabric dried out. "He couldn't possibly be a rake if he didn't appeal to women." She carefully removed Lady Carrington's hat, finding that the lady was examining her in the mirror. "I can tidy these curls, ma'am, or would you prefer me to twist them back?"

"Oh, I must have curls around my face. I would never wish to look severe." Lady Carrington gazed at her reflection. She wore a fussy style that suited her, being a rather spare woman otherwise, like her sister, the dowager countess. "I'm afraid I would be useless as a dresser. Miss Beeby must help you."

Anna took her place on the dressing stool. Owing to a natural curl, she didn't mind leaving the damp hair around her face to rearrange itself. The rest of her looked neat enough. She only needed to add her plaid shawl again to keep her shoulders warm and she was done. "Let me fix your hair now, Jonquil, though you look quite pretty the way you are. Here, I'll brush the tail back into the knot again, and you will be as good as new."

Each lady checked herself in the mirror. Anna laughed at the sight of them together, each as precious about their appearance as the other. "I can only hope the gentlemen are as careful with their presentation as we are."

"Don't doubt it," the countess said as she sailed out the door. "They, however, would never admit to it."

The gentlemen awaited them in the dining parlor, which was easily found by Anna because she had been in the house before. She smiled as she walked into the warmth. "Such luxury, a big crackling fire." Then she blushed, horrified that she might have revealed that the vicarage was rarely well heated other than in the vicar's study. "After travelling in the cold," she amended.

The gentlemen moved away from the fireplace, allowing the ladies to warm their hands. Anna glanced at the side table where knives and forks had been dropped in a heap. Judging by the fact that Mrs. Merriweather appeared to be the only indoor servant, and likely very much needed in the kitchen, Anna idly began making settings for each of the travelers. Naturally, the gentlemen hadn't thought to do this, but she didn't need to make a production out of acting the maid. She did this in the vicarage on most days, only glad she didn't have to cook meals. The life of a servant would be harder than anything she had ever known, and she didn't mean to contribute to making their lot worse.

Lord Delmore watched her, idly fingering his fob watch. She lowered her gaze. Even though he had kissed her, since then he had shown no interest in her other than as a neighbor. She, on the other hand, could not help but be attracted to the man. From his ruggedly handsome face to his magnificent physique, he was more male than any other gentleman she had met. His face, dominated by the provoking green of his eyes and his unwarranted eyelashes, was strong nosed and squared off by his manly jaw. Perfectly male as his features were, his lack of moral fortitude had given him a perpetual expression of vague amusement covered by cynicism. Unfortunately, this made him even more attractive to Anna.

If she had roguish dimples or a naughty smile, he might be more attracted to her, but even she knew she looked more like vicar's stepdaughter than a Cyprian. She sighed and rearranged a fork.

In no time, a tureen of soup was put on the table with fresh bread and butter, a great treat in this weather when bread took an age to rise. The countess served the soup, impressing Anna, who doubted that the countess had served soup herself before. In a pinch, and they were in a pinch, each of them could rise above it, the gentlemen feeding the fire as necessary.

Finally, the picnic basket was unpacked. A feast had been put together, wheels of cheese, stuffed boiled eggs, a leg of ham, a box of nuts, oranges, jellied eel, a spiced cake, preserves, and two bottles of wine. After the soup, Anna needed little, but she couldn't resist a walnut, which Jeremy cracked for her between his fingers. The room appeared to chill, and she glanced at the window, watching forlorn white flakes of snow drifting down. She dragged her shawl tighter around her shoulders.

Jonquil followed the direction of her gaze. "It's snowing," she said in a voice of wonder. "It hardly ever snows in late November. I hope this won't make our journey back difficult."

"You may well have to resign yourself to staying here overnight." Lord Delmore smoothed a crease from his buff wool waistcoat. "We don't yet know if the wheel of the chaise can be repaired today. We may be able to use the old landau to travel once the groom arrives back from the wainwright, but not if this snow continues. We couldn't risk another breakdown in this weather."

"In that case, we ought to preserve some of the food," Anna said in a light voice.

Jonquil frowned at Anna as if she was being willfully frivolous. "We have to go home. Mama will worry."

"Fortunately, Carrington and I are here to lend this adventure respectability." Lady Carrington served Jeremy a slice of fig and ginger cake, and then she glanced at his face. "Are any of the bedrooms prepared?"

Jeremy took his first mouthful before answering. "We

weren't expecting to stay but I imagine someone could make up a few bedrooms if needs must." He took another huge bite of his cake.

"Mrs. Merriweather would need another three sets of hands to be able to do that as well as run the kitchen without help." Anna brushed the nutshell crumbs onto her plate. "Let's pray the coach arrives back within a few hours attached to a new wheel. In the meantime, we should make ourselves cozy in the sitting room. One fire will be plenty to keep going." She heard herself organizing again and inwardly winced. She did this at home, because no one else would, but with virtual strangers she should have kept her mouth shut and let Sir Walter or Lady Carrington take the lead.

"Oh, dear," Lady Carrington said in a faint voice. "One of us will need to pack up the food in case of an emergency. Have you ever heard of such economy in all your lives?"

Anna smiled, certain Lady Carrington was being droll, but Jonquil took her words seriously. "I'll pack up the food. I have done such tasks before. Anna and I can also help in the kitchen."

"I could chop more wood," Jeremy said heroically. "Might keep me warm while I'm doing so."

"Since the lack of a nearby stream prevents me offering to catch fish," Lord Delmore said, glancing at Anna. "I expect I could be of use as a stable hand."

"We have two grooms, my lord," Anna reminded him. "You could forage for food, kill a boar or a deer, enough to feed this household for days."

His gaze hooded. "You flatter me, Anna."

Jeremy looked rueful. "I'm sure we can last a few hours

before we starve. We're in more danger of being bored to death, if we have to be holed up here."

"Do you want to risk the drive back home in the landau? I'm sure it wouldn't take more than two hours if it doesn't fall to pieces on the way." Lord Delmore toyed with the stem of his wineglass. "Better that than being left overnight with a pack of dead bores."

"You know I didn't mean that I would be bored. I simply meant that we don't have entertainment here. Should we take a vote? Who wants to try the trip back in the landau?"

"I certainly don't," Lady Carrington said, glancing at her husband. "The short trip here in that creaky old thing was bad enough. Rather a day in front of a warm fire than a marooning in the snow."

The only person who looked unsure was Jonquil.

"Right. We'll stay in this monstrosity of a house." Lord Delmore rose to his feet.

Jeremy stared at him. "Monstrosity? That's a little harsh. Better this than nothing."

Anna smiled wryly. Unlike her, Jeremy, of course, would never have nothing. As well as this small estate, he had the lands and income allowed to a second son. However, a second son with a small estate, the use of a town house whenever he pleased, and his own stable was certainly well placed.

After showing his brother a pair of autocratic eyebrows, Lord Delmore moved over to hold Lady Carrington's chair while she arose. Then he offered his arm to escort her into the sitting room.

Anna and Jonquil packed the leftover food into the basket.

"You don't think we shall really be forced to stay in this horrible old house overnight, do you?" Jonquil asked in a whisper.

"I have no idea, but what would it matter, other than not having our night attire handy? But fear not. The snow is sure to stop long before tonight. Someone can ride to the nearest village and hire a carriage if need be. Failing that, a rider could return to Hastings House and fetch another form of transport. We are not stranded miles from the nearest civilization, you know. Maldon is no more than a mile away."

"And Lord and Lady Carrington are here to chaperone us, after all." Jonquil laughed nervously.

"If they were not here, the situation would be rather more awkward." Anna carried the food into the kitchen. Reprehensible as her thought was, the idea of having a whole day and night to spar companionably with Lord Delmore would be enough to keep her smiling for days.

The gentlemen arose to their feet when she and Jonquil joined the others in the sitting room. "Since we've nothing better to do, shall I take you on a tour of the house?" Jeremy asked glancing at his brother.

"Excellent idea, old chap. Is the place haunted?" Lord Delmore glanced sideways at Jonquil, whose eyes rounded.

"Naughty boy." Lady Carrington rose to her feet and pulled her shawl tighter. "See, you have frightened Jonquil, Delmore. Of course, the place is not haunted. We should be gazing around and giving Jeremy advice as to the refurbishment. I might have liked a tour of the gardens, but we ill-advisedly chose the wrong weather. Miss Winters? You have already seen the place, have you not?"

Anna nodded.

"In that case, we'll leave you here in the warmth. Delmore, you shall stay with her. We can't all go trooping off and leave her alone. You can see the place any time you wish."

Lord Delmore offered Anna eyebrows comically tilted in alarm, which she accepted with an outward show of resignation, inwardly delighted to be left with him. His fine looks were not the only thing about him that stimulated her. She enjoyed his sardonic humor and the way he tried, and failed, to bait her. "The house will be quite delightful once it is dusted and polished," she said, repeating the same words she had offered to Jeremy a few weeks ago during her first visit.

"I think it may need more refurbishment than that." Lord Delmore opened the bottom buttons of his coat and leaned back in a puce velvet armchair, placing his elegant hands-on armrests worn by fifty years of grasping.

Anna shrugged. Any woman who became the mistress of this house would change the curtains first. The blue velvet had faded to ivory in the sections most exposed to the sunlight. "I'm sure Lady Delmore will have myriad ideas. Do you think there is a real chance of us being snowed in?"

"None of us has anything better to do than idle away here for days."

"Speak for yourself. We are not all dilettantes."

"You have no good opinion of me, do you?" He stretched out his long legs, meshed his fingers across his flat belly.

She tried to ignore the ironic tilt of his mouth. "On the contrary. My opinion of you is very favorable. You have certainly treated me with more civility than I could have imagined. No earl has kissed me in a stream before. And you are very kind to allow Jeremy to live in your house when he has one of his own. He stays because he thinks your mother depends on him. He knows she doesn't want to live here. Your house is far grander."

"So, I need to speak to the vicar's daughter to learn the wherewithal of my own family, do I?" His expression hooded.

"Perhaps if you spent more time at home and less gallivanting around with opera singers you would see for yourself."

"Do you realize you are an annoying woman?"

"That's right. Attack me for telling you the truth." She lifted her chin.

"I could strangle you, but I would far rather do something else entirely to you." He shook his head as if impatient with himself and thrummed one finger on the chair arm.

"Drown me in the stream?" she asked in a hopeful voice. Her imagination had run wild wondering what the something else might be. "Or kiss me again?"

"Kiss you?" he said, momentarily drawing his eyebrows together. "That's the very least of it."

"What's the most?" She almost breathed the words.

He threaded his fingers across his flat belly, staring down at his hands. His head lifted and his voice softened. "The usual. I want you, which you apparently know, but you are respectable, which you also know."

She needed to study a knot on the fringe of her shawl. "That is not true. Since you kissed me in the stream, I have had all sorts of far from respectable thoughts."

"And what exactly do you mean by that?" His gaze met and held hers.

"I would rather have an hour of pleasure than a lifetime of regret." Her heart thumped loudly enough to hear. No other man had tempted her to speak so freely, nor tempted her to think about her own wants.

"Pleasure?" His lips curved with a cynical smile. "Who is to say you shouldn't have a lifetime of pleasure?"

She glanced down again, unable to hold his gaze. "A lifetime of pleasure is not on the cards for me. In little over a month, I'm off to the city to be Jonquil's companion. I will be watching her enjoy the season I would have wished for myself. I will be watching her bat off suitors who wouldn't have looked twice at me. You may be surprised to hear, my lord, that you are the only man who has kissed me in my whole life."

"In that case, Jeremy is a fool."

"I'm a friend to Jeremy. He doesn't see me as a woman but a good-natured sounding board."

"I should succumb to your blandishments, Anna, but I can't do that to you."

"Because you must save me from myself?" She offered a wry smile.

His jaw tightened. "You don't know what you are saying. We should not be having this conversation."

"How do you usually choose your next mistress?" she asked in an interested voice. "Do you knock on her front door and make her an offer? Or do you meet in a stream and kiss her first?"

"We should not be having this conversation, either. There is only one woman I have kissed in a stream, and if I'd been entirely sober, I never would have kissed her. Ten to one, being in the vicar's part of the stream, she would have been respectable, and I had no business doing so."

"Alas, now she is no longer respectable." She creased her face and wrung her hands, if clasping them together could be described as wringing. She willed her voice to crack. "You have ruined her."

"You are greatly exaggerating, my girl," he said grimly. "If you are no longer respectable that's none of my doing."

"You put ideas in my head. Ideas I had never previously considered." She tried a tragic expression, trying not to smile, but the truth was that she was now considering an idea that ought to have shocked her.

He stared narrow-eyed at her for at least half a minute until he heaved a long-suffering sigh. "I see. This is a mighty heavy-handed application for the job as my mistress. You'll need to do better than that namby-pamby wronged-woman act. I engage only spirited mistresses. I don't have the patience to repair hurt feelings."

"Tch tch. If you are planning on being a bully, I'll rescind my application. I don't mistress for men with no sensitivity."

He gave a satisfied smile. "So, we don't suit."

"Apparently not. I can see I'll have to try another tack if I still want the job."

"You don't. I have it on the highest authority that I am

a selfish brute, that I have no use for women other than in my bed. I have no sensitivity whatsoever."

She considered, while her whole body thrummed. "You certainly know how to kiss, though."

"Anna, this will not happen. My brother would be devastated if I took up with you. As for my mother, she would disown me."

"She would be thrilled. She has never approved of me. For all I know the only reason Jeremy has continued to see me is because of that. He is completely loyal to those he calls his friends."

"My mother doesn't disapprove of you." He stared at her.

She shook her head. "She barely acknowledges my existence. She made sure of Jonquil joining this party and you as well. Neither of you need to be here. You might be colluding with her to lure me away from Jeremy for all I know."

"Not a minute ago, you told me you have no serious intentions toward him."

"Your mother doesn't believe that. She hasn't directly spoken to me in years. Haven't you noticed?"

"As a matter of fact, no."

"She would be delighted if you set me up as your mistress for then she would be rid of me for all time."

He frowned. "You forget. I can't set you up as my mistress, not when you are about to join society as your sister's companion."

Her heart fluttered. He appeared to be finding reasons not to consider her proposal rather than simply saying she didn't appeal to him. "I don't expect our association will last so long. I suspect you will forget me the moment you get back to town."

"Oh. You mean to be my country mistress."

"After you return to the city, I must go on with my life. First, I need to see Jonquil suitably married and then I'll settle down to be my mother's old age comfort if I can't find a gentleman farmer who might take me on."

"You would be better off married to Jeremy."

"Don't you understand? He has no intention of asking me and if he did, he would be ruined in the eyes of society. Doing that to someone I don't love is lowering, worse than staying to look after my mother and my stepfather. I couldn't do it. But I want something first, a taste of what life really is."

One of his shoulders lifted and dropped. "Your season in town might be the very thing, you know."

"You couldn't bring yourself to make love to me?"

"Not this way, Anna. I couldn't take you as my mistress even for an hour."

"What about as your lover?"

"The thought causes a certain stirring, but I am convinced this whole conversation was started to find out how disreputable I really am."

"Not exactly, but I did learn something."

"Do you plan to share your knowledge?"

"No, my lord. The essence of attack is surprise."

The expression in his eyes had softened and he looked so young and handsome, so joyful, that something inside her chest expanded. Her heart almost stopped. This man could very well be her everything if he could forget his scruples for a while. His shoulders were broad enough to carry the problems of the world without flinching. If he lost his youth and looks, he would still be the interesting and exciting man he was.

He and she shared the sort of rapport she hadn't experienced with another. Doomed as she was to spinsterhood or a marriage her mother would consider beneath her, she had mourned the lack of a kindred companion. Most people stared, trying to work out if what she said was ingenuous or ingenious and apparently concluded she was the social misfit they expected. Had this man been portly, older, and possessed of a modest income, she could have made a go of it with him.

He rose and took a poker to the fire without glancing at her. Voices echoed from outside. "Our merry band has returned and none too soon." He placed the poker back on the stand without glancing at her. "I was beginning to think we needed a chaperone."

"Not at all," she said, trying to quell her longing. "You warded me off beautifully. No doubt you've had practice."

The door opened a crick and his groom's head appeared. "S'cuse me, milord. Might I have word with you."

"Come in, Wilson," Lord Delmore said with impatience. "You're letting in a draught."

The rest of the man appeared but he remained with his back against the door. "Travers has arrived back from the village. The wheel can't be done today on account'a the wheelwright not wantin' to drive all the way out there while it's snowing," he said defensively. He took a deep breath. "And 'e fell off 'is horse and discombobulated his shoulder. I told him you could fix it."

"The disobliging wheelwright fell off his horse and he expects me to fix his shoulder?"

"No, Travers fell off the carriage horse that 'e were riding," the man said, frowning. "He's in the kitchen."

"Travers, not the horse," Anna put in.

Lord Delmore gave her a glance of overdone patience. He fingered his earlobe. "I can try with the shoulder, but it won't work if he has broken it. I'll need you to steady him while I pull his arm."

"You're surely not going to pull on the poor man's arm?" Anna covered her cheeks with her palms, sympathy for the groom turning her blood cold.

Lord Delmore turned to her. "If he has knocked the joint out of place, I have done so before with success."

"Let's go, then."

"Not you, Miss Winters. This is a job for a person with a strong stomach."

"And for a person with a kind heart. The least I can do for the poor man is make him a comforting posset."

"Lead the way, Wilson. I warn you Anna, if you show a sign of fainting, you will be left where you lie. We won't have time to coddle you."

"Such a shame. I'm due a very fine coddling," she said in an undertone.

He turned his leaf green eyes on her and heaved a breath, wisely saying nothing.

The warmth of the kitchen was overpowering compared to the draughty sitting room. Mrs. Merriweather curtseyed when she spotted Lord Delmore. "Good of you to come, my lord."

Lord Delmore turned to the cadaverous brown-haired

man sitting on a kitchen chair, and cupping his elbow in his hand, his face a picture of misery. Even his side-whiskers drooped.

Travers tried to smile at his supposed rescuer. "Won't want no ladies in here if you are about to twist me arm." He dragged in breath. "Might be a small amount of bad language."

"Make sure there's not," Lord Delmore answered in a severe tone. "Let me see what the problem is." He gently prodded the arm from the elbow to the shoulder, prodding more around the shoulder than the arm, which looked out of place, lumpish at the top. "Perhaps Miss Winters would start brewing a posset for you. She won't want to watch this."

"I suspect I'll be more use at the moment seeing to Travers' comfort."

Lord Delmore took Travers' lower arm and lifted. "Be brave, man," he said when Travers groaned. "As long as you don't have too much swelling, a small amount of pain now will save you a greater amount of pain later." He lifted the wrist level to the man's shoulder and pulled.

Travers made the sound of an animal caught in a trap. His face turned a deathly shade of white. He closed his eyes and then he breathed out. The silence in the room expanded. Finally, blue around the lips, he stared at Lord Delmore. "I think you done it, my lord," he said in a reedy voice. He glanced at his shoulder that no longer looked stiff and strange.

"Can you move your hand? Do you feel me do this?" Lord Delmore pressed his fingers into the man's flesh all the way up his arm.

Travers nodded. "Yes, I think you done it. My thanks to you, my lord." With that, Travers fainted.

"Now is the time to prepare a posset," Lord Delmore said with a wry glance at Anna. "Wilson, while he is out, make a sling for his arm. I'm sure the Merriweathers will find room for you both in their cottage." He left the room.

"Never seen that done before," Mrs. Merriweather said breathlessly. "You go on back to your fire, Miss. I'll make the posset."

"Do you have a spare room in your cottage, Mrs. Merriweather?"

"We'll make room for 'im and Mr. Wilson. It won't do for them to sleep in the stables, not tonight. Snow looks fit to last a while yet."

"That's very generous of you, Mrs. Merriweather." Anna followed Lord Delmore into the sitting room. "You are a miracle worker, my lord."

"I've had occasion to do that once or twice before on the hunting field. I've seen the harm that can happen if it's not done as soon as possible. The muscles tighten and the arm is lost forever. One minute of pain is better than a useless arm."

"I expect you can use that analogy for other situations as well. Best to dampen the hopes of a woman who wants you rather than let her dangle in suspense for weeks, imagining that you might want her."

He crossed his arms over his chest. "Or another analogy would be to shock a man by propositioning him, without warning, rather than hoping he will proposition you."

She heaved a sigh. "Do you think you would have?"

"Not when I discovered who you were," he said, shaking his head.

"But you are considering it now?"

Before he could answer, Lady Carrington sailed into the room, followed by Jonquil and the gentlemen. "A very satisfactory inspection. All of the furniture needs reupholstering and all the curtains replaced, but Sir Walter found no woodworm and Miss Beeby found no ghosts."

Jeremy chortled. "Ghosts are far more likely to haunt the house after midnight."

"According to the ghosts' manual?" Lord Delmore asked. "Did you find the bedrooms in order? From all appearances, the snowfall is increasing."

Jeremy's forehead wrinkled. "It won't be at all comfortable if we have to stay here overnight."

"That question has been answered. Travers arrived back with a word or two from the wheelwright. The snow is too heavy for him to come out and attach the wheel, though likely he can't fix it before dark, anyway."

"That's torn it." Jeremy clapped his palm on his head, glancing wryly at Anna.

The countess rustled her gown over to the chair closest to the fire and sat. "None of the beds are made up," she said dolefully. "And the sheets haven't been aired in a year. And with the way we are situated, I suspect we'll have to sleep the gentlemen in one room and the ladies in another. Chaperonage, you see."

"Lord Delmore was just saying the same thing to me." Anna shot a sideways glance at London's most fascinatingly elusive earl. "Chaperonage is rather more important to him. It wouldn't do for him to be in any way compromised."

"Oh, I would wriggle my way out of it somehow, Anna. A lady might not have as easy a task. My reputation protects me but endangers her."

"Tosh," Jeremy said. "No one would ever suspect the lady of putting a foot out of place. If you were speaking of Anna." He queried Lord Delmore with his gaze.

"Not specifically, no. In general, yes. We have two single gentlemen here and two single ladies. We need to make sure our behavior is circumspect."

Chapter Five

Anna Winters puzzled Delmore. The woman was a delight and she had completely outfaced him. He liked nothing better than verbal sparring. Few of his mistresses had talents other than in the bedroom. Truth to tell, once the deed was done, he rarely saw the need to stay and gossip. Anna's charms didn't rely on her face or her body, but her fascinating mind. Had she been a courtesan, he wouldn't have waited for her to make an offer. She would have been in his arms and his bed by now.

An illicit association between them was, of course, out of the question. She was gently born; unquestionably a lady, the sort of woman who could run a household and a clutch of servants without resorting to complaints and tantrums. Although he had come to believe his mother wouldn't countenance a match between Anna and his brother, he didn't quite credit that she was unmarriageable. An enchanting woman like her would never be left to remain on the shelf. Once she hit London, she would soon see that. She would captivate everyone she met, the way she had him. At this stage, he could not consider stepping in and taking her as his mistress, no matter how much the idea of bedding her appealed to him.

Dissolute he might be, but not lost to all decency.

He had enough experience to ward her off, but temptation sat on his shoulder, urging him to stay within her reach. Rubbing the back of his neck, he turned to his brother. "Added to the problem is that Travers dislocated his shoulder. We are now one groom short."

Anna's face creased with sympathy. "I believe the ill-fitting saddle slipped and he fell. Lord Delmore put the bone back in place not ten minutes ago, but I'm sure it will still ache for some time, poor man."

Jeremy blinked at her. "I'm very sorry to hear that one of my mother's grooms is in a fix. Wilson will need to take over from him in the stables."

"He already has my two to look after." Delmore said, slightly surprised by Jeremy's edict. "I'll give him a hand if need be. I can't say I'm booked for a cotillion tonight."

Jeremy had the grace to look abashed. "We're cutting it fine for an overnight stay here. We have no one to prepare the bedrooms for us, either. Not if we need to keep Mrs. Merriweather in the kitchen."

"How many would be fit for occupancy?" Delmore dropped another log on the fire, watching the sparks fly up the chimney.

"Well, two. Aunt Bodger's bedroom and Bodger's. He didn't waste money on the others because he never had guests. As her ladyship said, the bed coverings are in poor condition."

"And my love." Sir Walter turned to his wife. "I will not

be shoved into a bedroom with these two young bucks. Likely they would snore the tiles off the roof."

"I wouldn't wish to burden them with you, my dear husband. Your own snoring must only be borne by one who loves you."

"In that case," Sir Walter said in a satisfied voice, "I will sleep with my lady love in one of the bedrooms and the ladies will use the other. As a punishment for putting us in this predicament, Delmore and Jeremy shall sleep in the stables."

"With six incontinent horses? If you don't mind, uncle, I will occupy the couch in this room." Delmore glanced repressively at Sir Walter.

Jeremy frowned. "None of these other dashed chairs are big enough to hold me."

"We could put two of the armchairs together," Delmore suggested, stony faced, hoping he sounded serious.

Jeremy's face lit with indignation. "I would have to sleep sitting up."

"I'm sure you have done so before."

"Not intentionally." Jeremy's face relaxed. "But if I had Temple to tell me about his last trip to Brighton and how he took every bend in the road, I would nod off in an instant. But there's a leather couch in the library that should suit me rather well."

"You didn't show us the library, Jeremy," Jonquil said sounding wistful. "Is it stocked?"

"It's full of dusty old books, if that's what you mean."

"Books. Dear me. Being the expert on wines that I am, I think I ought to check your cellar." Sir Walter brushed the front of his jacket with his hand, as if smartening up for an inspection. "If we are about to spend the night here, we'll want to remain jolly. I'll warrant Bodger-the-codger kept himself well supplied."

"Go ahead, Uncle. Jonquil, if you want to choose a book now is the time."

"I don't see anything else to do."

Anna stared after her sister as she wandered off. "I expect we'll want supper tonight. I think I ought to confer with Mrs. Merriweather as to what we might find to eat."

"As long as she has eggs, we'll be right and tight. I have a light hand with a soufflé, if need be," Aunt Carrington said, surprising Delmore, who hadn't imagined the lady could cook. "I expect Mrs. Merriweather has a hen house if we want a chicken or two, but I'm hoping that the remains in the picnic basket will be enough to satisfy us for tonight."

Jeremy sighed. "I might see if I can find an interesting book, too." He left and while the ladies discussed food, Delmore watched the snow add a layer to the carriage sweep. Perhaps he had been selfish to reserve the only heated room for the night, but he couldn't see any of the others sleeping on the dilapidated couch. By morning, when they awoke and wanted a warm room to sit in, he would be in the stables checking the horses. If he could get the late Mr. Bodger's old creaker greased and oiled, and if the snow eased up, they could leave tomorrow. Then he could send someone from Delmore House to repair and collect the chaise from the roadside. As a last resort he could take his phaeton back to Delmore House and have a carriage sent to get the rest of the party.

Anna and the countess disappeared while he was mentally exploring all other options. The door opened.

Jeremy and Jonquil returned, the latter's face expressing glee. "We found a game of spillikins and a pack of cards. That's better than a book any day." She settled on a chair beside the card table. Jeremy sat opposite.

"Don't tell me you two are playing old maid." Delmore placed his hands on his hips.

"Haven't played for years," Jeremy answered defensively. "I can hardly fleece Jonquil while she is my guest."

"Aside from that, I don't have any money." She examined her cards.

Delmore needed to see how Travers had settled in. First, he made his way to the cellar where his uncle stood, his eyeglass trained on the label of a bottle with a moth-eaten label. "Chambertin. He has two dozen here. I'm sure he can spare a couple to me."

"I doubt he knows what he has, but do you see any brandy?"

His uncle took two steps and retrieved a dusty bottle he had put aside. "Don't drink it all, my lad. I wouldn't mind a drop or two of this one myself."

"I'm taking it to the groom who dislocated his shoulder. I want him to sleep well tonight. Tomorrow is bound to be a long and hard day."

"Good idea, but if it's sleeping he means to do, he'll want something easier to toss down." Carrington plucked a bottle out of a higher rack and went back to examining labels.

Clutching the bottle by the neck, Delmore strolled back through the kitchen where his aunt was picking through shelves in a corner cupboard. "Do you have any vanilla?"

she called to Mrs. Merriweather who was pounding pastry on the central table.

"There's a jar of pods on the top shelf. Yes, that side, my lady."

Delmore stood in front of the frazzled cook. "If you don't mind me visiting your cottage, I'll check on Travers," he said to her, as she wiped her hot face with her floury wrist.

She appeared dazed. "Please do, my lord. Take a weatherproof from the lobby. The cottage is just past the stables."

Ignoring her advice, he trudged outside, past the high stone-wall of the stables, inside which horses clattered around, blowing out pleasant horsey sounds of satisfaction. Wilson now had six to manage when he normally had the aid of two other grooms and a stable boy—no holiday for him while they were stranded on this derelict property. Delmore knocked on the door of the cottage and entered the three-room dwelling.

The small front parlor had been hastily furnished with two truckle beds pushed up against a couple of saggy chairs, and a set of drawers holding large pot of sprouting greenery, no doubt an experiment pulled from the garden. Anna stood by Travers who sat on one bed, nursing his wrist. "My lord." He started to rise to his feet.

Carefully evading Anna's enquiring gaze, Delmore lightly rested his hand on the man's uninjured shoulder, preventing him from standing. "I expect it's aching like the devil," he said, sympathetically. "I thought a bottle of brandy would help." He glanced at the label surprised that he hadn't given a thought to brandy for himself. Not since lunch had he taken a drink. Anna had diverted him from his usual course.

The man's face brightened. "Very generous of you, my lord, though Miss Winters has made me more comfortable with this here sling."

"That is very good of you, Miss Winters. Should I suspect you're not too handy in the kitchen?"

"I'm handier in the kitchen than with slings, but he didn't look at all comfortable after Wilson had dealt with him. The brandy will help, no doubt."

"Share a little with Wilson, would you, Travers?"

"Certainly, my lord. Though if the countess, your mother, hears of it ..."

"She won't. In the meantime, rest. We'll work out how to get you back safely tomorrow after we've all had a good night's sleep."

Anna glanced at him, her skin porcelain perfect in the late afternoon gloom. "Since I'm needed here no longer, I shall now be helpful in the kitchen." After the last word, her mouth pursed. He dropped the idea of keeping her at a distance. One kiss should satisfy him—but no more than that, for he hadn't yet stifled his last ounce of decency. Three or four brandies should dull his need for her.

His shoulders relaxing, Delmore inclined his head and held the door open for her. He could ease his surprising need to hold her close before he drank himself into his normal state of inebriety. With the house filled with four family members and a servant or two, he shouldn't be alone with her, but he wanted to let her know that his rejection of her hadn't been easy. A brief moment with the delightful creature would go a long way toward appeasing his unusual restlessness and the slow ache of his desire. Unfortunately, his best option for privacy was with six horses and a groom. The last, he could easily dispense with a high-handed order.

"Would you care to inspect the stables with me?" he said, noting the soft pink of her cheeks and the way the light turned the blue of her eyes to silver.

"I'm not at all handy in the stables." She looked puzzled.

Each time he glanced at her, he saw more: the humor expressed by her arching eyebrows, the intelligence in her eyes, the slight hint of a dimple in her chin, and the soft sensuousness of her lips. Clearly the current situation brought out the romantic in him.

"I think you might let me be the judge of that," he said, gazing at her while he guided her toward the main stable entrance.

He leaned against the smaller of the doors. The stench of horse was decidedly unromantic, and he saw the error of his ways when she pinched her nostrils with her hand.

"You'll soon get used to the smell." He smiled and reached out to touch her soft hair.

She stood, staring at him. "Doubtless, were I to be at all interested in horses, but apart from seeing them from behind while they pull a conveyance, I have little experience of them."

"You don't ride?"

"I don't possess a horse, my lord. The only riding horse in the family belongs to my stepfather. Our stable boy takes care of her along with the single horse that pulls Mr. Beeby's trap which, occasionally, the ladies of the house are permitted to use."

"You don't live a life of luxury, do you? Beeby sounds like a rare old miser."

"If it isn't for his comfort, he sees no need for it. One might have thought my mother could have influenced him for the better, but instead she goes along with his whims. Not for me, that sort of marriage. I'm not saying women should be equal, but I do think we should be equally considered."

"I think I should kiss you to show that I am equally considering you."

"You turned my remarks to your benefit very quickly. This points to you having a lot of experience—"

He cut her words short. Barely inside the door, which was still chinked open, he caught her into his arms. He stared down at her to make sure of her willingness, saw no objection, and eased her against his body, his hands on her waist and his gaze on hers. With aching slowness, he lowered his mouth to hers.

She caught her breath and slid her hands up his chest to his shoulders, standing on tiptoes so that her body pressed full length against his. His body hardened and heated and the kiss went deeper. She shifted her fingers into the hair on the back of his head, and his mouth opened over hers.

A cough sounded from behind him. "Scuse, me, my lord. I think Travers might need my attention."

Anna pulled back, breathing heavily, her face pink with embarrassment.

"Quite right," Delmore said and waited until the door closed behind Wilson before taking Anna into a close hold. "Where were we?"

"Where we shouldn't be." She leaned back, her palms hard against his upper chest. "Not at this time."

"Perhaps not, but surely we can take a few minutes of pleasure for ourselves." He examined her expression.

"Although I would be glad if you pleasured me, my first place of choice isn't in the stables. I rather thought you might have a luxurious boudoir, with red velvet curtains and a fur rug."

"I do, naturally, but I didn't bring them with me this trip. The best I can offer you at this time is a furtive roll in the hay." He winced, doubting she would find that amusing. Fortunately, she had given him time to think. A kiss or two wouldn't do him. Not at all. He wanted more and she said she did too. Where would be the harm? He needed to think. "You must stop propositioning gentlemen. Someday, one will take you seriously."

"I wish you would, for I am serious. There is no point in kissing if it leads nowhere."

"Let's be content with kissing for the time being, shall we?"

"I can't when there is so much else to do. You may be able to stand in a stable dallying in the middle of a snowstorm, but I need to make up beds and prepare food. We have servants to think of as well as ourselves, you know. We put them in this predicament, and we shouldn't be leaving them to get us out of it."

"You are quite right." He straightened, narrowing his gaze on her. "One more kiss will give me the motivation to muck out some of these stalls and work my way back into Wilson's good graces."

She relaxed. "One more?"

"One more." This time he didn't hold her body so close to him. He savored her lips and enjoyed the fact that her breathing sped up. He didn't enjoy his own body's reaction when he knew he could go no farther, but after no more than a minute or two, he dropped his hold on her. For a moment she didn't appear to notice and then she sagged just a little, which he appreciated was an equal reluctance to stop the kiss. "Back to housework for you, and stable work for me."

She raised a hand to his cheek while staring right into his eyes. "Thank you for not trying to change my mind."

"What would be the point when you are right?" He turned. The slip of her heels told him she left.

He forked straw out of an empty stall and was about to toss in new bedding when Wilson arrived back. "Not a word," he said to his groom.

Wilson smiled dourly and nodded. Side by side master and man cleaned and refreshed the stalls that would house the restive chaise team.

Anna found she quite enjoyed being marooned. At home, likely she would have been doing the same work as here, only slightly more efficiently because she knew where to find the ingredients and utensils needed. Not so the baroness. She acted like a woman with a new lease of life, making suggestions about food that might please the others.

"Plenty of ham here, ma'am." Mrs. Merriweather

looked puzzled. "With bread and cheese, that would make a mighty fine supper."

"But boiled eggs chopped with chives and parsley would be a treat with the bread, wouldn't it?"

"Yes ma'am. But you could feed an army with the remains of that fruitcake."

"What about tomorrow, then?"

Mrs. Merriweather frowned about food being wanted for tomorrow. "Likely the snow will have stopped, and Mr. Wheelwright will have your wheel ready."

"We need to be prepared for a siege," Lady Carrington announced in a hearty voice. "I haven't had such an adventure since '94 when the ..." She glanced quickly at Anna and swallowed the rest of her words. "We were rather nervous in those days, not knowing if civil war might break out."

Anna offered a blank smile. She had decided long ago not to react whenever the subject was mentioned, and so far, she had been left in peace. She hadn't even met her father, and yet his deeds followed her wherever she went. But for him, she would be marriageable. "Before I was born, my lady. I'm sorry you were frightened."

The baroness evaded her gaze. "A storm in a teacup, as it happened. I think I should put a fresh cloth on the supper table now. Will this one fit, Mrs. Merriweather?" She pulled out the top one from the napery chest.

"They all fit, my lady." Mrs. Merriweather concentrated on her bread dough. Tonight, this would be left to rise in the warmth of the kitchen to bake for breakfast. "You have lap napkins there should you want some, too."

The baroness gathered up an armload of napery and left after a guilty glance at Anna.

"Don't know why she thinks everyone will want sweet omelets, not when there's enough sugar in that cake of Lady 'astings' to keep everyone awake for hours," Mrs. Merriweather muttered.

"She is used to partaking of larger meals later into the night. She doesn't live the country lifestyle the way we do, Mrs. Merriweather. I think everyone will appreciate the fact that she thought to feed them, don't you?"

"If you say so, Miss. No doubt, I couldn't manage to cook for us all, me not being a cook but an 'ousekeeper."

"The snowstorm was badly timed. Doubtless, we will be able to leave you in peace in the morning." Anna cut the ham thinly, slice after slice, making sure none overlapped another too far. Then she made curled pats of butter and piled them high on a dish.

Mrs. Merriweather set out a board for the cheese, and flower painted pots for various pickles, which Anna filled with supplies from the larder. How old these may have been she couldn't tell. "Do you mind if I take a box of these candles, Mrs. Merriweather?" she asked when the baroness arrived back to fluff up her eggs. The rest of the meal sat ready to present.

Given permission, she pressed the candles into the holders in the dining parlor. She saw more holders in the old dresser in the sitting room, and she filled each one. Later they would need the candlesticks to light them to their rooms. She and Jonquil found a chest of sheets in the hall. Also accustomed to this job, they shook out the sheets to air them and made up the beds in the rooms, speculating about whether Lord Delmore and Jeremy would want sheeting. Jeremy had decided to sleep on the library couch.

Deciding that feather quilts would do the two, Anna huffed a bundle into each room, leaving the options on a chair.

By six, the stranded party sat down to a simple but tasty meal, completed by the sweet fluffy omelets, which had used up Mrs. Merriweather's whole supply of eggs. "Made by the fair hands of the baroness," Anna said as she passed the dish.

"My love." Sir Walter stared at his wife in amazement. "Had I realized your culinary talents I would have put you to work in the kitchens at Fairways."

"Later tonight, you may wish you hadn't said that," his wife answered sweetly, as she bit into her delicate concoction.

Finally, everyone sat back, replete. "Who's for a game of whist?" Jeremy asked as the party prepared to leave the table.

The baroness glanced at him, but Sir Walter took her arm. "Let the young people play. We can sit and doze by the fire. You may like to taste the Chambertin I found in the cellars."

"I would rather taste a sherry."

"There is no accounting for some people, but you shall have your wish, my dear. I brought a bottle of sherry from the cellars too; in case I couldn't please you with the Chambertin. Delmore, you'll have a Chambertin, will you?"

"Thank you."

"Jeremy?"

"Sherry for me too. Anna?"

"A small glass."

"Are you not planning to offer sherry to me, too, Jeremy?" Jonquil sounded put out.

"Would your mama approve?"

Jonquil gave a loud sigh. "I'm about to make my come out. I'll be offered ratafia everywhere in a month or more. Does that answer your question?"

Jeremy raised his eyebrows and poured four glasses of sherry. He passed the first to the baroness. Lord Delmore poured himself a wine, a very full one, and placed it on the card table, ready for a game of whist.

Anna's gaze met Jonquil's and with shared amusement, they sat opposite each other for the first game, winning the first hand. "We play this at home all the time," Anna explained when Jeremy expressed surprise.

"I'll have you for my partner next. Delmore let me down very badly."

Delmore did not react to his brother's competitiveness. Next, he took Jonquil as his partner. They won the following game but Anna didn't let Jeremy down. He was the least skilled player though his enthusiasm was unmatched. The third game was won by Delmore and Anna. She stood, stretching, and walked over to the fire. "I'm not used to sitting so long in one place."

"What do you normally do during the evening?" Delmore asked, pulling out his chair and standing. He refilled his glass to the brim again and walked over to the window through which he gazed out into the darkening night.

"I attend to the household accounts. You might think my mother should, but she is tired after helping my stepfather with the parish business and likes to attend to her own letter writing or embroidery in peace. Then there is always a pile of mending, and of course the bread dough. I'm up and down the whole time. The servants arise early in the morning to lay the fires. I make sure of enough spills, and enough candles. Is my list long enough to show I am not usually so idle?"

He turned to sit on the windowsill. "More than enough. And Jonquil, what do you do?"

Jonquil made a face of dissatisfaction. "I'm learning the harp of all things. And embroidery, and everything a lady need to know to run a household, including how to make soap and candles."

"Our mother is a lady. Does she know how to make soap and candles?" Jeremy asked Delmore.

"I expect so, though why she would is a mystery to me."

"A woman should be able to do anything around the house that needs doing," Jonquil said with an annoyingly pious expression on her face because she was simply repeating Anna's mother's words to her.

"Do you know how to make soap and candles?" Jeremy asked Lady Carrington.

"In theory, yes, but I can't play the harp and sing like an angel the way Miss Beeby does. I must have other talents. What talents do I have, my love?" She poked her husband in the ribs.

He almost lost his grip on the stem of his glass, through which he was peering to admire the color of the wine. "Many. Too many to enumerate. You are a very skilled woman and I bless the day I found you."

Delmore grinned. When he did, he looked young and charming, so very appealing to Anna who found that whenever his gaze caught hers, her belly constricted, causing a delightful clutch lower down. She wanted him so badly that she ached, but she couldn't marry him, and he would never ask her, any more than Jeremy would. Surely a night or two in his bed wouldn't be too much to ask after twenty-four years of spotless virtue and a loveless life ahead.

Delmore's lips said no but his body said yes. She couldn't deny she knew the cause of the rising in his breeches, and she wouldn't be unlucky enough to start a baby her first time. No one did, according to Morag. Beware the second time, she'd said fiercely because she thought Anna had her first time a few years ago with Jeremy. No matter how often she said she hadn't, Morag persisted. Jeremy won't marry you. He knows about your father. At that stage, Anna hadn't but Morag enlightened her. That was the day when she understood Jeremy's mother's aversion to her. Lady Delmore was frightened Jeremy would ruin himself with an unacceptable wife.

Anna had made sure from that day forward of never encouraging Jeremy: of treating him how a sister might. They remained firm friends, but he knew she saw him as no more than that. Fortunately, she could never be Delmore's friend, which would make being his lover so perfectly transient; lover one moment, aloof neighbor the next.

A sudden burst of laughter broke into her musings. Jonquil had started a game of spillikins, and Jeremy had knocked half the spills onto the floor. "My win," she said, her face a picture of innocent young mischief.

"You've probably playing this for years while I've had other kittens to fry, fish to fry I mean. Here, let me set them up this time."

"Oh no. A man who fries kittens should be outside with the other kitten fryers in the snow." Jonquil held the spillikins out of his reach. Anna had never seen her step-sister as animated before.

"I meant to say other fish to fry, and you know it. Afraid of being beaten, are you?"

"No one beats me at spillikins. No one at home has the patience to play."

"We're all far too old here," Delmore said in a cynical voice from his position on the other side of the room. He twirled the stem of his glass. "I'm not sure of the last time I played. Shall we join them, Anna?" He scoffed his wine and then poured another for himself and Sir Walter.

For a man who hadn't played for years, Delmore showed a great amount of style. He won, of course. His concentration was the steadiest despite his heavy drinking. Jonquil kept giggling, which normally annoyed Anna but tonight she enjoyed seeing the younger woman happy. Jonquil too often sulked. Tonight, she was on her best behavior, strange when the night ahead was bound to be uncomfortable, and the next day even worse if they couldn't have the chaise repaired, or if the snow continued to fall.

Finally, Sir Walter emptied the last few inches of wine from the last bottle into his own glass. He leaned back, his fingers clasped across his belly, glancing at the countess who sat perfectly upright on the couch beside him, her chin on her chest and her eyes closed. He nudged her awake. "Per-haps we can persuade these young people to make a night of it and then we can toddle off to bed, my dear."

She blinked twice, her forehead creasing. "Of course. Come along, young ladies. I'll walk you to your room." Arising, she groaned. "And then off to that cold room for us too, Walter. We must take a candle. Oh, it will be so miserable out in the hallway." She clutched her shawl tight around her shoulders, preparing for the onslaught of a dark and draughty corridor.

Anna took the candlesticks from the dresser and passed one to each person. Jeremy lit his from the candles on the table and passed on the flame. Delmore opened the door so that everyone could pass through.

Anna's bedroom could have grown icicles from the ceiling. She and Jonquil undressed quickly down to their shifts. Sleeping together prevented either from freezing to death but ... how much more wonderful it would have been to lie with Lord Delmore and experience the comfort of his big body.

Chapter Six

Delmore awoke just past dawn with a dull headache. His tongue struck to the roof of his mouth. A brandy gargle would cure that. Sitting up, he stared at the windowpanes. Rain smeared the glass. Beyond, the blurry pink sunrise pushed through the gray of the clouds. Groaning out the stiffness in his back caused by the uncomfortable couch, he cast his cover aside and eased on his boots. He found dregs in the brandy bottle, swilled out his mouth and swallowed. The fire needed replenishing and he coaxed out a wavering flame. After giving his jacket a hearty shake and smoothing the worst of the creases from his shirt, he dressed without the aid of his valet, a shave, or a mirror. Perhaps later, he would be able to borrow a razor from Jim Merriweather.

After using the necessary outside, he strolled back in through the kitchen where the stove was already warming the room. His groom and the outdoors' man sat at the table consuming what appeared to be half a loaf of bread between them and a glass of milk each. Wilson sprang to his feet.

Delmore concentrated his gaze on Travers. "How is the shoulder feeling this morning?"

"Not so bad, your lordship. An ache, no more."

"Good to hear. Wilson, today I plan to drive to Maldon to see the wheelwright. I want you to have the phaeton ready in an hour."

"Yes, my lord. Mrs. Merriweather will have you set up with breakfast right away."

"Fresh bread and ale will do nicely, thank you," he said to the housekeeper who nodded. "In the meantime, do you think you could supply me with hot water and a razor?"

"Yes, my lord. Where do you plan to shave?"

"Here will do."

Wilson busied himself with the hot water and stropping Jim's razor. He offered to shave Delmore who decided after noting his groom's rough shave that he could manage himself. That done, he sat alone in the gray lit morning parlor with bread and cheese and a jug of ale, all of which he called a very fine breakfast under the circumstances. Outside, the relentless drizzle spread and melted the worst of the snow.

A creak in the floorboards outside caused him to turn and smile at Anna who appeared in the doorway. No one would have suspected she had dressed without a maid. One might presume her light brown hair had been dragged through a brush one hundred times before she had made her usual shining loose knot on the back of her head. He appreciated the delicate, natural curling around her face, and the fresh pink of her cheeks. "An early riser, I see."

"I thought I might need to help in the kitchen. Everyone else will be up early. No one could have had a comfortable night's sleep on those lumpy mattresses. Even Jonquil began stirring before I left the room. Normally she sleeps most of the morning away."

"While you do all the household tasks?" Her dreary blue gown didn't do justice to her slender figure. Had he the keeping of her, he would put her in the hands of Madame Amalie in London, or he would have once, but now he would need to sell a few of the family jewels to do so.

"There's no doubt I'm hard done by, a slave to my family, a martyr to the last." She smiled as if to indicate she didn't mean a word she said but after the past day, he didn't doubt she took a heavier load than her thoughtless young sister. "I doubt we can expect Lady Carrington to spend another day in the kitchen. She and Sir Walter should be given hot water for a wash in the very least, after what I assume would have been a restless night."

"And you will do that?"

"Of course. Judging by the crumbs in front of you, Mrs. Merriweather arose early and baked. I possibly won't need to do another thing, other than to ferry water to the bedrooms."

He appreciated her willingness to help the day run smoothly. "Allow me to aid you while you eat your breakfast."

A smile lifted one side of her mouth. "Should the Earl of Delmore take hot water up to a young nobody and a couple he outranks?"

He inclined his head in assent. "Certainly, if you will

drive with me into Maldon this morning. I need to see to the chaise wheel. The snow appears to be melting. If all goes well, I should be able to arrange for the wheel to be fixed in time for us to arrive back at Delmore House this afternoon. Even should that be impossible, we must replenish the food supplies in this house. I'm sure Mrs. Merriweather will be happy to give you a list."

She nodded, her eyes gleaming with humor. "How clever of you to find a way to be alone with me."

"I thought so," he said, remaining expressionless. "Though the presence of Wilson may curb my impulse to act like a fool."

"I'm sure I would be able to push him off the phaeton should he be de trop."

"I hope he never hears you say that. He will be enough put out to have a female passenger." A strange warmth occupied his chest. He smiled at her, liking her far more than he thought possible, and desiring her more by the minute. His body warned him he might embarrass himself if she continued to stare at him with a smile in her beautiful calm eyes.

"Does he not approve of your mistresses?"

"He is far more fastidious than I. But then, he never sees the benefits the way I do. He only hears the orders or the tantrums. I doubt you will bother him with either."

"I could be encouraged to have a tantrum and I am quite partial to giving orders, but I will control myself in order to change his mind about my gender."

"You may well succeed if you manage not to have hysterics or to clutch at my arm while I'm cornering."

She raised her eyebrows. "Which mistress did that?"

"How many have you heard about?"

"Three," she said promptly. "How many haven't I heard about?"

"As a genteel lady you should have heard of none." He tried a severe lowering of his eyebrows, but her glinting eyes and her delighted smile had a tendency to draw out the ridiculousness of the conversation and relax him into being his younger self and not Lord Delmore, the heartless cynic. "And if you don't want me to snatch you into my arms and kiss you again, you need to leave this room at once."

She appeared to consider.

Too tempted, he took three long strides, reached out, and edged her in a light embrace. "Last night was rather painful for me." The slight enlarging of her pupils told him she knew to what he alluded.

She idly smoothed a forefinger down his hastily tied cravat. "I amused myself for some time thinking about creeping downstairs and accosting you on the couch."

"You would have found it highly uncomfortable, my dear. I had a broken spring in my back most of the night. Had you accosted me, I would have put you beneath me and suffered no longer."

Her lips pursed. "If you were as skilled a lover as purported, I may not have noticed."

"We'll never know." He dropped a kiss on the tip of her nose and reluctantly let her go.

"Never was a woman so beautifully scorned while being so dangerously tempted. You are far too well behaved for me, which I regret."

Trying to read her expression, he gazed at her deliberately limpid expression. "You are quite mistaken. You are scarcely a fallen woman despite your intention to shock me. Never imagine I don't desire you. However, I suspect you are toying with me."

"I'm finding you a sad disappointment, to tell the truth. You don't live up to your reputation. Or do you only want women you can't have?"

He drew a deep breath. She could be right. He certainly wanted her, but he had no choice other than to ignore her provocation. "Be ready in an hour."

At the designated time, Wilson brought the phaeton to the front of the house. Her pelisse flying behind, Anna pattered down the stairs to the hall where Delmore awaited her. She huffed to a stop. "I have permission to borrow Mrs. Merriweather's waterproof to wear in the phaeton," she said looking pleased with her forethought.

He held up Jeremy's greatcoat. "I have appropriated this for you. The capes will afford far more protection from the weather." He waited for her to place the weatherproof on the hall table and then turn and push her arms through the sleeves of the greatcoat. Then he adjusted the layers of capes. He stood back staring at her. The hem almost dragged on the floor and the sleeves covered her hands. "Your hat won't do. You will need Jeremy's as well." He pulled undone the ribbons of her bonnet and dragged her hat off. Then, he took the small, brimmed beaver and tested a square placement on her head. "Fortunately, you have enough hair to keep this from dropping down to your nose."

"I'm sure I look very odd, but at least I will be sheltered from the weather. Women's fashions don't allow for that. Now, Mrs. Merriweather has dictated the list of goods she needs. I told Lady Carrington I was going shopping with you. She looked pleased. Doubtless she will be glad to keep me out of the kitchen."

Jeremy appeared behind her. "And where do you think you are going in my coat and hat, Miss Anna Winters?" He stood, his back rigid and his chin jutted.

"Did Lord Delmore not ask you?"

Delmore half smiled at her. "The lad was snoring so loudly I thought he would sleep until noon. We're off to Maldon on an errand of mercy, Jeremy. I want to make sure the wheel is repaired, and we need more food."

A frown formed between Jeremy's eyebrows. "Take off my coat, Anna. It's too big for you, anyway. I'll go."

She glanced at Delmore. Her disappointment was palpable.

"You won't be any use to me," he told his brother. "I need Anna to purchase flour and ..." He checked the list. "By George, I don't know the half of it. Wax. Wicks. Butter. Oil. Flour. Sugar. Dried figs. I can't see you managing this order with any comfort."

Jeremy fingered his neck cloth. "She shouldn't go alone with you."

"In an open phaeton with a groom? Does she not travel about Danbury with you?" Delmore pulled on his gloves, keeping his tone neutral.

"No one gives a hoot. I'm not a ..."

"What?"

"I don't have a reputation with the ladies." Jeremy glanced away.

"Nor do I, dear boy. Not with ladies. Wearing your

greatcoat and beaver, she more resembles a short man. But Anna is a lady, is she not?"

Jeremy looked sulky. "Well, make sure you take good care of her."

Delmore carefully placed his hat on his head and escorted Anna to the phaeton.

Wilson stood square shouldered, his face stiffening when he noted Anna. "If you are taking up a lady, mind you hold onto them leaders and don't get distracted," the groom said to Delmore in a tight voice.

Well aware Wilson had seen him kiss Anna in the stables, Delmore clamped his lips. "Thank you for the reminder, Wilson. Make sure you sit in the back seat, facing the road behind, and do not move. You may not listen to my conversations or try to butt in. If you do either, I will find another groom, believe me." His tone implacable, he handed Anna up to the high seat where she arranged the layers of the coat around her. Then he stepped up and crossed in front to her other side. "If we don't slide into any drifts, we should be safe enough."

"I don't doubt I'm in good hands."

His body began to thrum, realizing she had again been suggestive in her words. "You can't know that since you have not yet been in my hands." He reached under the seat and pulled out a travelling blanket, which he placed carefully around her knees.

"Meaning I have something to look forward to?" She glanced at him.

He made no answer, instead passing her a woolen muffler. Satisfied he had done his best to shield her from the intemperate weather, he grabbed up the reins and took the chestnuts into a smart trot around the carriage sweep. Within minutes and without speaking, he pulled onto the main road, determined not to let her blatant provocation affect him. "The sweetest fruit is invariably out of reach," he eventually said, staring straight ahead.

"So, I have found. I should stop reaching but I don't have it in me to give up. Do you think I should settle for sour, easily reached fruit?"

"You are reminding me that is what I have done for years, but even less so. I haven't bothered to reach—I have simply dangled my money."

"I have wondered why you stoop to buying affection. You are well born, wealthy, and not least of all, very pleasing to the eye. And yet you think no one would love you for yourself?"

"Wealth and position tends to dull a man's tastes. I am well aware that the prettiest young ladies are presented to me each season, despite my reputation. Mothers are perfectly happy to match me with their young virgins, not because I might make a decent husband, but because of my outward trappings, my estates and my title."

"But you prefer elderly experienced women. I quite understand your reasoning. Older women are more grateful, more inclined to overlook the deficiencies in you. Whereas a younger lady might worry that you would develop a belly long before she did, or that you would prefer to sit night after night with a few bottles of Chambertin within your reach rather than attend every masque and every fashionable ball."

"Elderly?"

"It has been whispered that La Gloriosa was a year or

two over twenty-five. Elderly. Almost doddering in fact." She leaned into him, slipping her hand beneath his elbow, as if confiding her words to a reliable older person.

At first offended by having his taste criticized, he realized that again, she deliberately goaded him. He gave a short laugh, keeping the horses at a trot. In this weather, with slippery roads, he couldn't afford a mishap. "In her dodder-age," he agreed in a comfortable voice. He didn't miss his mistress one bit. She knew what to do with her hands, but she never quite understood wry humor the way Anna did. She couldn't relax him in the same way while keeping him edgy and wanting her.

"I am twenty-four, old enough to be sensible but young enough to appreciate a man with experience, having none of my own. You might say I am the right age for a man in your position."

"Self recommendation is no recommendation."

"I can hardly ask someone to recommend me to you as your temporary mistress." She sounded indignant.

"Can you never be serious?"

"I spend most of my days being serious. I love having an opportunity to be frivolous. I don't have many. Once I'm a respectable companion, I will have to keep my words to myself, other than to say yes ma'am and no sir."

"You have your priorities right at least. I hope you would continue to say no sir, not that you have ever said those words to me."

"I haven't yet had cause. Be sure I will when I do. Will you drop me off at the markets while you browbeat the wheelwright?"

He blinked at the quick change of subject. "Is that what you wish me to do?"

"I see no sense in us wasting time. We want the chaise fixed as soon as possible and I expect Travers didn't brag to the wheelwright about being in an earl's employ."

"He is my mother's coachman, not mine."

"A countess has less consequence than an earl. The wheelwright will soon see that, especially if you have a gold sovereign for him."

"Thank you for your hint. Do you manage Jeremy this way?"

"Have I been managing? I beg your pardon. I am used to organizing servants and the tradesmen we deal with on a daily basis."

"Do you perform every task at home?" He assumed so, since her mother seemed ineffectual and her sister self centered, and wondered why he asked because she would never admit to being the family drudge.

"Jonquil is too young," she answered, confirming his suspicions. "Mama is too distracted. She does every task the vicar asks of her. To have found a husband who would take her daughter as well as herself has obligated her beyond bearing." She blinked rapidly, clearly impatient with herself for saying so much.

"You need to get married and away from there," he said in a rough voice, hardening his face.

"Eventually I will give in and accept anyone who will have me, the same way my mother did. First though, I will live vicariously through Jonquil and her come out. I hear I am allowed a new gown, which is more than I have had for two years."

If he took her as his mistress, she could have twenty new gowns, even if he had to sell the Gainsborough to do so. Given her traitorous, father she could never be more than respectably married, unless Delmore could buy a husband for her. Others had done so with cherished mistresses. But even if he had the funds, taking her as his mistress was not on the cards. He wouldn't do that to a woman for whom he had a deal of respect. "Who knows?" He managed a shrug. "You might find yourself a husband. You're not unattractive and you have a rather addictive charm."

"Oh, my. A compliment from the dastardly earl."

He smiled, keeping a steady eye on his team. In no time he passed the few small outlying farms and reached the village of Maldon, a tidy hamlet with one wide main street that curved past stone buildings and opened into a central market square sheltered by a tall roof. He pulled up the phaeton. And waited. "Wilson, go to the horses' heads, please."

"Oh, we're here, are we?" The groom spoke with blistering sarcasm. The phaeton lifted slightly as he sprang off and passed to the front, his head down, his under-lip forward. "How's a man to know when all he can see is the road behind?" he grumbled.

"I didn't hear that, Wilson. Hand down Miss Winters, please." Delmore found two guineas in his fob pocket and placed them in Anna's palm. "That should do you. I'll be back as soon as I have beaten the wheelwright into submission." He watched as she stepped down, taking Wilson's hand as her foot reached the step.

She thanked him and turned to smile at Delmore before swiftly moving past barrows laden with pumpkins, cabbages, and fresh greens, the capes of Jeremy's coat almost dwarfing her. Jeremy's hat sat at a jaunty angle as she disappeared.

Wilson swung up behind. Farther ahead, a group of buildings proclaimed a fodder store, a chandler, and a butchery, until eventually on the outskirts, he noted a sign painted white on black and tacked to an old wheel, advertising Hicks the Wainwright. Delmore stopped outside a tall wooden building with a straw thatch. Wilson went to the horse's heads, and Delmore left to find the wheelmaker.

A fire crackled in the centre of the barn-like space and a burly, red-faced male in his late thirties or older stopped beating his hammer against a metal wheel rim. He stared open mouthed at Delmore's greatcoat and tall hat.

"Good morning," Delmore said, glancing around. Wheels of a size to fit every vehicle stood propped against three walls along with a carriage door or two. Rounds of metal and lengths of wood sat in stacks. An old leather carriage seat sat in a corner. Smoke hovered in the air. "Doubtless, you have Lady Delmore's wheel here among these others." He raised his eyebrows.

The man cleared his throat. "The lads brung it here yesterday, sir."

"Today I would like the wheel replaced on the countess's chaise. I realize you may have prior orders, but I have a gold coin for you if you can deliver the repaired vehicle to Drake House before midday."

The man's jaw dropped at mention of at least a month's wages. "Yes, milord. I'll work on the wheel right away. I'll need to find me lads …"

"Do that," Delmore said in a bored voice, and left. He allowed himself to smile cynically as he climbed into his phaeton again, but although money worked wonders, so too did having enough to feed a family. Now he only needed to pick up Anna, and his good deeds for the day were done, or almost.

Perhaps he could satisfy Anna's curiosity about the needs of a red-blooded male. Likely if she knew part, she may not wish to discover the whole. Part would possibly stop his craving for her and send him off to find someone more experienced. If he repelled her, she would stop offering herself and leading him into the worst sort of temptation, that of taking a woman simply because he could.

Anna bit into the cut piece of apple the fruiterer wanted her to taste. Stocking up on the Beeby household's food had always been her favorite task, not that she often had the time. One of life's true delights for her was to wander around a produce market, meeting cheery and interesting stallholders, most of whom offered fresh wares to try, using funny quips and enormous smiles. "Delicious," she said. "Not like our apples at home." In the vicarage they stored the apples, eating the oldest first. Anyone who wanted a fresh apple needed to be a little sneaky, which was not beyond her.

The grocer shuffled the fruiterer aside, his gaze shifting behind Anna. "This'll be your pa come to check on you," he said in a lowered tone. Then he plastered a welcoming smile on his face. "Good morning, sir. The lad 'as done a right proper job of collectin' the 'ousehold supplies."

Anna swiveled to face Delmore, trying to suppress her amusement, hoping her expression conveyed a message that she was going along with the grocer's inability to recognize her gender. Not for a moment had she imagined the stall-holders might take her for a lad, but Jeremy's hat confused them, and the coat confirmed the impression. The novelty of passing as male tickled her sense of humor.

For the past quarter hour, she had enjoyed playing the role of an earnest young stripling. Standing hipshot, as she had seen Jeremy and his friends do so often, helped to disguise the fact that she wore a gown beneath the huge coat. "I have done very well, my lord," she said in the hesitant voice she had adopted. "Mr. Samuel here says I'm as good as a housewife any day. Not that I want to be a housewife, but a man should be able to do everything his servants can do, you told me."

"I said no such thing." The casualness of Delmore's tone showed he was apparently comfortable with Anna's ruse. "What would happen to this great nation if every master was as good as his man?"

"In an emergency it would be helpful," she said in a mock miserable voice. "And today is an emergency. You said we couldn't send the housekeeper out in this wicked weather."

"Nor we could. Someone has to be preparing the meals. Now, have you completed the list she gave you?"

"Not yet. I wasn't expecting you to be finished so soon. We still need ..." She referred to the list. "Well, it's not here, but I'm sure we need a bag of sugared almonds."

Delmore gave a long-suffering sigh and raised his eyebrows at Mr. Samuels. "A small bag," he said in an indulgent voice. "And have someone put the parcels into my phaeton."

"I'll hold the almonds," Anna said, trying not to laugh.

Delmore frowned at her. "Make sure you don't give yourself a bellyache."

Anna smiled at the grocer who smiled back. "E's a good lad," he said to Delmore. "No 'arm in lettin' them have treats now and again."

Delmore nodded sagely and the grocer offered Anna a conspiring smile. The goods were loaded into the phaeton and tucked under the front seat. Anna held the almonds, taking one and sucking the toffee. She couldn't think of the last time she'd eaten anything so frivolous, and she offered the bag to Delmore, who declined.

"What was that about?" He stood by the step of the phaeton.

"You're the one who suggested I wear Jeremy's clothes. Don't be surprised that everyone in that market assumed I was male. I could have explained and embarrassed everyone who mistook me, or I could have enjoyed myself. I am but a weak woman."

He shook his head slowly. "A less weak woman have I ever met, but now you're established as a male, we can drop into the tavern for a glass of ale, for which I am greatly in need."

"I don't like ale."

"In that case, you'll have to watch me drink, either that or sit in the phaeton while Wilson attends to the horses."

Wilson placed himself in front of Delmore, his thin face

tense and his hands on his hips. "I'm not mindin' no woman while I look to the horses."

"Of course you're not." Anna tried to sound equally outraged. "I'll watch Lord Delmore drink. At least I'll be able to make sure he doesn't overdo his tippling."

"My lord don't never overdo the tippling." Wilson's expression darkened. "Not when he has the 'orses to think of. You don't want to listen to no one 'oo says 'e does."

"I wouldn't be so silly, not when I can see the facts for myself." She turned her back on Wilson mainly because she had the terrible urge to laugh. The poor man didn't know whether to defend or defy his master. Delmore had that effect on people. Anyone could see he drank too much, but he never appeared to be drunk, or even unsteady. That, of course, showed him to be a perpetual over-imbiber, which wasn't good for a man.

"Since I can't have you sitting in my phaeton while I'm in the tavern and I can't have you lined up in the tap room, regardless of how you are dressed, I will take a private room." Delmore nodded, answering his own question.

"I can't say a warm drink wouldn't be welcome," Anna said uncertainly. "Yes. Thank you. And at least I won't be seen by anyone I know."

"Unless you are in the habit of dressing like a male."

"It is the first time I have done so." She frowned at him.

"Let's hope my reputation will stand up to me using a private room to drink with a boy." Delmore smiled wickedly and her heart skipped a beat.

Just a month, just a week, just a day, just an hour—she would take any time with him that she could. She didn't doubt for a second that she was achingly besotted with this man. No one before him had understood her so well. No one before him laughed when she laughed. In every circumstance he remained in control, never ruffled, never bested. These traits made him a man among men, a natural leader, and a man to admire. Why on earth no smart woman had snapped him up by now was a puzzle to her. She walked beside him through the door into the tavern.

The host came out after Delmore had glanced into the taproom. "We'll take ale and a pot of tea in a private room, if you please." He glanced at Anna. "Make that a pot of tea and a light repast," he said slowly. "Forget the ale."

The beefy host, a man with bristling gray hair nodded. "Perhaps the young master would like a piece of my wife's apple pie?"

"I'm sure he would enjoy that. Would you take ale and cheese out to my groom? We'll want to be on our way within half an hour." Lord Delmore unbuttoned his greatcoat.

The host opened a door to a small room in the other side of the passage and then walked backwards until he reached the door to the kitchen, which he scurried through.

"You would think he had met royalty by the way he behaved," Anna said walking ahead of Delmore into a room furnished with a cozy armchair, a fire, and an eating bench with a long seat. She sat at the bench.

Lord Delmore sank beside her, removing his hat. "The man expects a good price for a private room. I doubt it would be used too often in this farming area."

"Did you leave the wheelwright in a pool of tears and apologies?" She unbuttoned her coat.

He gave her a glance of reproof. "The wheel will be attached and the conveyance at Drake House by midday."

"Then, why on earth are we here? We ought to be there helping to pack up."

"Pack up what? We only have ourselves. You only have to tell me you don't want to be alone with me, which I would find confusing when you have been propositioning me almost since the moment we met." His smile twisted.

She swallowed. "I doubt we can do much dallying when we know the tavern keeper will be in and out of this room."

"Once he has been in, I shall pay him to be out."

She carefully removed Jeremy's hat. "My guess is I look rather unappealing at the moment, and please don't tell me the truth."

"You look like old mother Hubbard, your hair is standing on end, and I'm sorry I kissed you."

"Really? Could you make yourself sorry again?"

"Do you mean that? I never know when you are serious or if you are playing with me."

"Nor do I," she said, lifting her shoulders. "You are so lovely to play with that I don't know how to stop."

"Oh, my dear one. I know how to stop and of course I wouldn't cross the line in a dingy room in an inn."

He put a finger under her chin and pressed his lips softly on hers. Her eyes closed and she enjoyed this tender moment a little too long. Her hand reached out and clutched the back of his neck and he drew her into his body. As she twined her arms around his neck, her hat dropped off. At the same moment, the landlord walked into the room with a plateful of apple pie. "Deary me," he said. "Well, at least he's not a boy."

Anna adopted her dowager glance. "Thank you, my good man. I will take that as a compliment. Yes, put the tray there please." The moment had been lost but perhaps that was for the best. Who knows what she may have been tempted to do? The man left and she poured the tea, her hands slightly unsteady.

Delmore glanced at her, a strange expression on his face. "I wonder if it's honest to eat that whole plate of apple pie, bearing in mind that you are not the lad the innkeeper thought you were."

She surprised herself by breaking into laughter. "Perhaps not. I think I may have an obligation to share it now that I have been unmasked." She slid the plate toward him knowing her opportunity had been lost.

After the teapot had been well and truly emptied and pie plate sat forlorn, they left for Drake House.

Chapter Seven

Delmore kept his chestnuts to a slow trot, unwillingly grateful that the innkeeper had interrupted his moment of insanity with Anna. They'd had a time in the stables yesterday when he could possibly have sated his need, but she saw that as the wrong time. Half an hour ago, he may well have thrown caution to the winds and hired a room had matters progressed the way his body had been insisting.

Every time was wrong. He had no idea why she, of all people, so attracted him. Although he liked her calm demeanor and appreciated that in a room full of women, she wouldn't be the last noticed, she was no raving beauty who would turn heads. Instead, she simply had a smile started in her eyes and slowly moved to her mouth, where the corners tickled up. Her body was curvaceous, but not overly.

He certainly liked her mind, but none of his mistresses had minds, and he had been happy enough to bed each for a certain time. He clearly didn't require a woman with a mind, but thus far Anna hadn't made herself into a dead bore by asking what he meant when he had added a dry comment. More than likely she would cap his by one of her own. Perhaps a flamboyant body was not an essential for him, either. Anna's, sight unseen, was bound to be beautiful. If not, he doubted he would care if he had her in his bed.

He wanted her past reasoning why. But, unless he was willing to accept responsibility for her, he couldn't take her, not a respectable woman with her whole life ahead of her. She deserved so much better than a sot and a wastrel who couldn't stop drinking long enough to work out how to run his property at a profit. If he didn't change his way of life, he would lose his inheritance.

He groaned into his muffler. Perhaps the lessening of his brandy intake during the past two days was playing havoc with his brain. He didn't have to have Anna at all. He'd always had a perfectly capable hand. And then she shared the carriage blanket with him. The drip from an overhanging tree trickled from the brim of his hat onto his nose, and the closeness of Anna was causing an unnecessary stirring of his cock.

He glanced at her, and her hand slid underneath to his knee. She said nothing. She stared straight ahead while her hand shifted from his knee to his thigh to the juncture between his legs. His horses bumped each other as he inadvertently jerked the reins. Trying to control a pair was quite a task when his concentration suddenly switched to a place other than the road ahead.

"Keep that up if you want to cause an accident," he said in a voice that rasped.

"I take it that you are interested in having an accident caused."

"What makes you think that?"

She leaned right into him. "This." On top of his trousers, her hand completely covered his cock, her thumb and fingers measuring the length, which tried to outgrow her hand. "I had to know. In the stables 'this' pressed against my body. I know enough about the bulls and the stallions to know what the lengthening means. You want me."

"I do, but I don't plan to take you."

"Please, let me learn a little about your body. I promise not to a take advantage of you."

His mouth curled wryly. Many a young virgin had heard those words, and he knew the truth was somewhat stretched. If she wanted to know about a man's body, now was the time to find out, when he could do no more than submit to her ministrations. He would pay her back in kind, because that was what she needed; not a good tupping, not a ruining of her, and not a lesson about men who couldn't marry her. All she needed was almost pure and simple womanly pleasure.

He brought his horses back to a walk. Taking the reins and his whip into one hand, he used the other to move her palm off him and undo his flap buttons. "Take off your glove." He used a low voice, not wanting Wilson's interest piqued. She did so, staring at him, and he took her hand inside his trousers, leaving her to find whatever she wished. This way, she had the choice to pleasure him or to be repulsed.

Beneath his trousers he wore his carefully tucked shirt.

"I'm sure I'll never get this arrangement back the way it was." Her voice sounded strange; low and husky, intimate.

"Of necessity, I need to free myself a certain number of times during the day and won't require your help dressing. The only thing I want from you is exactly what you are doing to me."

Although once she had latched onto the idea and him, she seemed perfectly happy to tease him to death. He was damned if he would give her instructions, but the horses acted out all their fantasies, bumping each other, tossing their heads, snorting, pulling and otherwise suiting them-selves. Finally, she grasped the width of him and ran her thumb lightly over his tip. His cock made an involuntary twitch. She gave a soft laugh into his shoulder and did the same motion three more times. "Does it always do that?"

"I suspect so."

"Why?"

"No idea. But if you keep doing that I'm going to have to stop and take to the bushes for a while."

"Why?"

"You are pushing me to the limit, and you may not like the result. It's a trifle messy." How he managed to speak was a matter of wonder to him when he could barely breathe. At the same moment, Wilson called out, "What's 'appening, Milord. Phaeton is going every which way."

Anna quickly removed her grip on Delmore and raised a slightly flushed and guilty face to his and then to the back of the phaeton. "He let me have control for a moment, Wilson, and I'm afraid I'm a mere beginner."

Delmore laughed. His cock throbbed like the very devil but at least he had come to his senses. "I'll take over now and you can be easy, Wilson." He quickly rearranged his shirt and buttoned his flap, shifting slightly in his seat, waiting for his erection to subside. For the rest of the way back to Drake House he enjoyed the pleasurable throb of a half erection and Anna's hand lightly resting on his knee. While being inexperienced, she certainly knew how to maintain a fellow's interest.

He pulled up his rig outside the stable and sent Wilson to the house with the supplies. Travers arrived and held the horses while Delmore climbed down, assisting Anna when he had walked around to her side.

She stripped off Jeremy's hat and smiled up at Delmore. "That was quite an adventure. I've never been a boy before. Boys are allowed far more liberties than women."

"Is that your excuse?" He smiled down at her and took her toward the back entry of the house.

She blushed. "I must say, my lord, that you are very free with your favors."

"We have unfinished business, you and I." He walked her into the kitchen lobby and passed through, hoping to find Mrs. Merriweather. As usual, she stood over the stove, while speaking to Wilson who was unpacking the bag of goods. "Help Travers with the horses, Wilson. They'll want a rubbing down. With any luck, we should be on our way back home this afternoon."

Wilson scooted off. Anna looked ready to go to work preparing food for everyone, again. He had in mind pleasuring her instead.

"Could you tell me the way to the servant's wing, Mrs. Merriweather," he asked in a careful voice.

"The place is empty, my lord. Me and Jim are the only

servants."

"I would like to inspect the place before we leave. I'm sure Mr. Hastings and my mother would like to know how many he has placements for."

Mrs. Merriweather lifted her head, smiling. "Will he be moving in soon?"

"As soon as we can arrange."

She poked at her hair. "Go up the flight of stairs leading from the lobby. You will find another flight, narrower. Two floors up, my lord, you will find very nice quarters for servants, only needing a little dusting and a fresh linen for the beds."

"Thank you." Delmore ushered Anna to the flight of stairs. "Up you go."

She didn't question him. As she reached the top, she stopped and glanced around a rather small sitting room containing one sofa, four single chairs upholstered in mismatched fabrics, and a large and perfect spider's web in the far corner. A narrow passage led to the bedrooms. She inspected the first, which contained a single, iron framed bed with a bare mattress. "The place hasn't been dusted for months, but the staff left the rooms tidy. Will your mother need to know anything else?"

"I have no idea. I thought this would be the best place for us to spend some time alone. I can't imagine anyone coming up to disturb us, can you?" He stared at her, hoping that she would find the servant's old quarters preferable to the stables.

"I can't imagine that anyone even knows of this place."

"Nor I." He shrugged. "I'm nothing if not inventive. Now my dear, we have to take up where we left off."

"We do?"

The hope on her face was his undoing. He took her into his arms, smiling into her eyes. She guarded her expression. Very slowly, keeping her gaze on his, she slid her hands to his shoulders. Jeremy's hat brim poked into Delmore's cheek and so he knocked the thing off, sending his own hat flying after, both skittering across the bare wooden floor. Then, of course, he couldn't hold her close with both Jeremy's and his greatcoat in the way. "Let's have this off you," he said as he lifted and pushed the coat from her shoulders.

She stepped out of the puddle of fabric. He opened his own coat and took her inside with him. Her beautiful body pressed up close and the heavy pounding of her heart was shared with him. Overcome by tenderness, he pressed his cheek against hers. A last glance into her beautiful shining eyes, and he took her lips with his. The softness of her skin, the fresh coolness of her cheek, the tickle of her hair on his forehead—all that and a woman who wanted him simply because she did. Her arms clasped around his waist, and he gave her a kiss that stopped and started. He could have done nothing but kiss her for hours, but they didn't have hours to spare. Sooner or later, the rest of the houseguests would wonder where he and Anna had gone. He wanted no whispering about her.

"I very much enjoyed what you did to me in the phaeton." he murmured close to her ear.

"Do you want me to do that again?"

He shook his head. "I must repay the favor."

"What do you mean?"

"I think it is time I pleasured you, Anna." He rested his chin against her face.

Her fingers briefly smoothed over his jaw. "Does this mean I will be your mistress?"

"It means you will be my love. This is the only time we have. May I know you as you know me?" He slid his hands from her waist up to the place where her ribcage met the softness of her breasts.

She drew in a sharp breath, and nodded, her eyes full of questions. He found the hardness of her nipples and brushed a thumb across each. She gasped and she didn't stop him. Then he leaned down and placed a kiss on each swell, on top of the material of her dull blue gown. Her fingers combed into his hair and again he took her lips while holding one soft breast in each of his hands.

His own body reacted urgently, but this was her time, not his. Letting her go for a moment, he shrugged his coat off his shoulders and swung the whole like a cape onto the bed mattress. With a soft laugh, he scooped her up and placed her atop the silk lining.

Although her face held a touch of wariness, she took a half breath and smiled at him. "My, do you have a masterful way about you." She shaded her expression, placing both arms around his neck. With her almost beneath him, his cock threatened to burst his breeches. He tugged the material of her skirt and petticoats up and found her beautiful rounded naked bottom. She tensed.

"I let you touch me," he said in a somewhat husky chiding tone. "Now you must let me touch you."

"I'm not quite sure what you are going to do." She evaded his gaze.

"I wasn't quite sure what you were going to do to me in the phaeton, but I trusted you."

"You beast. You knew what I was going to do to you far more than I did. I was guessing." Her voice, already soft and gentle, so un-Anna-like, almost reached a whisper. "And you encouraged me, you know you did."

He moved his hand to her hip and then to her belly. "Encourage me."

"Dear Lord Delmore, please do as you think right."

He made a wry face. He certainly didn't intend to do wrong but perhaps he also didn't intend to be wise. "I will do you no harm, Anna. You will go to your husband a virgin, but one who has known pleasure."

She raised her mouth to his. "I know pleasure at this moment. I love your hand on my bare flesh, I love you touching my nipples, and I adore you kissing my mouth."

As he found her soft womanly place, he kissed her lips. As he found her secret little nub, he swallowed her gasps. As she came to her completion, he breathed with her, enjoying her every writhe of pleasure. He longed to take his pleasure too, but without a doubt she had come to him a virgin and he would leave her in that same state.

She lay back, her cheeks flushed, her mouth red and soft, and her eyes slumberous. "I don't believe I did that to you."

"You meant to, there's no doubt, but I'm afraid men are not as unobtrusive at showing their delight as women."

"Should you do that now?" She stared at the urgent length of his covered erection.

He almost agreed but deep down he knew if he dallied and gained his own completion, he may well have lost another scruple, which would lead, as he knew, to losing the next and the next. "We must gather up our senses, my dear one. We have been to Maldon and now we are back. Best you step into being Anna Winters and not Delmore's delight." He breathed out, trying to concentrate. Somehow, she had buried herself deep into his mind and that would not do at all. A woman that he couldn't possibly marry must stay a passing fancy and no more.

She sat up, her lovely eyes filled with trust. "If I am Delmore's delight," she said softly, "you are Anna's adoration."

He forced a smile and swung himself off the bed. While she put on Jeremy's coat, he donned his own and his hat. She carried Jeremy's hat as she stepped down the stairs and into the main house. He followed. They met no one.

She walked into the sitting room. "You're back," Jonquil said in a dissatisfied voice, and Delmore left to tidy himself.

He could be proud of one thing, only. The husband she was certain to find in London would find her completely intact.

Tall overhanging trees splattered raindrops onto the chaise rooftop. In the cozy comfort of the newly repaired vehicle, Anna sat with Lady Carrington on the forward seat. Jonquil sat on the backward one with Travers. To spare Travers' arm, muffling himself in his scarf and greatcoat, Delmore sat on the driver's seat. He had volunteered to take the vehicle back to Danbury. Trailing behind, Jeremy managed Lord Delmore's phaeton under the strict supervision of Wilson and Sir Walter.

While the baroness and Jonquil discussed the rooms in Drake House and the likely improvements, Anna had time to dwell on her ravishment, if the intimacy she participated in could be called ravishment. Even now her cheeks heated as she remembered she'd had the temerity to rest her hand on Delmore's rising on the journey back from Maldon. From there, matters had proceeded at a great rate, which had caused her not to regret a single one of her actions.

When Delmore had unbuttoned one side of his falls, she was a lost woman. Touching his male part, of a size and hardness she hadn't expected, caused an unexpected rush through her body. Lord preserve her. She experienced the same rush right then, and clamped her legs together, trying not to lean her head back and savor the moment. Cock, he called the appendage no one in her family ever referred to although every man had one. Although she didn't like the term greatly at least she gained some amusement. She would have called it his ahem because that was the only word she had in reference other than a pleasure stick, which one of the maids had said in her presence. Afterwards, Anna had bent over and silently laughed in the corridor outside the kitchen.

A fine sort of mistress she would make if she didn't know the name of his most precious possession. Even then, she didn't know if her handling was right, but she could tell he liked what she did. And when he did the same to her not half an hour later, his breath came as fast as his urgent kisses, which he spread from her mouth to her neck and back to her mouth. She couldn't forget the excitement of what she had done to Delmore and what he had done to her.

Her private parts throbbed. Lost in gloriously lurid thoughts, she almost jumped when Lady Carrington nudged her. "Jeremy will need to hire more servants. I don't know what the lad is about not to get that quite fine house in order. I hope Carrington is discussing this with him right now. He is the closest thing to a father that Jeremy has now, not that his own father took a scrap of notice of him."

"The house could be quite smart." Jonquil glanced at Anna. "I suppose his mama would want to choose the new curtain fabrics."

Anna blinked and took a deep breath. "Likely she would but he might be better off to wait until he marries so that his new bride can do so." Her voice sounded husky.

Jonquil's lashes lowered. "What color would you prefer?"

Anna frowned as she tried to concentrate. "I haven't given it a thought. What color would you prefer?"

Jonquil gave her a puzzled glance and went off into a soliloquy about fabrics while Anna recalled Delmore handling her little nub until she made a dreadful groan of pleasure. And embarrassed herself below, which appeared to please him greatly. His mistresses were lucky. She stared out the window, envying each one of them.

"I don't know what your mother is going to say about us being held overnight at Drake House." Jonquil glanced at Travers who stared out the window, scrupulously trying to distance himself from the conversations.

"Do you know, I haven't given a thought to my mother or your father. I suppose they would have been worried."

Lady Carrington creased her forehead. "Let's hope they realized that if neither a carriage nor Delmore's phaeton had arrived back yesterday that something of a weather nature must have occurred. We'll take you home first so that I can explain to your parents and let them know that you were both chaperoned at all times."

"Anna wasn't, not this morning when she went to Maldon with Lord Delmore," Jonquil said, her stubborn chin jutting.

"Of course she was. They had the groom, and the phaeton is open. I doubt your mother would cavil at that. And very good of Anna, it was, to make sure that the Merriweathers were provisioned."

Anna blushed with guilt. To be praised for going with Delmore when her motives had not been at all pure was hard to hear. "I doubt Mama would mind. She thinks I'm past my last gasp as it is." Being considered too old to be eligible before she ever had been so was also hard, but not her mother's fault any more than her own. Poor Mama. To have married a foolish young man like her father had been a mistake but the shame had destroyed her mother who now lived as a shadow. Anna had been forced into the background in the same way.

When they reached the vicarage, she saw how worried her mother had been. She hurried outside, her expression a picture of downtrodden womanhood. One-handed, Travers opened the door and let down the chaise steps. He leapt down, holding his one hand out to steady Jonquil while she descended.

Mama kissed her on the cheek. "I'm so pleased to see you all safe and sound, my dears. Mr. Beeby thought you might have been caught in the snowstorm and I tried to hold onto that belief."

Lady Carrington leaned forward. "We weren't at all discomforted, Elizabeth. The carriage broke a wheel and we had to stay overnight at Drake House. All adequately chaperoned as you can see."

Anna alighted and kissed her mother on the cheek. "Refreshment," she whispered into her mother's ear.

Her mother blinked. "Would you like to step inside for a cup of tea, Alice?"

"Thank you for the kind thought, but we must get back. My poor sister has been without her sons for two days and she is surely worried."

"You looked after my girls. I'm indebted to you." Mama glanced at Jonquil, who wore her innocent angel expression. "I do hope you behaved yourself?" She only asked Jonquil. Apparently, she trusted to Anna's good sense. A flush of guilt touched Anna's cheeks. Jonquil could have been up to all sorts of mischief while Anna was fascinating herself with Delmore. She would have to be far more watchful when she was in London. Possibly she could be. Delmore hadn't mentioned he would be going back then.

Jonquil tilted up her pert nose. "Of course I did. Everyone was very kind to me."

Mr. Beeby came out too. He shook coachman Travers' hand, clearly not knowing who he was. Lady Carrington didn't enlighten him. Neither he nor Mama appeared to notice Delmore on the driver's seat, and the chaise proceeded back to Hastings House. Anna wanted to wave goodbye to Delmore or at least glance at him one last time, but he remained on the box muffled to his ears, staring in the other direction. She didn't know when she might see him again and she still had more mistress-ing to learn.

<h1 style="text-align:center">Chapter Eight</h1>

When Delmore arrived home, he saw two grooms dragging his phaeton into the carriage house. Wilson had already fed and watered the team. His mother had done her fussing over Jeremy and seemed unprepared to fuss over Delmore. A blow-by-blow description of the past twenty-four hours was then given to her by his aunt. Anna's part seemed largely, but strangely, ignored which although unfair, suited him.

"Jonquil was a real trooper," Jeremy managed to tell his parent before going upstairs to change. "You wouldn't think anyone related to old Beeby could have a sense of humor, would you? Well, she has. She kept me entertained with childish card games. She even made Delmore laugh a time or two."

Delmore didn't remember anything about Jonquil's part in the entertainment. He couldn't look past Anna and was astonished that Jeremy could. Anna lit up every room. Had she been here, he wouldn't have noticed for the first time how shabby the entrance hall appeared. He wouldn't have seen the dust on the mirror.

In fact, while driving the carriage down the sweep, he noticed for the first time that the trees along the edge needed trimming and that the hedges had lost their usual crisp lines. "Do we employ the normal complement of gardeners?" he asked his mother as he passed his hat and coat to the footman.

She blinked. "The house is my province. You would have to ask the steward."

He sat in his study for a long time, wanting Anna Winters and knowing he could never have her. She was no courtesan, and she was no light woman. She was simply herself, a delightful person who deserved a home and family of her own. The sooner she left for town, the better. In London, she would meet many a respectable man, surely one good enough for her, though her father had made this difficult. As a traitor to the crown, he had destroyed her chances of marrying into the ton. Any time she stood in a London ballroom, the friends and companions of the Prince of Wales would judge her and gossip about the events of 1794.

Being a companion to her sister while in the city would be difficult, but a woman with her natural grace would manage. He shouldn't make her chances even worse by acting the frustrated lover. Nor would he. One day, he too expected to marry. As a peer with a history of youthful indiscretions, he would need to choose a woman whose antecedents were respected in society, who could hold her head high in any company. This would help build in any of his hoped-for children the moral rectitude that had been absent in his family for the past few generations.

He poured himself a glass of sack and gulped down two without thinking. As he reached for the bottle again, he paused. Drinking numbed his brain and he needed to think. He pushed the bottle aside, sat with his elbows on his desk, leaning forward with his fingers massaging his scalp.

He had to finally face a fact that he had done his best to ignore during this past month. His ancestral home no longer hummed with activity. The floors didn't gleam, the windows looked dull, and the bells took an age to be answered. He employed the usual number of staff according to his steward and to his mother. He certainly signed off on the same wage bill. Perhaps he simply employed the laziest servants.

If so, that was his fault. He shouldn't have left his steward and his man of business to make all the decisions while he stayed in town enjoying the pleasures of the flesh. In that time, he had drunk himself into a stupor night after night, for no reason other than that his father had done the same before him. Although Delmore knew an earl had responsibilities, he had left his mother to run the household the way she had always done.

Perhaps she resented this. Perhaps she wanted a life of her own, unencumbered by the duties of the wife of an earl. He had never given a thought to her needs. Perhaps he should have moved her into the dower house when he had inherited the responsibilities he had refused to take. The time had come to discuss this and a few other matters with her.

He lifted his head and for the first time, he concentrated

on the dust on the top of the mirror above the fireplace. Was the whole house beset by dust? To check, he walked over to the glass fronted bookcase and reached up to the molding. Even before he noted the gritty texture, he sneezed. Since the butler remained unchanged, perhaps he too had grown less diligent.

He rang the bell and had the butler send Pickering to him.

His valet stood in front of his desk, a querying smile on his face.

"Are the meals downstairs up to scratch?"

Pickering hesitated. "Good nourishing food. Well cooked. Why do you ask, my lord?"

"Would you say we had adequate staff to run the house?"

"Adequate as to numbers, or adequate as to skill?"

"Both." Delmore leaned back as he tried to read the expression on his valet's wooden face.

"I wouldn't question the skill," Pickering said eventually. "Your cook is by way of being a genius, given what he has to work with. Your footmen are efficient."

Delmore narrowed his eyes. "What are you not saying?"

"You could do with more housemaids, my lord. No one likes to perform jobs beneath their dignity. The housekeeper will dust, but she doesn't have all day, or so she says. The head footman will clean silver but not if he has to act as the boot-boy. The butler will serve drinks, but not meals."

Delmore drummed his fingers on his desk. "Thank you, Pickering." The stiff-backed valet left. Servants never liked to reveal the below-stairs gossip, whether they were part of the normal household or not.

On a usual day, if he wanted to speak to Wilson, he would go to the stables to find him. Today, he rang the bell again and sent the butler off to find the groom. A few minutes later, his boots hastily wiped, Wilson stood before him, a rebellious expression on his old/young face. "If them 'orses have taken harm, you need to look to your brother. Anxious hands he has, not like yours."

"I haven't yet inspected the horses, Wilson, and if the horses have taken harm, we, you and I, will coddle them until they have regained their spirits. I want to speak to you on another matter. Are you finding the stables here everything that you would expect?"

Wilson blinked. "They're not like ours in town. Everyone is willin' enough but stable boys do the work of grooms. Ain't much mucking out done. Maybe we oughta 'ave brought our own grooms and the stable boys could do their work they way they ought."

"Perhaps so. They have little enough to do while we're not there. That will be all."

Clearly Delmore had been derelict in his duty. He had looked over the garden and seen a change was needed, but he had left the house to his mother and ignored the stables. He arose and made his way to the steward's office, a space in the vast downstairs area. Most of this was dedicated to the running of the house: kitchens, larders, wine cellars, the game room, and the servants' accommodation. The steward's office faced the bleak garden and could be entered from an outside door or from a passage inside. He chose the inside.

The two rooms, one a working space and the other an area furnished with cabinets, drawers, and a central table, were unattended. He gazed out the window, staring at a garden whose trees needed a winter pruning, whose lawns needed scything, whose beds needed weeding, the whole a metaphor of his life.

He was as derelict as his property.

He had no real interests other than trying to keep boredom at bay. He had no real role other than spending the money that his ancestors had made for him. His wine bill the last quarter had come close to rivaling his gambling losses. His man of business had informed him that finding the wherewithal to keep Delmore's bills paid had become a nightmare. Delmore had ignored him, deciding his man of business was needlessly fussing over incidentals.

Taking the books for the last quarter back to his study, he reached for the bottle of sack as he entered the room. For a minute or two he stared at his empty glass, and then he sighed. He put the glass and the bottle on a tray and rang for the butler again. "Remove all the wine from my study, please."

Westerfield's heavy gray eyebrows hit his hairline. "All, my lord?"

"Every scrap. Wine will be served at meals but at no time during the day to anyone."

"Sir Waldo?"

"Will be treated as a guest. My brother and I will not drink other than at meals."

"Very good, my lord." Like every butler Delmore had seen, Westerfield kept his expression blank. As he should. His business was to serve. Delmore's from now on was not to rely on drinking to decide his moods.

Jeremy didn't appear to be a tippler and he wouldn't

notice the lack of sherry during the afternoon or the brandy after dinner. His mother might even approve. She had ignored Delmore's habit of drinking ale in the morning, a bottle of wine with his midday repast, and various refreshment during the day, but she had offered a frowning glance at the footman when he had presented three kinds of wine with the evening meal. Possibly he tippled constantly because his father had. The day at Drake House, being occupied with others and their wants, had shown him how often he expected to take a drink.

Uneasily, he sat with the steward's accounting in front of him. Until he heard voices in the hall, his mother and his aunt and uncle arriving back from the daily grind of morning calls, he didn't notice anything other than the disturbing figures in the books in front of him. His concentration now lost, he stared at the late afternoon gloom outside the window. He stretched his back. He wanted Anna, but like a glass of brandy, she was not for him.

He rubbed his forehead, doubting she believed him when he told her that the affair he hadn't started would now end.

The Christmas festivities, like the heavy fruit pudding, were now finished. Anna sat in the front parlor embroidering the last of the tiny white flowers onto the border of the yellow voile she and Jonquil had purchased two months ago—the day that Delmore had been respectably introduced to Anna.

The warmth from the fire barely reached her, although

she had pulled up a chair to one side. For years, embroidery had been her greatest pleasure. Being off her feet doubled her enjoyment. Having recently completed Jonquil's pink gown, she diligently plied her needle, trying to savor an activity that had formerly been her only joy.

One tear wandered out of her eye and dripped down the side of her nose. She used the back of her hand to wipe up the spill. In the past four weeks she had heard nothing from Delmore. She had hoped for a meeting, or an invitation, or even a social call. Clearly, she had been mistaken in his interest. She was apparently just another woman to him.

The door opened and Jonquil glided across the room to warm her hands by the fire. She glanced down at the embroidery. "You're so kind to do that for me, Anna. It's lovely."

Anna cleared her throat, keeping her gaze on the work, although she doubted that a single passing tear had reddened her eyes. "Thank you, but you know I love doing this fine work. Morag has finished sewing the under-gown for you. She grumbled to me for half an hour this morning about the lack of fullness in the skirt, but I explained for the third time that we needed to cater for the current fashions."

"Could you put more lace on the sleeves?"

"If you have more, the voile overdress will look too fussy."

Jonquil flopped down onto the settee, prepared to argue, when the knocker sounded at the front door. Morag's heavy footsteps plodded down the hallway and back. The parlor door cricked open. Jeremy wandered in. He had been by almost every second day since the unfortunate stranding at Drake House, keeping the vicarage informed as to his latest doings, mainly sporting events attended by him with John and Rodney.

"Delmore has run mad." He tossed his hat onto the side table. By rights, Morag should have taken his hat as he entered, but her memory wasn't the best these days.

Jonquil looked interested. "In what way?" She arranged herself on the settee, ankles primly together, hands clasped on her lap. Before the visit to Drake House, she had usually left the room whenever Jeremy came to call on Anna. Now she hastened into the room whenever she heard his curricle outside.

He turned the other single chair by the fire to face her and Anna and sat. "I can't really say, but he spent yesterday on the home farm and today he is off to stick his nose into the affairs of his tenants."

"Isn't that a good thing?" Anna kept her gaze on her embroidery.

"What does he know about running the home farm or the seeds the tenants ought to be planting? He pays a steward to handle all that sort of rubbish."

Anna made a triple knot for the stamen of the flower. "Perhaps you ought to be doing the same at Drake House."

"The codger likely knew what was what. He ran the estate for fifty years and my rents seem to be quite healthy." He stared at Anna.

"You would never guess by the look of the place."

Jonquil clicked her tongue in reproof. "When he moves in, the house will be refurbished, won't it, Jeremy? You plan to make it look nice."

"Eventually." He smiled absently at Jonquil. "I have no need to rush. First there's the London season to be dealt with. I wouldn't want to turn the house on end when I plan to be in town for the balls and all the other entertainments you and Anna might be attending."

"Will you be staying with Rodney again?"

He shrugged. "I would prefer to stay in Delmore House but unless my mother goes for the season, the place is not opened."

"Does Delmore not use the house?" Anna's voice trailed forlornly. Delmore had not mentioned that he might see her in London. He had never made a single assignation. Perhaps he had another mistress anxiously awaiting his arrival.

"Oh, he doesn't bother with the place. He has one of his own. He thinks Delmore House is too big for a bachelor."

"Perhaps he simply leaves Delmore House for you and his mother." Anna snipped off her thread.

"That's what he said but he really prefers being on his own. Her Ladyship says she isn't interested in the season. Perhaps she would be if she was on the hunt for another husband, who knows?" Jeremy made a face of wild speculation and huffed out a laugh.

"Would you want a new papa, Jeremy?"

He turned to Jonquil. "Depends on who he is. If he's someone with a place of his own, that would suit her. She doesn't care to move into the dower house."

"It's a sweet little place." Anna stared at Jeremy. "Not that I've seen inside but from the outside it's lovely with those climbing roses up the side and the pretty green lawn."

"She prefers Hastings House. She has lived there for more than thirty years."

Anna absorbed the fact that Lady Delmore hadn't lived in town with her husband while he was alive. He had died a few years after Anna had moved into the vicarage, but she didn't recall ever seeing him in the district. Jeremy had rarely mentioned him, but young aristocrats seemed to be brought up by servants and tutors. Not having a father herself, Anna accepted the late earl's casual treatment of his sons as relatively normal. "Will she stay when Delmore marries?"

"That's a joke, Delmore thinking about marriage. Our father didn't marry until he was forty."

Anna's back stiffened. "He doesn't have to do everything your father did."

"He has for most of his life. He went to the same schools, spent the same amount of time at Oxford, got send down, fathered his first child when he was twenty-two, which our father also did ... I shouldn't have said that in front of Jonquil, should I?" He glanced at Anna with remorse.

"It's said now." Anna knew about the farmer's daughter. The whole district knew. Gossip said Delmore had been gulled. The girl looked nothing like him but apparently, he had never made a fuss. "You have heard the gossip before, haven't you Jonquil?"

"No one believes it." Jonquil folded her hands in lap. "But his payment speaks of a guilty conscience and so no one bothers about praising him."

"He probably has others that he doesn't support. That's why." Jeremy raised his chin.

"Guilty without a trial because he lives the same lifestyle as your father with his mistresses and his gambling." Anna deliberately sounded prosaic. She couldn't fault the gossip because Delmore was well on the way to being profligate, but she saw a good man beneath his rakish exterior. He still supported his family. Jeremy should have been planning to set up his own household as soon as he had come into his inheritance last year, but he still lived on his brother's largesse. Lady Delmore doubtless had her own income and by rights should have moved into the dower house, but more than likely she was needed to run the big house. After all, Delmore showed no sign of settling down in the near future. He still had more mistresses to take, or at least one more.

He had said, "You will be my love. This is the time we have, only now." Had she misunderstood? Did he not plan to accept her offer? Another tear tried to drip but she had the presence of mind to discard her sewing for a moment and find her handkerchief. Fortunately, she wasn't crying, only a little blinky in the eye area.

"He's a good chap when all is done," Jeremy said in a serious voice. "Not that my uncle agrees. He has to drink alone because Delmore has taken up sobriety for the time being. Apparently, he is currently enjoying raging headaches."

"In that case, sobriety would help." Jonquil nodded as if she knew. "When I tasted the tiniest glassful of papa's brandy some years ago, I certainly had a headache later. At the time, though, despite the strong taste, I quite enjoyed the woozy feeling."

Anna gave a shadowy laugh. "Your papa gave me quite a lecture. He presumed I encouraged you to drink the brandy."

"You tasted it first, Anna."

"That's the magic word. I sipped. You gulped."

"I see I'm in the company of two dedicated tipplers." Jeremy leaned back, resting his hands on his thighs.

Jonquil giggled. Anna picked up her embroidery again, more focused on Delmore's sudden change of lifestyle than on the silly conversation. She wondered what he was up to. Eventually Jeremy left and she convinced Jonquil to knot a fringe for her new reticule.

Every little bit helped. As well as the pink gown, Mama and Morag had made Jonquil a pink spencer and a sprigged muslin day gown. New underwear had been cut ready to sew but Morag kept muttering about the indecency of the skimpy fabric and wearing only single petticoats. Anna had cut out two more gowns for Jonquil, and her stepfather had allowed her a length of material to make a gown for herself. Not being a sweet young eligible, she had chosen a strong color, a dark green on which she planned to add a patterned hem border of pale yellow. Her best blue gown would be trimmed with cream on the shoulders and the hem. She would, of course, take her usual day gowns, which could be spruced up, one with a patterned spencer and another with a patterned trim. Her aim was to look self possessed rather than fashionable.

She hoped she had enough hours in the day to finish her gowns before she was whisked off to London to be the old maid companion to her pretty younger sister.

Delmore entered his mother's rooms. Nine years ago, with his father, she had occupied the suite he now called his own. After his father had died, she had relegated herself to the suite of rooms her own husband's mother had formerly taken in an older part of the house. Her small area was furnished with delicate Chippendale chairs and side-tables, and comfortable couches upholstered in pale blue velvet in the old-fashioned style of her mother-in-law. She had made no changes for herself other than to shift a few minor paintings of roses from various parts of the main house.

Seen as a twenty-year-old male, these rooms appeared to be quite a tolerable area in which his mother could spend her time. Now as a closer to thirty-year-old earl who had finally investigated exactly how he earned his income, his gaze rested on furniture desperate for another coat of shellac and carpets layered on top of each other to hide the worn patches in the one beneath.

His mother indicated an elegant high-backed chair in a shabby blue for him to seat himself. "How delightful to have your company." She put down the book she was reading and folded her hands neatly in her lap.

He sat in the chair nearest to her, never assuming for a moment that she meant those words. His relationship with her was cordial but never close. He scarcely knew her. At the age of six, he had been sent off to Eton and from then he had spent most of his life in the city studying to be his father, without ever learning how to take his place. As the next earl, he knew politicians, princes, aristocrats, and gentlemen with influence. He knew how to gamble, how to set up a series of mistresses, how to avoid the French disease, and how to treat a lady like his mother with courtesy.

She in turn had taught Jeremy how to revere his father, how to charm debutants, and how to love her. In the game of life, Jeremy was an early winner. Delmore knew he had missed quite a few of life's practical lessons and he seemed to be running on the spot trying to catch normality, if anyone could describe life in this household as normal.

In recent years, his conversations with his mother had been polite but impartial words about the latest political shenanigans, or comments on the doings of Prinny and his set. Delmore conversed with her in passing, or during meals, but on a personal level, he knew nothing about her. Yet, he respected her and, deep down, loved her. "My maturing has been a long time coming. Thank you for taking care of my inheritance for me."

"My dear boy ..." She straightened. "I could do no less than my duty."

"And you did no less than your duty to my father, too." He reached across and took her hands in his.

Her gaze met his in query, but she left her hands in his keeping. "Although he would never admit to it, I suspect that's why he married me."

"I hope I haven't burned too many bridges to be able to find the wife who will live up to your example. I'll be sure not to spend more than my estates earn from now on."

One side of her mouth lifted. "I'm not certain how you will manage that."

"For a start, I'll return the staff from the city that I haplessly acquired from here." He let her take her hands back and she picked up her sewing again.

"And then how will you afford your own?" She peered at her bundle of threads, searching for a new color.

"I plan to sell Packham Place and use Delmore House as my city abode. How easy it seems now I have realized I can't afford to keep both houses running. I have no idea why I thought I could."

"You thought you could afford both because your father did." She wet the end her embroidery silk between her lips and poked the thread through her needle.

"Clearly he was a better manager than I."

She raised her gaze. "Your father never bothered about managing. He borrowed money from the estate's accounts so that he could keep his respectable life, and also enjoy his fancy women and his card parties. Delmore House for the family, and Packham Place to impress Prinny." She sounded impartial.

"And I carried on his tradition." He set his uneasy palms together and concentrated on meshing his fingers. "Despite the fact that I'm not one of the Prince of Wales' cronies." He glanced at her. "You never seem to go to town these days. And Jeremy stays with friends whenever he does. I have staff in both houses that are underemployed while we need more staff here. Were you assuming I would wake up to this one day?"

Her head inclined slightly. "My advice was not solicited. My duty is now and has always been to keep doing the best I can."

He wanted to reach out and take her hand again, but shows of affection had always been discouraged. The last time he had hugged her had been the day he had been sent off to school some twenty years ago. His father had told him to behave like a man and The Honorable Calder John Hastings, as he had been then, had squared his shoulders and, bereft, let his mother go. "At least I have discovered why my tenants hold me in contempt. I should have been investing money in the estate instead of raising the rents. You'll be pleased to hear that I plan to sell off any carriage that is standing idle."

"You will, I hope, leave me with my barouche."

"I will leave you with whatever you wish. Mine is the profligacy. I have any number of vehicles in the city, a team of four idle chestnuts, four sturdy carriage horses, too many riding horses, and a commensurate number of stable boys and grooms. When I go back to town, I'll sort out the essentials from the money wasters.' He tried a smile. "Soon, you'll have this house fully staffed again."

"That will be a blessing. Thank you." Her eyes shiny bright, she met his gaze.

"Are you happy living in these rooms?"

"I'm not unhappy."

"That isn't what I asked," he said, for the first time, understanding the expression of wariness in her eyes.

"Where else should I live? Your father spent my dowry money. Unless I marry a man of subsequence, here is where I will stay."

He stared at her, hearing the strain in her tone. Why had he never considered that she might want to marry again? By his calculations she was now not quite fifty. Her jaw line was firm, her figure was still slender, and even a son could admit she had kept her looks. "I'll be sending some of the staff from Packham Place to Delmore House instead, if you wish to stay in town for the season."

She breathed out. "I would certainly enjoy that, Calder. I'm sure Jeremy would bear me company. I know he means to go. Do you plan to go, too?"

"I think not. I have much to learn about being a landowner. One of my tenants has expressed interest in experimenting with crops. Apparently, he brought up the matter with my steward some years ago, but my man of business decided we couldn't allow that while I needed every penny to pay my excessive bills. If I can manage to live within my income, I should be able to make a difference here." He rose to his feet. "Now, I have taken up much of your time and must get back to work."

"Work?" Her mouth lifted on one side as he stood.

"I'm redefining boundaries today, a task that I must admit I find interesting, to say the least." He left quite amazed that field sizes, crop yields, and weather patterns had begun to absorb him. If he didn't watch himself, he would turn into a gnarled old farmer who could only discuss sewing wheat and digging ditches—which reminded him of Lord Grantham.

As he changed into working clothes and his old sturdy boots, he recalled how often he had seen their neighbor sitting in the morning parlor or trailing the widowed Lady Delmore around the garden. However, a man who had sold off most of his lands to a rich industrialist and had barely managed to keep his old pile warm these days, couldn't afford to offer for a woman who had no prospects.

If the dowager Lady Delmore had her lost dowry replaced, she may well be a catch for a man who already seemed besotted.

Chapter Nine

Rugged up against the cold and frosty morning, his hat brim low across his forehead, Delmore drove his phaeton out to the Forster's farm, the tenancy he had presented to his first love for the man who was willing to marry Delmore's spoiled goods. After only a moderate flurry, his mother and brother had left for the London season, leaving him distraction free and with the chance to make the first meaningful changes to his life.

Wilson held the horses while he knocked on the door of the neat little cottage where Isla lived with her farmer.

"My lord," she said, curtseying and indicating the front parlor. She didn't look the way he remembered. Nowadays she was decidedly plump but still very pretty. Her redheaded daughter sat near the fire, peeling apples, a bowl of the cut fruit in her lap, staring curiously at Delmore.

"Do you want an audience, my dear?" he asked Isla, after quick glance at the neatly aproned child.

"Go out and help your father, Missy."

The child slid off her chair, placed the bowl on the floor, and left without a word.

"Her father? At least you aren't telling her the lie you told everyone else."

She shrugged. "What else would she call him even if she had been yours? He would still be known as her father. Have you come to oust us?"

He glanced around the small room, noting the cozy fire, and the single polished side table, clean linen neatly folded atop, awaiting another destination, perhaps. "Believe me, I need all the good tenants I can get. I would simply like the record straight. My name is on her birth certificate. I believe that can be amended if we both agree."

She backed slightly, folding her arms. "Will you take back the tenancy if I don't?"

"Not while your husband is doing such a fine job of running this farm. I simply want one less deed on my list of sins." He waited, trying to read her expression.

Finally, the suspicion faded from her eyes. "I will go with you to change the papers whenever you like. I think Mr. Forster will be pleased. Missy has neither a brother nor a sister. And truly, you were never a sinner. I liked you very much. Sadly, I also liked Mr. Forster very much before I liked you."

Strangely touched, he smiled and reached out to take her hidden hand. "Thank you, Isla. I liked you too but now I plan to start again and be the man I should have been."

Strolling out of the cottage, he was tempted to do a merry jig. Wilson glanced at him but said nothing until they reached the crossroads. "I kept a watch for her 'usband.

Lookin' after the little girl kept him away. If he had tried to bother you, he would 'ave had to deal with me."

Despite Wilson being half the size of the farmer, Delmore believed his groom. Touched by the fierce loyalty in Wilson's tone, he said, "Fortunately Mrs. Forster and I sorted out matters. It won't change a thing for either of us but perhaps the little girl will appreciate being known as the daughter of her father."

~

LONDON

Anna sat in a plush red chair beside her aunt on the sidelines of the Meridan's ballroom. Shepherds cavorted with nymphs on the gilded paneling of the walls. Anna cavorted with no one, glad not to be dancing, or so she told herself. The ballroom floor juddered with the pounding of feet. The musicians at the other end of the long room competed with the conversations, adding to the general gaiety.

Lady Prescott fanned herself and moved her lips closer to Anna's ear. "She looks very lovely, so sweet and young." Aunt Lucy's gaze indicated Jonquil, who beautifully performed the complicated steps of the cotillion she had been learning for the past month. "I suspect it's due to you. You always had an eye for style."

"She looks pretty in yellow, but she looks pretty in everything."

"You look rather regal yourself." Aunt's dimples showed when she smiled. Unlike her younger sister, Anna's mother, Aunt Lucy was outrageous in the way she dressed. No color was bright enough for her and tonight she wore a pink gown with four rows of red ruffling on the hem. The same ran in two rows from her high waist to her shoulders and down to the waist at the back. Only a few flat curls around her face showed beneath her enormous blue headdress from which three peacock feathers sprang. On someone else, her style might be overdone. On aunt overdone looked perfect.

Anna laughed. "That's one benefit of not being a debutante. I can wear the darker colors that suit me. I only wish that I could wear a turban like you."

"When you are older, my dear. Your hair is still pretty enough to feature. I do like that style on you. The upsweep is very elegant."

"You were so kind to take us both for the season." Anna laid her hand on her aunt's for a moment. "I sincerely hope we are not being too much bother."

"I wanted you for your own debut, my dear, but your mama didn't think ..." Lady Prescott's cheerful face wrinkled with regret. "So, I snatched this chance instead. We can call you a companion as much as we like, but chaperonage is my role, not yours. You are meant to be enjoying yourself as well. You should have accepted your young man's invitation to dance."

"Jeremy will ask again, never fear. I thought it was more important for Jonquil to be on the floor for the first dance, and she is comfortable with him." If Delmore were here, she would love to be dancing with him, but Delmore was still at Hasting's House in Danbury. She hadn't seen him for almost two months. If she hadn't been so forward ... but then she would have regretted never having kissed him, never having touched him, never having been pleasured by him. Clearly he had decided not to give her another chance. "Oh, no. Here comes John Temple. Surely, he knows a few other ladies here?"

John Temple stood in front of her with an expression of abstraction on his round boyish face. "Anna, would you allow me the honor of a dance with you tonight. The next country dance would do me."

"Well, then, John, the first country dance is yours, though I'm sure you are only asking me so that I will remind you of your steps."

"Not at all." He gave her an offended glance. "I want to join Jonquil's set and I'll have a better chance if I partner you."

"Very wise." After he left, she turned to her aunt. "In case I think I'm looking rather smart tonight, that is my reminder about being Jonquil's companion." She gave a soft laugh.

Lady Prescott clicked her tongue. "The young man is sadly callow. You wouldn't want him courting you."

"Oh, no. I fear I must settle for a much older man." One of about twenty-nine years-old would do nicely, one with dangerous green eyes, dark hair, and a smile so reluctant that one needed to coax the action out of him. The one who could never marry her and who had not said he would require her as a mistress. "Oh, no. Here comes Rodney Toddington. Jeremy must have lined up all his friends as he threatened."

Rodney also booked a dance with her. When the cotillion finished, Jeremy brought Jonquil back. A young friend of his soon snapped her up while Jeremy stood watching as she was guided back onto the floor again. "I may not have to try to find more partners for her. Which is a relief. Now, this is my dance with you, Anna."

She enjoyed herself on the floor again while wondering what society thought of a companion agreeing to dance almost as often as her charge. No sooner had she sat beside her aunt again than Lady Delmore herself arrived with a gentleman in tow, apparently a contemporary of Delmore's. Despite being astonished that the dowager was willing to introduce partners to her, she greeted both with a smile.

"Delighted to make your acquaintance, Miss Winters." Mr. Robert Fieldhouse bowed. "Do you waltz?" A well set-up man of about thirty with pleasant features, Mr. Field-house could boast a full head of light brown hair fashionably cropped and brushed forward.

"My waltzing is very rudimentary, Mr. Fieldhouse, practiced only rurally."

"Could I interest you in a town partner, Miss Winters? This is my self-effacing way of asking the most elegant young lady in the room to waltz with me." He held out his hand, confidently waiting for hers.

"Do accept, Anna." Her aunt gave a mischievous smile. "Mr. Fieldhouse is an excellent dancer."

He nodded politely at Aunt Lucy and turned back to Anna. "I believe you live in Danbury?"

She studied him, noting his perfectly cut black jacket and his fashionably tied white cravat. "My step-father is the vicar."

"Imagine Delmore being acquainted with a vicar." He shook his head, pretending shock. "The mind reels."

She smiled back. "I'm not sure if either know who the other is. My stepfather is notoriously vague."

"And Delmore is simply notorious?"

She laughed. "Not in Danbury. He is most respectable. One would hardly believe he is considered a very dashing fellow."

"He is considered a rake, Miss Winters. His father was one of the Carleton House set and Delmore is a la mode with the friends of the Regent."

She nodded and rested her hand on his. "I would be delighted to waltz with an acquaintance of the rakish earl. That is, as long as you don't mind my inexperience."

"Not at all," he said smoothly, moving her onto the floor. "A fellow never minds inexperience in women. We delight in teaching, you know." His smile came with half hooded eyes. A flirtatious man, his comment about the regent's friendship had reminded her about Delmore's responsibilities, but she already knew a sanctioned match between her, and a member of the Hastings' family was impossible. The words only served to depress her. She could never have him as her husband, and he didn't want her as a mistress.

Mr. Fieldhouse waltzed divinely, and she enjoyed the novelty of dancing with an expert. When he delivered her back to Lady Prescott, he bowed. "May I have the honor of the supper dance too, Miss Winters?"

She glanced at her aunt.

"Miss Winters would be honored, Mr. Fieldhouse." Aunt prodded Anna in the side when he left. "One conquest. How many to follow, I wonder?" She smiled roguishly.

"I would hardly compare a polite request to eat supper together as a conquest."

"He has only been on the market for a year, and he is quite a catch. He's worth some ten thousand a year."

"Perhaps we ought to introduce him to Jonquil. Mama would like ten thousand a year."

Aunt Lucy shook her head. "The child is too young for an experienced man. His wife died two years ago, and he has two young children."

"Ah, he wants a new mother for them. I can quite see that I am more suitable in that case. Does he know about my father?"

"Everyone does, Anna, if you don't mind me being truthful. But Mr. Fieldhouse isn't a close acquaintance of Prinny's and can marry wherever he likes. Oh, here's Jonquil again, and young Mr. Toddington." She aimed a severe glance at Rodney as he seated Jonquil on the other side of her. "Have you come to take Anna to the floor, sir?"

"I d-did book this next dance." Rodney Toddington was possibly the most outrageously handsome of Jeremy's friends, with soft brown eyes and unruly hair as dark as midnight. He currently wore his perfectly arched eyebrows lowered in a frown. "Can't have Anna sitting with the dowdies. Beg your pardon, Ma'am." He blushed and hung his head. Why a man of such fortunate looks had no confidence was a mystery to Anna.

"How can I resist such a gallant rescue attempt? Aunt, you ought to have worn the orange gown as I advised, then no one would have the right to call you dowdy."

"No ma'am, indeed, I didn't mean you. I meant the

group here, all the chaperones, not the ..." He swallowed, belatedly realizing he was only digging his hole deeper.

Anna took pity on him. "Come along. This is the dance before the country-dance where John wants to partner me so that he can join Jonquil's set. Perhaps he might have asked to partner Jonquil, but I expect he didn't think of that."

"He didn't," Jonquil said, butting in. She used her pouty smile. Her sweetest dimples appeared as she glanced at Rodney. "And so, I have lost John to you as well. Now I might not be in a set, myself." She folded her arms across her chest, eyeing poor besotted Rodney sideways. Only the fact that he had already danced with her stopped him from changing partners midstream.

Fortunately, Jeremy came to the rescue with a partner for Jonquil. She accepted the new gentleman with grace, watching Jeremy leave to partner Miss Goodings, the lady held to be the most beauteous this season. After tonight, she might be deposed by Jonquil who was certainly turning peoples' heads. Jonquil herself didn't seem as overjoyed with the new young man as she should have been. Although she managed to be on the floor for every dance, she seemed her most animated when Jeremy was present.

The stranding at Drake House had changed the relationship between the two. He no longer tried to avoid her and, as she had done at home, she made sure of being Anna's chaperone whenever he came to call. These days he seemed so at ease with Jonquil that he didn't make a face when she arrived hot on his trail. Then again, she no longer butted into conversations. She participated the way a young lady should.

After a very pleasant supper dance with Mr. Fieldhouse, Anna agreed to have him call on her the next day. Aunt nodded with satisfaction. "We'll have a list of admirers for you by the end of the season, see if we don't."

Anna smiled but she doubted she would make a good match for Mr. Fieldhouse. He lacked green smiling eyes. He couldn't match her sense of humor with droll repartee. He didn't make her heart race and she would never offer to be his mistress. She had lost her heart to a rake and doubted she would get it back.

Chapter Ten

ESSEX

Now that Delmore had corrected the problem with his now unneeded staff moved back to Hastings House, he had a dust free study warmed by a glowing fire. A polished silver tray on his desk held a silver tea service and a rose painted china cup. A proper earl like his father would have a bottle of wine or brandy presented at this time of day. Today his son drank tea. He sipped, not acquiring the taste but not objecting to the tang either. The benefit of drinking tea was that it didn't influence his thinking and these days he didn't particularly object to thinking.

Apparently, the clean country air made a man want to change, to be responsible and care about his family and his estate. He couldn't say he had increased his income, but he could say that his income no longer decreased. In fact, he saw every possibility of remaining on an even keel until he managed a hoped-for turnaround.

Yesterday, he had driven over to his paternal grand-mother's house. The place had been bleeding money for years. He needed another call on his purse as much as he wanted a stagnant pond in the sheep pastures. Since the crumbling pile was not part of the estate, he had decided to sell so that he had the money to repair the Hastings' dower house for his mother. The roof of the dower house leaked, and the kitchens needed upgrading. With luck the renovations would be started before she arrived back from London.

"You wanted me, my lord?" Wilson stood in the doorway, his expression truculent.

"I have decided to go up to London tomorrow." Delmore carefully replaced his cup in his saucer.

"I thought we was going to be stuck 'ere forever," Wilson said, his expression lightening.

"Does country life not suit you?" Delmore folded his hands.

"Suits me well enough but I'm worried about them grays."

"I plan to sell them. Since no one else has four matched grays, I will make a tidy profit. I will also be disposing of my father's travelling carriage. I don't remember the last time it was used."

"You ain't never used it while I've been with you. Catching dust, it is."

"Aside from that, I won't have the room for many more carriages at Delmore House." Delmore sipped his tea. "I'll be transferring all my livestock from Packham Place before the month is up."

Wilson's forehead creased and he focused on Delmore's face. "You're set on selling, are you, Gov? Are we broke?"

"Not yet. But I was heading in a downward direction. If

you know of any other economies I can practices in the stables, let me know."

"I knows right enough. Wait till we gets back. You've got a stable master needs getting rid of too."

"And you haven't told me before this?" Delmore raised his eyebrows.

"Would you 'ave listened? No, you wouldn't." Wilson folded his arms across his narrow chest.

"No, I wouldn't. I thought I had all the money in the world, while all I had was no sense." Delmore took his quill out of the holder.

A shadow of a smile crossed Wilson's face. "I wouldn't say that 'zactly."

"What would you say?"

"You was doing what your pa did. You didn't know no better. And I won't say no more. I wants to keep me job." With a smug grin, Wilson left.

Delmore smiled reluctantly. The groom was right. Delmore had followed in the footsteps of his father. Perhaps he would never have questioned his lifestyle but for his mistress's temper tantrum, which had decided him to leave London for a few weeks. Pure selfishness had caused him to note the diminishment in his comfort while away from London; showed him the dearth of servants to keep the family estate running in the manner he expected.

Coming back to Hastings House had woken him up to the fact that he used alcoholic beverages to support him to continue his self-defeating behavior. When tempted to misbehave with Anna Winter, he had taken the first step, which his previous life had taught him would lead to the next irretrievable step. In the normal run of events, he would eventually have taken her, regardless of the consequences. However, neither that day nor the one before had he consumed his regular portion of wine. His mind had been a little less clouded than usual. Despite Anna's wholehearted willingness to be his plaything, he had managed to summon up a previously unknown skerrick of decency.

Even he knew he didn't deserve a naturally charming, completely honest woman like Anna. He deserved the women he consorted with, the unfaithful wives, the easy women, the mistresses who would as soon offer their lovely bodies and empty minds to the next candidate. To take Anna as his mistress would be a travesty of all that was right. She should be respectably married to a man who deserved a bright and beautiful wife.

One day he might be that sort of man but first he had to learn to live without mindlessly drinking himself into oblivion, or taking a new woman whenever the last began to bore him. The country stay had cleared his brain somewhat and he knew he didn't intend to end up a man like his father, an overweight wheezy reprobate, like the prince regent. Delmore had gone down far enough and now was the time to pull up and aim somewhat higher.

After steadily gazing out the window, watching as heavy clouds darkened the sky, he squeezed at his forehead between this thumb and his fingers. Beginning slowly, he cleared up the papers on his desk. Next, he pulled a batch of worn journals down from a high shelf. All the information about the farming practices that other landholders had decided made good money needed to be investigated. His eyes began to skim and finally focused on the facts he needed.

Two weeks of sobriety later, with his tenants now willing to meet his gaze, he left for London.

~

LONDON

Mr. Fieldhouse took Anna onto the floor for the first waltz. He presumed he could have the first dance and since Jeremy hadn't yet arrived at the Prescott's ball with his friends, she had no plausible excuse to refuse. Although she appreciated having a suitor, she disliked his assumption that she had accepted him as an aspiring contender.

"I had no idea Aunt Lucy could fit a hundred people in her ballroom, let alone the orchestra," she said to him as he walked her onto the floor.

"More than a hundred people have arrived, already."

"That can't be so. She only sent out a hundred invitations."

"Your sister has many suitors. I suspect even those not invited have come to see if she stands up to her beauteous description."

"Now you have cast me down. I thought so many arrived because of me."

He blinked with puzzlement. "If the young men knew what a treasure you are, you would certainly be the rage. But you treat men like people rather than prospective suitors. You don't flirt enough."

"I'm a failure, to be sure."

"You are delightful, Miss Winters, and you must know it."

She sighed. She quite liked Mr. Fieldhouse. He had scrupulous manners, a good income, he dressed well, and he didn't lack charm. She didn't object to him. She didn't object to him having children. And, tonight, he even managed plain speaking rather than flattery.

The music began and she followed the steps. Truth to tell, she liked dancing, but she enjoyed interesting conversations far more. Mr. Fieldhouse hadn't yet attempted to supply the latter. Mama wouldn't have wished more for her than an aspirant to her hand such as he. Mama should have married a man like him herself, one who wasn't so imprudent as to follow the Stuart cause and betray his rightful king. Her father had been a rash young man who hadn't given a thought to anyone but himself. The repercussions of his actions had almost destroyed his pregnant young wife's life. She had been questioned and bullied after her husband had died, in case she too had harbored traitorous intentions.

Poor Mama. Perhaps once she might have been an intrepid young lady, but that experience had left her timorous enough to accept being her new husband's slave, willing to give up her life for him, because the selfish creature grandly accepted the responsibility for Anna as well.

Anna would never be like her mother, and she certainly wasn't like her father. She was herself, apolitical and proud. She would rather be the mistress of the man she loved than the wife of one who thought she would be useful to him. In that way, she might be like her father, unrealistic, but she hoped not. She simply wanted to be a woman with enough strength to live her life without being reliant on any man who would consider marrying her.

The set finished and Mr. Fieldhouse tucked her hand under his arm to escort her back to Lady Prescott. The noise of the guests almost drowned out his words. She leaned an ear closer to him, gazing across the floor ... and her eyes met Delmore's.

The shock caused her to straighten. She stood frozen to the spot; having had no idea he would be here tonight. While her heartbeat thudded in her throat, her delighted smile began and stopped. The earl hadn't bothered with her for three months. More than likely, he didn't mean to acknowledge her tonight. The lightness in her chest changed to a heavy-breathing disappointment.

He lowered his gaze and turned back to the beautiful woman with flame red hair who had her hand in his arm. Anna immediately tightened her grip on Mr. Fieldhouse and began to nod in agreement to whatever he said, although she couldn't concentrate on a single word.

In a daze, she let Mr. Fieldhouse take her back to Lady Prescott's side, forcing herself not to glance in Delmore's direction. Although she had never had him, she had lost him. In no time he would be back with his old friends, living his unsavory lifestyle without the most caring mistress a man could have. But she couldn't afford to look downcast. She wouldn't give him the satisfaction that he could add her lost hopes to his list.

Before she could say a word, her aunt grabbed her, smiling from ear to ear. "Lord Delmore's here. What a coup? You and Jonquil are now made. You are the success of the season even if he never even speaks to you." She squeezed Anna's hand.

"Did you invite him?" Anna asked politely, her throat aching.

"You don't invite Delmore." Mr. Fieldhouse looked amused.

Aunt patted her chest. "You wait and hope and, oh my goodness, he is walking toward us."

Anna refused to turn and stare like a gawping country spinster. "I'm glad he has the manners to introduce himself to the lady holding the ball that he came uninvited to."

"To which he came uninvited." Delmore's deep voice came from behind her. "If you wish to be correct."

"I have always wished to be correct." Jaw tight, Anna turned to face him. "But often events conspire against me. Lady Prescott, may I introduce you to our nearest neighbor in Danbury, Lord Delmore?"

"The honor is mine." He gently took Aunt's hand, smiling into her eyes. The dangerously charming Lord Delmore to the letter. "I believe my mother is here somewhere and I'm sure my brother is not too far away, bearing in mind Anna's presence. Fieldhouse, good evening."

Mr. Fieldhouse gave Delmore a common bow while Aunt began to fan herself, possibly because Delmore used Anna's name.

She frowned at him. "You should call me Miss Winters."

"Since we are such old friends, don't you think that might be a trifle ridiculous?"

Aunt looked faint. "I had no idea. I may have recently said a few words you could have taken amiss, my dear."

"You certainly didn't. The whole village of Danbury knows about Lord Delmore's dastardly deeds."

Delmore's eyes glinted. No wonder she couldn't resist the wretch. He never failed to show his amusement when she spoke, which had given her an elevated opinion of her place in his life.

Jeremy appeared. "Delmore, you're up from the country! Good show. Does mother know? Are you staying with us?"

"In order, yes, yes, no, yes. Now Anna, may I have the honor of a waltz with you?"

"I think I'm fully booked." She gazed in the other direction.

"You may have my waltz, Calder," Jeremy said with unusual gallantry. "I may be able to persuade Miss Goodings to dance with me instead."

"I'm not to be traded away like a horse." Anna lifted her chin.

Delmore raised his and folded his arms but his eyes gleamed and his mouth twitched.

Mr. Fieldhouse turned to Jeremy. "If you don't want to dance with her, I would be delighted to partner her again."

"See what you have done, Anna?" Delmore held out his hand. "In seconds this has become an auction."

Idiotically, she accepted the invitation she craved, to waltz with dear Delmore one single time. "It's a shame arrogant doesn't start with D or as a word it would be applied to you." She moved onto the floor with him, well aware of the stares.

"I couldn't see you paired with Fieldhouse again," Delmore said in a low voice. "He is not for you."

"That's for me to say." She stared straight ahead. If she

met his gaze, he would guess how much she wanted him and only him.

"Your taste is shocking. I mean that literally. I am shocked that you would consider a man with two small children." He took her right hand and placed his arm around her waist. The moment he stepped into her, she was waltzing.

She knew he would make a wonderful partner. He understood the ebb and flow of the music and he made a dizzying pattern for them both around the floor. She finally turned her face to him. "What made you come up to town?"

"I have to attend to business matters. I didn't intend to ask you to dance but the thought of Fieldhouse having you annoyed me."

She met his gaze. "I can't imagine why."

"He would take advantage of you in a second. The man has no moral code."

"And you do?"

"In certain circumstances, yes."

"I have found the man to be scrupulously polite."

"You haven't been in bed with him."

"And you have?"

"In a manner of speaking. We have shared women." He averted his gaze.

She didn't know what he meant. "Are there not enough women to go around that you need to share?"

"In some circles—Fieldhouse's—sharing is a titillation. I'm not proud of what I have done but I was very young and foolish at the time. At least I have learned better. Fieldhouse hasn't."

"How could you possibly know that?"

"Women talk."

"Women certainly talk about you. I haven't heard a word of gossip about him. Even Aunt thinks he will do nicely for me."

"He is not good enough for you."

"Tiddlepish. I am reliably informed that he has ten thousand a year."

His gaze met hers. "I had no idea you were fortune-hunting." He clamped his lips.

"Well, now you know. I wouldn't let myself go for any less."

"And yet you offered yourself to me for nothing." His eyebrows flattened.

"You might note that I didn't offer myself in marriage."

"No, you didn't." He swept her past two couples, into the centre of the floor and out again.

Never had she been partnered with a man as skilled, and had she not been displeased with him she would have been in raptures. When she found the breath to speak again, she asked, "Are you making a spectacle of me?"

"I assume so. I thought you might like that, being a fortune hunter. You would be more noticeable."

"We fortune hunters prefer to be discreet. I don't want you to scare away any other prospects I may have."

"Now that I have waltzed with you, you will be much sought after. You might note that I haven't danced with another woman. That will be noticed."

"You think much of yourself, my lord."

"When a man doesn't interest himself in respectable woman, he is noticed when he does. And so, the woman is noticed. Then people wonder why and insist on finding out for themselves. In no time you will have a crowd around you."

"And that will gratify me immensely, since I am meant to be a companion and not a blushing debutante," she said crossly. "If Jonquil suffers for your folly ..."

"Neither of you will suffer from this." With that, he took her back to her aunt.

Chapter Eleven

Delmore had been surprisingly angered by the thought of Filthy Fieldhouse laying a finger on Anna. He should have realized other men would be as attracted to her as he was. Without a doubt, he couldn't compete with the man's money. His own fault. He had been a fool, and he couldn't turn his life around in an instant. The woman surely wouldn't wait for him to catch up to her aspirations.

Showing his feelings wouldn't help one bit. He spotted his mother and his Aunt Carrington gossiping on the other side of the room, and he stalked over. After bowing formally to each, he stared back toward Anna who was surrounded by Jeremy's friends. He hardened his expression. "I came here to let you know that I arrived in town some hours ago," he said stiffly. "I am putting Packham Place up for sale and I will be staying in Delmore House with you while I organize the shift."

His mother examined his face and placed a kiss on his cheek, an action she hadn't performed for many years. "You are selling Packham Place right away? In that event, Jeremy and I will be delighted to have your company at Delmore House." She frowned. "Though, we might have to ask Westerfield to send up more servants from Hastings House."

Delmore shrugged. "If you wish, but I have a skeleton staff at Packham Place who will need to be redeployed."

"We'll discuss this tomorrow if you can spare the time."

"Of course, he can spare the time," Aunt Carrington said, tapping her fan lightly on his shoulder. "What else does he have to do? A pleasure to see you here, Delmore, and well done. If Jeremy had danced one more time with Miss Anna Winters, people would be enjoying themselves with unhelpful gossip."

He blinked at them, having lost the train of the conversation. "How many times has he danced with her?" At that very moment, Anna was about to grace the floor for a country-dance with Temple. Did the woman not know how to behave like a companion?

"Twice so far," his mother said with a worried pucker of her face. "People are asking me if he has any intentions there. I said the family history precludes that. And I made sure of introducing her to Mr. Fieldhouse. If she is hanging out for a husband, he would suit, I think, don't you, Alice?"

"He is a fine-looking gentleman, Mary. And his little girls need a caring mother. I found Anna to be most helpful when we were snowed in. She would make any man a good wife."

"You introduced Fieldhouse to Anna?" He stared at his mother, breathing hard. "To keep her away from Jeremy?"

He had to concentrate to keep his voice relaxed. Fieldhouse was the one man in the room that he could not tolerate.

A few years ago, the man had married an eighteen-year-old innocent. He had given her two babies in quick succession. She had died in childbed with the last. In the meantime, he had maintained his lifestyle, which included a mistress who invited whores to join her in his bed as a titillation for him. He enjoyed group performances. A previous mistress of Delmore's said the man needed to make up for his thumb-sized appendage.

"I've been trying to keep her away from Jeremy for years, Calder. I thought if he moved out into his own house, he would be forever at hers. If he stays with me, I can keep an eye on him, at least, and make sure he doesn't allow himself to see her as a suitable alliance."

Delmore frowned. "Does he know this?"

"He knows why I don't approve of her. Like father, like daughter. Her father was a very foolish young man. I don't doubt she is the same and prone to rushing about impulsively."

Nor did Delmore. Anna presumed he would take her as his mistress if she demonstrated her willingness. Possibly she expected him to give her a house, but his house presenting days were over. Even his father hadn't given away more than two. "I'm glad to be of service," he said with a curt nod. "I may be more use if I know what is happening. I have never seen either him or her look any more than friendly toward each other or heard either say a world that would lead me to assume she is a danger to his heart, or her to his. Tonight, he is doing as I did at his age, scanning all the eligible young ladies to see who might suit best.

Though, possibly he has marriage in mind, whereas nothing could have been further from my thoughts at his age."

"But, my dear, it's not natural for a man and a woman to remain platonic friends." His mother glanced at him, her expression curious. "Do you have any platonic female friends?"

"I had a few friends with wives I liked, but I don't think I can describe any of them as particular friends."

His mother and her sister exchanged glances. "Lady Somerville is not a platonic friend?"

Lady Somerville had accosted him as he was trying to make his way to Anna. The beautiful redhead had accosted him a time or two before, usually out of sight, and once in the garden of her own husband's townhouse. The woman had no scruples and at that time, a little over six months ago, nor did he. "Her husband is not a friend of mine, my lady. I think he was a friend of my father. And I wouldn't call her a friend. More as a casual acquaintance." His behavior with Lady Somerville had never caused him the slightest touch of regret before tonight.

"As I thought." His mother and his aunt exchanged another glance. "Please don't closet yourself with her tonight. Lady Prescott has never brought out a young lady before and you causing gossip at young Jonquil's debut ball wouldn't suit her one bit. Nor young Jonquil. She, at least, has a chance of a respectable marriage and poor Elizabeth Beeby can't be left with the two of them."

His aunt nodded in agreement with his mother. "They're attending our ball, too. Sweet creatures, both of them. They behaved beautifully when we were marooned at Drake House, though Carrington thinks Anna is the more attractive. He likes her plain speaking. It really is such a pity about her father." Her face screwed up with sympathy.

Delmore set his shoulders square. "Do people say that about me? That it's a pity about my father?" He stared at his mother, whose husband had certainly been no saint.

"Of course not. Your father had his shortcomings, but he was never a traitor. He was one of Prinny's best friends." Dropping her gaze, Mother positioned her largest diamond ring squarely over her glove.

That done, her eyes met his. He tried to read her expression, a hopeless task in which he had never succeeded. The dowager had always been a mystery to him, cold in her affections, and rigid in her opinions.

"And my father was the one who informed on Anna's father." He clamped his lips, watching the dancers on the floor form an arbor for skipping couples to pass under. He couldn't spot Anna.

His mother heaved a breath, which she slowly let out. "We never expected to have Elizabeth Winters living in our parish. She had been a great friend of ours in the days when we were making our own debuts." Her mouth twisted. "It was most unfortunate that she took Horace Beeby, the vicar of our very own parish, as her husband after Richard Winters died. We were quite disturbed when we discovered we would be living near her after all those years."

"I fail to see why you expect her to take the blame for her husband's foolishness."

"No one imagines she knew about her husband's plan, but ..." She sighed.

"And her daughter, who had not yet been born, is somehow treated as though she were complicit."

His mother glanced away again. "I don't doubt Elizabeth had a hard time after Winters died. He left her nothing. She would have been in dire straits but for the help from her family. Marrying Beeby was the wisest thing she could do."

"Done in desperation, more than likely." Delmore clipped out his words. Only desperation would force a woman to marry a ranting bore like Beeby. The scandal must have humiliated her beyond bearing. To have to bear that because her first husband had been involved in the Popgun Plot, a traitorous idea thought up by three members of the London Corresponding Society. The plan had been to assassinate King George III by means of a poison dart.

After the arrest of these gentlemen, Winters, younger than Jeremy at the time, in the hearing of Delmore's father, had bragged about his involvement. Before he had quite sobered up, rather than face imminent arrest, Winters escaped by jumping out of an upstairs window and breaking his foolish neck.

Naturally, recriminations had flown between Anna's paternal grandparents and Delmore's father. Delmore heard all this when the new Mrs. Beeby moved into the vicarage. He'd been down from Oxford. According to his father, words had been said that could never be taken back, words that started with "traitor" and ended with "you, sir, are little better than a murderer." His father had taken violent exception to that.

Ten years ago, Delmore had thought the story a serious matter. These days he saw the whole thing as a tragedy. Richard Winters had indeed been a young idealist. While

Delmore lost himself in thought, Lady Somerville accosted him again. To show Anna that some women didn't argue with him, contradict him, or insist on having the last word, he joined the country-dance with her as his partner. He might also join her in the garden for a quick tête-à-tête later. She had no objection to lifting her skirts for a man with an insatiable ache.

But before he could follow up her invitation, he needed Anna to notice. She studiously avoided glancing in his direction. Therefore, he left for home, and paced the formal rooms of Delmore house alone, waiting for his mother and brother to return.

For reasons unknown, Rodney had swerved his attentions from Jonquil to Anna. She had known him for ten years and had seen no evidence that he had a brain in his head, but he was adorably handsome, and he had a streak of gallantry a mile wide. Without knowing, he kept her from glancing Lord Delmore's way for quite some time. When she finally had a chance to inspect the room, the dastardly earl had left. Good riddance. She never could abide a man who gave her orders.

The last guest departed, and she and Jonquil retired for the night. The two shared a bedroom, which meant that Anna had to continually tell her stepsister if this or that suited her. Her white nightgown suited her but no one other than Anna saw how sweet and young Jonquil looked in the pin-pleated cotton.

After the maid had left the room, as Jonquil plaited her

hair for sleeping, she said, "You were flirting with Rodney, Anna, you know you were." Her voice had taken a saintly tone and she evaded Anna's gaze.

"I may have been." Anna brushed her hair and prepared three sections for her own long plait. "It's my job as your companion to make sure you are not overwhelmed by suitors. I'm taking the least favored off your hands." She smiled, finding humor in that at least.

"Take John Temple." Jonquil's nose tilted up. "I would rather have sweet Rodney than him. Though, I wouldn't care to be married to a man who has no conversation."

"I suspect Rodney will age badly. Such dark hair is likely to turn gray overnight."

Jonquil glanced up with a frown. "He will look wonderful with gray hair, and you know it. Not that I want a plain man for a husband and neither do you. Jeremy's features will always look distinguished. He is rather like Lord Delmore, who might be old but is still handsome. How people stared when he danced with Lady Somerville. What a scandalous pair. Everyone knows she is married."

Anna drew in a deep breath. "I suspect a relationship with her is convenient for him. He won't be forced to marry her."

"He won't be forced to marry anyone. He's a man. They choose, we consent." Jonquil tossed her plait over her shoulder. She turned, blinking with concentration. "What do you think of Mr. Fieldhouse? He is very rich, isn't he?" She folded down the covers on her side of the bed.

"So, I heard." Anna tried to sound noncommittal. She swiped the warming pan over the sheets on her side before sliding into the cozy spot. "And of course, that's what every woman wants—a good income for life."

"You're assured that." Jonquil flumped in beside her. "Judging by the way Jeremy behaves toward you, I suspect he'll be popping the question any moment now." Leaning back against the headboard, she crossed her arms.

"Not to me, he won't," Anna said, fluffing her pillows into shape. "His mother would be most distressed if he did. She disapproves of me; you must know that." She scratched at her eyebrow; her belly knotted with frustration. Nothing she could do would ever change Lady Delmore's mind about her. Although Anna didn't relish coming between a woman and her son, Lady Delmore had made an unfortunate decision, which Jeremy duly ignored. In the same situation, Anna would do the same, for she certainly would not give up a friend because her mother's prejudgements.

"She was very nice to you tonight. She complimented your gown. She took no notice of mine although mine is far prettier. Everyone else says so."

Since Anna had chosen the fabric for Jonquil's gown, she knew how beautifully the color flattered Jonquil. The soft pink made her look young and fresh and innocent. "She introduced me to Mr. Fieldhouse, but I think she was merely bringing his attention to me to sidetrack Jeremy. Mr. Fieldhouse then had no choice other than to remark on my gown. I really don't take this sort of mention seriously, and neither should you."

"It seems to me that you have attached Jeremy, Rodney, and Mr. Fieldhouse."

Anna laughed. "They were being courteous. I certainly don't take that amiss."

Jonquil slumped down under the covers until only her head and shoulders showed. "People seemed to think it was your debut, not mine." Her expression looked petulant.

"In a way it was. I thought they were kind to make a fuss of me, but no one did so to your detriment. What is this about?"

"Nothing." Jonquil lifted her eyebrows. "But you seem to have at least three suitors and I only have dancing partners."

"You can't measure your success by trying to compare it with others. I don't see any of them as suitors."

"Not even Mr. Fieldhouse? Do you think he is too old?" Jonquil covered the bottom of her face with the sheet.

"For marriage? Of course not, though he does have two children. That might be a drawback."

"He is awfully rich. His children would have nannies and governesses. I don't think one should worry about that. And who wouldn't love to be married to a rich man." Jonquil blew out her candle and slid down under the covers.

Anna blinked. She and Jonquil had been talking at cross-purposes. Jonquil had been interested in the older man with two children and a very fine income. How strange. But should that be so, Anna must treat Mr. Fieldhouse with more caution. She wouldn't want to spoil Jonquil's prospects. "Go to sleep, Jonquil. Tomorrow we will be inundated with callers. You need to look your best."

Anna tried to sleep but she replayed her conversation with Delmore a number of times without coming up with any reason to hope that he would change. Women abounded and too many wanted him. He had no moral code to abide by, like his father. If he wanted a woman, he would take her.

Except he wouldn't take Anna.

Clearly, he preferred meek and mild women who existed only to be female, not people in their own right. If she craved him badly enough, she would have to simper and importune him.

Never would she do that.

Delmore, annoyingly refreshed after a good night's sleep without the benefit of a drop of wine, awaited his family of laggards in the morning parlor. He had served himself from a large plate of ham. His mother arrived first. He had been reliably informed she'd taken hot chocolate in her room earlier.

"Good morning, Calder." She sat at her usual place at the foot of the table awaiting her usual pot of tea. More food began to arrive from the kitchen, a plate of scrambled eggs and a steaming loaf of hot bread with a dish of butter pats.

He made a note to himself to have a few leaves of the long table removed, for the formality of distance no longer appealed to him, if it ever had. Formality had appealed to his father, who never had much time for his family. "Good morning, Mother. You came in rather late last night."

"Jeremy wanted to stay until the end," she said comfortably, pouring milk into her tea. "He had promised the last dance to Anna, and he never breaks a promise." A footman arrived with a dish of buttered vegetables, which he placed in front of her. She toyed with her fork.

"I don't doubt he wanted to stay until the end." Delmore shrugged. Unlike him at the same age, Jeremy didn't plan to meet his friends at balls to go carousing later, sometimes to exclusive brothels, sometimes to gambling dens, but more than likely to both. "He's a fine young man. I missed that stage of my development," he added in a dry voice.

Jeremy wandered in wearing a velvet-collared dressing robe over his breeches and took his place in the middle of the seating. "What did you do instead?" He waited for the footman to present him with the ham.

"You'll understand that I wasn't invited to many balls after I rode a donkey through Lord Haversham's while my friends picked up supper dishes and hurled them at each other. I also recall another ball where opera dancers were tossed into the fountain and the odd duke or earl joined them. Naming no names."

His mother sighed. "Surely not, Calder?"

"Doubtless being disruptive is out of mode," he said wryly, adding butter to a crusty slice of bread.

"I certainly hope so." She began her eggs. "Will you be sending over the new servants from Packham Place today? We could certainly do with another footman if not a few maids."

"I'll keep on a footman and the butler until I organize the sale, but I'll want a slew of maids sent back from here to there to do a final clean up."

"You surely won't leave the house empty." His mother

looked aghast. "The place will invite mould if it's not kept warm."

"It will have to be minimally staffed until it's sold. I want to get the stables sorted out. Do I have any horse or coach either of you wants to keep?"

Jeremy lifted his head. "I would pay you for Father's travelling coach. When I move to Drake House, I will need one."

"You can have that. If you want a team, you'll have to pay for it, though. I bought all my horses during the last few years."

"I wouldn't mind the grays."

"They're too good for the coach. I'll be selling them."

Jeremy scratched his head. "But you will lend me Wilson to help me choose others?"

"I said so, didn't I? Perhaps we could go to Tattersall's today."

Jeremy shot him such a look of blinding gratitude that Delmore blinked. For a moment both sat in silence, Delmore recalling that when his father died, Jeremy had only been sixteen. During his Oxford days and later, he had no older male to advise him. Delmore certainly hadn't bothered. He'd been too busy wasting money and his life. It was time he made up for this.

"I can be ready in an hour." Jeremy rose to his feet.

"We'll meet in the sitting room."

After Jeremy left, the countess folded up her table napkin. "That was very kind of you, Calder. Perhaps you could extend your kindness to advising him about Anna Winters."

"He wouldn't take anything I had to say about her as a

kindness. Aside from that, I don't intend to interfere in his or her life."

He thought he meant his words.

During the day, Delmore discovered that Jeremy had a careful way with horses. Wilson chose two high stepping bays for him, the first of which immediately snuffled around Jeremy's pockets, discovering that Jeremy indeed kept lumps of sugar handy. The horse then allowed his nose to be patted and the other pushed in looking equally hopeful. "That's enough of that," Wilson said sternly. "These are workin' 'orses, not pets."

Jeremy gave a guilty smile and desisted. After Wilson took the horses back to the stables at Delmore House, Delmore and his brother went to the racetrack where Delmore resisted the lure to place a bet on a very fine black, which eventually won his race. Annoyingly. "I should have had money on that horse," he said to Jeremy, disgruntled.

"I'm surprised you didn't. Turning over a new leaf?" Jeremy laughed in a way that showed his disbelief.

"Perhaps. A fellow can only waste his time for so long before diversions become boring in themselves. I find I rather like racketing around in the country interfering in my tenant's business."

"You didn't." Jeremy looked shocked. "Don't tell Mother. She might expect me to do the same at Drake House."

"It wouldn't do you any harm now you have a comfortable inheritance. Drake House is calling for good management. I suspect you could handle it. You can't live in Mother's pocket forever."

"Perhaps if she could count on you, I wouldn't have to," Jeremy shot back. "You can't expect the woman to sit alone in that big house for the rest of her life."

"No." Delmore pushed his hands in his pockets. "I don't. Since she is not about to be presented with grandchildren any time soon, I'm having the dower house renovated and she can live there."

"She will dislike not having the big house to supervise." Jeremy watched his new bays being led back to the stables.

"She might not for all you know. She's an attractive woman. She may marry again."

Jeremy mulled those words. "Speaking of marriage, what do you think of Fieldhouse?"

"He's a commoner," Delmore said with contempt. "You're surely not thinking of marrying him."

"I'm thinking of him as a prospect for Anna." Jeremy aimed a rueful smile at him. "His birth is respectable, and his fortune can't be sneezed at. He is paying attention to her but somehow that bothers me."

Delmore stared at the gray sky. The tips of the nearby trees shivered in the breeze. Soon spring would arrive, and the air would warm. "She is too sensible to have her head turned."

"I don't like the way he looks at Jonquil either."

"Is he looking at her? I would have thought she was too innocent for his tastes."

"I can't say I know much about him. He's more your contemporary than mine."

"He neither drinks to excess nor gambles. He runs his

estates well. To a prospective bride he would appear to be a good bet. Perhaps he would be a good husband. Some men can separate their home life from their interests. He may be such a one."

"And what are these interests?"

Delmore moistened his lips. "He likes to use the whip on women to flog up his appetites. He likes to watch spectacles of a titillating type. He likes to join in groups participating in the same. In a whorehouse, he will order two or three women at a time."

Jeremy's eyes widened. "He must be an insatiable performer." He sounded almost admiring.

"I gather not," Delmore said wryly. "He enjoys inflicting pain. Women of a certain type of gossip. He is charged double, and he pays."

"So, you have been told this by women of a certain type?"

Delmore picked a length of straw from the sleeve of his jacket. "I may not have always acted wisely myself, and perhaps having more than one woman at a time is not unique, but a man who needs to hurt a woman to be able to perform is not a man I can admire. These acts should be enjoyable or not considered."

Jeremy's forehead creased. "And are they enjoyable?"

"Initially. However, it's a jaded man who looks for this sort of fling constantly. If you are thinking of trying it, let me introduce you to the right houses where the women are clean, and choose to perform for a certain consideration."

"Monetary?"

"Of course, though you will find enthusiastic amateurs at various country house parties. To my way of thinking, it's best to hire professionals. You never know when you might be caught with the wrong wife or wrong daughter and then there's hell to pay."

Jeremy shifted uncomfortably. "I'm thinking I'll stick to my own little ladybird. She would be upset if I wandered around trying to experiment with others."

"You have a little ladybird? Your father would be proud of you," Delmore said cynically.

"Everyone has one. I only see her when I'm in town." Jeremy lowered his eyes bashfully. "A man needs relief, of course, but I'll give her up when I marry. Our father humiliated our mother with his women. I wouldn't do that."

"Nor I." Delmore stared at his polished boots, frowning. As usual, Pickering had sent him out impeccably dressed. Until not too long ago, he had assumed he would marry to produce an heir and he would continue on with his rackety lifestyle, living in the city and keeping his wife in the country, producing babies, the same way his father had. Now he realized he didn't want that sort of life. He didn't have to be like his father if he chose not to. "And now that we've had the father/son conversation you missed, remember that you can come to me for more any time you choose." He managed a devil-may-care smile.

"Thank you, Calder. I may take you up on that another time. Now, let's get those bays home and try them out with my curricle. I have a morning call to make."

Delmore pondered. Jeremy had seemed interested in a pretty chestnut-haired debutante last night. "It's perhaps not wise to follow up your flirts too soon. Let them look for you, instead."

"Says the dashing rake. No, if you are referring to Miss

Goodings, she told me they were making calls tomorrow and wouldn't be at home. I'm off to see Anna. Last night was her debutante ball, though officially the fuss was to be made over Jonquil. I want to see how Anna held up."

Delmore glanced at his fingernails, and then flicked his gloves, preparatory to donning the pair. "You don't have any real leanings in that direction, do you?"

"Leanings like marriage? Did mother ask you to ask me?"

"She seems to be worried."

"Let her worry. She would be mighty lucky to end up with a woman as interesting as Anna for her daughter-in-law."

Delmore couldn't make himself push any further. Nothing would make him believe that Anna would have experimented with him if she had any feelings for Jeremy.

Chapter Twelve

The Prescott household had barely removed the empty plates left by the first of the morning callers—the mothers with their debutante daughters—before the young men, clearly not early risers, began to trickle into the drawing room. John Temple arrived with Jeremy.

Anna rose to her feet, smiling. She took Jeremy's hand first. "If you had come sooner, you would have seen Miss Goodings. Good morning, John. Do take this seat, if you please." She indicated one across the room from Jonquil, hoping to leave the space on the sofa alongside her for someone with whom she would rather flirt.

Jonquil shot her a quelling glance. "Do sit with me, John, and tell me how much you enjoyed last night."

John flashed a smile of gratitude before plonking himself down in the space allotted, sitting up straight and clasping his hands in his lap like a boy trying to please his tutor.

Jeremy walked with Anna toward the quiet of the bay window. "He bewailed her lack of attention to him last night and today I will now be regaled with the opposite," he said in an undertone. "He will be in transports of delight about her hair and her nose."

"In particular?"

He nodded, standing with his back to the outside view. "He read a book of poetry, I presume, because he can now count the different colors in each strand of her hair. And her nose is like a petal. A petal? Not a dandelion petal, I am supposing."

"It would be a rose, I'm sure. That rhymes with nose. A nose like the petal of a rose."

"You read the same book," he said in a tone of accusation. "That is what he said. I think she has a nose more like an uppercase L."

"I hope you never expect to court a woman, Jeremy. You do not understand the romance of poetry."

He grinned. "Delmore took me to Tattersall's earlier. That's more my style. On his advice, I bought a pair of high-stepping bays. I'll have to take you up for a drive in the park, but first look outside and tell me what you think." Turning, he lifted the lace curtain aside.

She peered into the street, spotting a pair of elegant horses being held by Jeremy's ancient groom. "Delmore has an unerring eye, is what I think. They're wondrous, Jeremy. Though, would I be allowed to drive with you unchaperoned in town?"

"You would. The curricle is open, and no one minds. Oh, good lord. Look who is walking to the door."

At first Anna could only see the top of a tall hat and the beautifully cut shoulders of a blue jacket. Her heart leapt, but a slight turn of the caller's head as he lifted a hand to the knocker showed her Mr. Fieldhouse's dark chin. She sighed. "He said he would call today. Rodney is in the street right behind him. I hope we have enough pastries."

"Is that a posy I see in Toddie's hand?" Jeremy gave a snort of derision. "I've been lax. I didn't think of bringing flowers."

"I didn't like to mention your omission. Then again, since you often bring flowers for my mother, I imagine we have been spoiled enough."

"I can't wait to see him present a posy to Jonquil. He'll blush and stammer although he has known her all his life." He sat on the windowsill and watched the door for Rodney's entrance.

A footman let in the two gentlemen. Rodney strode past Mr. Fieldhouse, arm extended with his posy held in front, and headed straight toward Anna. He offered her a dignified bow. "I hope you will accept these, Miss Winters."

Anna placed a palm on her chest, surprised. She accepted the delicate bouquet of tiny white lilies surrounded by fern with a grateful smile. "For me, Rodney? How utterly delightful. What a lovely thought." Jeremy snickered behind her. "Good morning, Mr. Fieldhouse."

Mr. Fieldhouse took her other hand and bowed. "I see you are well this morning."

Rodney gave him a glance of dislike. "Anna is always well. She's not the sort of female to fade away after midnight."

Mr. Fieldhouse tugged his ear lobe and gave Anna a complicit glance. "So, you don't see her as Cinderella?" he said in a patronizing voice. "She may be offended to hear that, Mr. Toddington. Miss Winters is a beautiful and intelligent young lady who deserves our admiration."

Anna's smile tightened. Rodney had shown exceptional thoughtfulness by presenting her with the posy, which she certainly appreciated. Mr. Fieldhouse had no right to treat him like the village idiot. He had always been a shy lad because of his stammer, which she knew frustrated him as much as his listeners. "Not at all. A gentleman who thinks to bring a mere companion a beautiful posy has a courteous and generous nature. I thank you, Rodney. You might teach Jeremy a few lessons."

Rodney blushed. "Perhaps I will when he begins to turn his mind to ladies rather than ... rather than horses."

"I like you both, and John, just the way you are." She took his arm and moved him to the chair closest to Jonquil's sofa. If Jonquil preferred Rodney to John, she could now take a moment to chat with him. Jonquil looked pleased. John frowned. Mr. Fieldhouse, after inspecting the trio with pursed lips, indicated the chair opposite for Anna. His autocratic manner brought her eyebrows together, but to refuse to sit in an offered chair would be unmannerly. Then he shifted another to seat himself beside her.

Jeremy, not one to manipulate a situation like Mr. Fieldhouse, engaged the other young lady in conversation by seating himself at her end of the room with her mother and Aunt Lucy. Fortunately, another mother with a daughter in tow arrived, allowing Anna a chance to give up her seat and also leave Mr. Fieldhouse to engage with Jonquil. Her duty as a companion done, if her duty including surrounding her charge with prospective suitors, she left to join her aunt and the other two chaperones as she should.

Aunt, in the middle of a conversation with the young ladies' mothers, turned to Anna. "Could you pull the bell, my dear niece? We need more refreshments for our guests."

Anna took the opportunity to give up her posy for the maid to place in a vase. Anna wouldn't want the only one she'd been offered in her whole life to wilt and die. Fresh tea arrived with tiny, sugared pastries. The gentlemen left the latter for the ladies, who had no intention of collecting cream on their chins, or crumbs between their teeth. Anna snatched up one, making up for a missed breakfast.

Finally, the ladyfinger sandwiches arrived. The silver tray emptied quickly. Jeremy took John to their next unnamed appointment. Rodney moved to talk to Anna. Mr. Fieldhouse shifted to Jonquil's side. Finally, the morning calls ended, with Anna satisfied that Jonquil had managed to flirt with each gentleman in turn. Tonight, she would have another opportunity to charm young gentlemen.

After dinner, Anna changed into a blue evening gown, one refurbished only a week before she left Danbury. On the hem and the bottom of the sleeves, she had added a quilted pattern strip that she had made some years ago but hadn't been brave enough to use. The colors of orange and pale green had always seemed too bright for a modest, penniless spinster. Tonight, she didn't mind, for she would likely wander unregarded at the biggest ball of the season.

Her hosts for the night, Lord and Lady Sneddon, had more money than sense, according to Aunt Lucy. Anna didn't mind going unnoticed. At least in a full room, people wouldn't point her out as the daughter of a traitor to the crown, an embarrassment she had suffered a few times already during her visit to town. She collected the pale green Merino shawl borrowed from her mother, pulled on her long white gloves, and pattered down the main stairs.

Lady Prescott and her husband, the delightful Sir Arthur, stood by the fire in the drawing room, as interestingly dressed a couple as she had seen. If only one day she could meet a man so perfect for her, marry, and live happily ever after. The couple only lacked children, which had caused them great disappointment. Anna tried to act as a daughter and had been kindly accepted as a substitute. "You are carrying that pretty beaded reticule I sent for your coming out in the country. How sweet," Aunt Lucy said, hugging Anna.

"I made sure of the orange in the decoration of my gown so that I could. It's such a lovely reticule that I could not keep it in the drawer any longer. Jonquil will be here soon. She needed a curl re-pinned."

Jonquil arrived in a flurry, fussing about her hair. In fact, she looked lovely. The embroidered border of white jonquils on her yellow voile overskirt, the decoration that had taken Anna many hours of sewing, suitably brightened up her modest white gown.

After adding muffs and cloaks to their outfits, the cobbled-together family left and arrived in a street full of coaches. Each stopped to let out the passengers and was quickly hurried along so that the carriage behind could also unload guests.

Anna doubted that among the invited guests, she would see anyone she knew. The invitees to this ball had dressed opulently in velvet cloaks or furs. Once inside the main doors of the house, the waft of perfume replaced the stench of the manure in the streets and the hovering smoke of a thousand fires. Crystal chandeliers lit by hundreds of candles reflected on glittering diamond tiaras and necklaces. Each voice drowned out the next.

The relief of leaving the receiving line was replaced by the inevitability of being crushed in the ballroom. How Jonquil would be noticed in this crowd, Anna couldn't imagine. Aunt waved to her friends on the far side of the room and hurried her husband and nieces over. Now safe and secure with people they knew, the Prescott group stared at the newcomers, discussed in a running commentary by Aunt. This one has an eligible son. This one has an unmarried daughter. This one was involved with a most unsuitable female. Finally, Aunt drew a breath. "Mr. Toddington has arrived," she said, smiling at Jonquil. "One of your flirts. Shall we beckon him over?"

"He's not my flirt," Jonquil said with an upward tilt of her L shaped nose. "He's Anna's."

"Truly, Anna?" Aunt queried her with her eyebrows.

"Of course not. He is simply an acquaintance. He has seen me in a faded gown picking apples, he has pushed me into a pond, and he laughed his silly head off when Farmer Johnson's pig chased me through Danbury. How could anyone have romantic feelings after that, let alone that I have contradicted him a number of times?"

"The latter is a sure way to lose a suitor," said a slow, deep masculine voice behind her. She couldn't turn. Her legs turned to jelly. "Any man who has seen you wet ..." Delmore's amused voice faded.

She drew a deep breath. A true gentleman would never allude to a private matter in public. "I expect I don't look any more bedraggled than any other person."

He moved to her side, bowed to Sir Arthur and Aunt Lucy, nodded at Jonquil, and turned his face to Anna. "Of course not. Had you left me to finish, I would have paid you a compliment."

She lifted her chin. "In that case, please proceed." Her extended family stood motionless, watching them. Had he not let her down so badly by not wanting her, she would not have considered challenging him. Remembering her manners, she curtsied. "If you please, Lord Delmore. For me, compliments are rare and welcome."

"Any man who has seen you wet would be as charmed as those of us who have also seen you dry."

Also. He had been unable to resist hinting at a secret. "Thank you, my lord. I am most grateful for your opinion."

Aunt's eyes narrowed. "We must move along. No use standing here on the outskirts if we wish to find dancing partners for our little debutante, eh, Anna?"

"No use at all." She repositioned her shawl, ignoring Delmore. Since he hadn't ruined her, he would not be allowed to pay her spurious compliments.

Delmore stood foursquare, his face pale and set. "May I have the honor of the first waltz, Miss Winters?"

She frowned. In front of others, she couldn't refuse, but being held by him in front of more than five hundred people was not a fate she relished. "You may, my lord," she said begrudgingly. Far better to be held by him in the silence of the night, when she could feel loved and desired.

"Since I have lost you for the first waltz, Miss Winters, may I book the second?"

The voice came from behind her. She swiveled to face Mr. Fieldhouse. Tonight, he wore a diamond pin on the lapel of his black evening jacket. "You may, sir."

He directed his gaze to Jonquil. "And Miss Beeby. Do you have a dance free for me?"

Jonquil blinked. "I have not yet been booked for any dance, Mr. Fieldhouse. You may take your choice."

"In that case, should your chaperone permit, I will take the first waltz." He looked at Lady Prescott for permission.

Aunt mulled her answer. "Indeed Mr. Fieldhouse, I am not sure that Jonquil should be waltzing."

"I waltzed at the balls in Danbury." Jonquil crossed her arms under her bosom and pouted.

Mr. Fieldhouse's gaze dropped to her cleavage.

"In that case, we shouldn't mind, should we, Anna?" Aunt's voice sounded hesitant.

Anna moistened her lips. "I'm sorry Mr. Fieldhouse, but until Jonquil has been presented ..."

"You know that as well as I, Fieldhouse." Lord Delmore frowned. "Young ladies cannot waltz until they have been approved by one of the patronesses of Almacks."

Mr. Fieldhouse bowed. "Bearing that in mind, I would be honored by the first cotillion, Miss Beeby."

Jonquil shot eye-daggers at Anna. She tilted her nose in the air and aimed a blinding smile at Mr. Fieldhouse. "Thank you, sir."

Mr. Fieldhouse showed every inclination to stay, which should have pleased Anna, but she didn't like the way he furtively glanced at Jonquil's breasts. She glanced up at Delmore. "You may leave, sir. Your frown is scaring off any aspirants for Jonquil's first dance. Oh, here is Rodney Toddington, Jonquil."

However, Rodney asked Anna to grace the floor with him for the country-dance, while staring with hostility at Mr. Fieldhouse, who made a vain attempt to edge Lord Delmore aside. Lord Delmore stood his ground, fiddling with the buttons on his jacket, talking about the weather of all things. When Jeremy finally arrived, Anna wished the music would begin so that all the superfluous gentlemen would leave. Clearly none intended to request Jonquil's participation in the country-dance. Fortunately, John scooted over just in time and asked Jonquil to be his partner. Anna had never been so relieved.

Performing the intricate country-dance with Rodney improved her mood, the most delightful part being that he didn't attempt to talk. He danced the steps beautifully, clearly enjoying the exercise. Someday he would make some lucky lady a very fine husband.

A queue formed in front of Jonquil for the next two dances, giving Anna a chance to stare at her fingers until the first waltz struck up. Waltzing with Lord Delmore would be painful, to be held in his arms, knowing he didn't want her. The man had no business teasing her this way. Any man with a scrap of conscience would ignore a woman he refused to make his mistress. If she wasn't good enough for his bed, she oughtn't be good enough for the ballroom. Doubtless he had bedded other women he danced with,

Lady Somerville for one. Why could Lady Somerville have him in bed and also on the ballroom floor?

How had Anna twisted herself into this ridiculous knot? She ought to be glad he treated her with respect. By the time he stood in front of her, holding out his gloved hand, she had convinced herself that he had offered to dance with her because everyone knew she came from Danbury and noblesse oblige had possibly been taught to him in the schoolroom.

Her chin high, and glancing neither to the left or the right, she stood with him on the floor. The music began and he took her into his arms, sweeping her almost off her feet. In a trice, she matched his long steps, back straight, head to the left, not glancing at him. The music enchanted her, the exercise stimulated her, and the man intoxicated her. His warm breath brushed her cheek. His masterful arms held her. He smelled of shaving soap mixed with peppermint. The last would be to disguise the brandy, or wine, or whichever alcohol he had consumed today, for the name Delmore was synonymous with the consumption of the grape, overconsumption in his father's case. She had never seen Delmore himself under the influence. "Are you enjoying your stay in town?" she asked politely.

"It's been productive. I found I couldn't stay away for as long as I wished."

"I had the idea you thought the country was slow."

"Initially. After you left, I found enough to occupy my time."

"Implying that I wasted your time?"

"Not at all. I wasted my own time. I have done so for years."

"Isn't that the role of the Earl of Delmore?"

"I thought so, previously."

She glanced at his handsome, resolute face. His skin had a more healthy glow, or did she imagine that? "And the good, cold country air brought about a great change in you?"

"So, to speak." He smiled down at her. "You look very beautiful tonight, Anna. I ought to give you a sapphire necklace to go with that gown."

"That's the sort of thing you say to mistresses."

"I forgot myself."

"Or you are thinking of taking up my offer."

"I'm not."

"I would love sapphires," she said ruminatively.

"I don't intend to proceed with this conversation I ought not to have started." His eyebrows lifted. "Forgive me for thinking you deserve jewels rather than a bare neck."

"No one deserves jewels." She glanced at the roomful of bejeweled women whose diamonds outshone the crystal glasses many held. "People buy them because they have money."

"Some people inherit them. My mother has a lovely set of sapphires that my father gave her. They belong to the estate. Should I marry, she will no longer be the possessor."

"I find that sad."

"Surely not. That's the way of the world. The young replace the old."

"Stripping her of her jeweler would make her hate her daughter-in-law, if they should be given to the younger woman."

"Only if Mother loved the sapphires and had no other

jewels of her own. She does both hate the sapphires and have other jewels." He took the corner in silence.

Anna gazed at the people she waltzed past, some staring curiously at her, but most absorbed in their own world. As was she. Being with Lord Delmore hurt when she knew she couldn't have him. "With what did you occupy yourself in the country?"

He remained silent for so long that she assumed her question had bored him and he had decided not to answer. "You know the gossip about the child I fathered?" he said, eventually, after he had waited for a more boisterous couple to circle past.

"It has been said that she looks more like her mother's husband."

"I cleared that up. Her birth certificate will be changed so that her real father is acknowledged."

"That is the last thing I imagined you would do. I would have expected any man to be outraged that he had been so used. No one would blame you for banishing the family from your estates."

"The man is a good tenant, despite being aware that he acted dishonestly, but until the child was born, he had a right to be outraged. I had, with the power of my money and birth, taken his ladylove from him. He could only save face by appearing to act nobly and marry the woman when I wouldn't."

"I think you acted nobly, my lord. You accepted being laughed at for years."

"I had no choice, Anna. Drinking helped me forget my foolishness."

"And perhaps led you into more foolishness."

Somehow, he waltzed her to the edge of the room and before she realized where she was, the crowd on the outskirts surrounded her. He still had her hand and he tugged her through the crush. When they reached the entrance, he dropped his grip on her hand, bowed, and tucked that same hand beneath his elbow. Without a single word, he escorted her along the gallery that circled above the vast entrance hall. He stopped at the second door, which he opened, glanced inside, and indicated she should enter.

Lamps in sconces lit the area. Books surrounded the room on three sides, including the doorway. Luxurious red velvet curtain shrouded the window. In the centre of the room, a comfortable seating area of low couches had been arranged, and he clearly wished her to seat herself. He sat beside her. "I hope you are not engaged for the next dance."

"And if I should be?"

"I will attempt to speak faster. Drinking did, indeed, lead me into foolishness. I'm trying, Anna—trying not to drink myself into a mindless state. I don't want to be the man I have been. I don't plan to drink myself into obliviousness night after night. I wish to run my properties efficiently so that I can support my people. I am not my father and I hope to prove this."

She examined the backs of her hands. "My loss, then," she said, tonelessly. "And one I will mourn."

"You surely didn't want to bed a drunken sot who would leave you sleeping while he found the next wheel on which to lose his money, or the next frog to be the first to jump into the fountain? You deserve so much more. You are a beautiful, intelligent woman. You should aim to be a man's wife and not his mistress."

"Until I had this chance to be in London, my aim was to have a little fling before I settled down in the vicarage as the invaluable spinster daughter who could run all the parish errands, leaving the vicar and his wife to run the parish."

"And now you have other options?" He raised his eyebrows.

"I have no idea. Is Rodney courting me to gain Jonquil's attention, or does Mr. Fieldhouse want a mother for his children?"

He sat silently; one curled hand covered by the palm of the other. "Toddington is your best bet. Even if he never sees the Marquisate, he is a good lad, perhaps even worthy of you, who knows?"

"I could manage on his income, but I am afraid I would also manage him."

"He might surprise you."

She laughed. "He already has. To have a man with his looks and assets showing interest is certainly a coup. Though, I think he would make a better match for Jonquil—two beauties side by side would be breathtaking."

"And yet, was she beautiful for years before anyone noticed?"

"Females seem to come into their own at about sixteen or seventeen years of age, though she dressed badly when she was younger. She needed to wear colors that suited her for her true beauty to shine."

"I can't imagine your mother noticing that. I think she sees nothing but Beeby."

"I managed to turn my mother's mind to my way of thinking and when I offered to make Jonquil prettier gowns, Mama consented. I only wish I could interest Jonquil in sewing for herself."

"Did you make your gown too?"

"Of course. I always have."

He enclosed one curled fist with his other hand, gazing at the floor between his knees. "I am not my father, and you are not yours."

She stared at him in disbelief. "You won't get anyone to believe the latter. And even if they did, I would still be no one because I have no money, no beauty, and no expectations. The best I can expect is a respectable marriage, and this year is my only chance."

He abruptly rose to his feet, holding out his hand to help her up. "Damn their eyes for thinking you would ever be no one," he said in a tight voice. "Walk proudly and follow my lead."

As proudly as she could, and hiding an amount of trepidation, for she had no idea of his plan, she re-entered the ballroom. Delmore stopped by the first group and introduced her to everyone. "Miss Anna Winters, my neighbor from Danbury." He gave her a moment to dabble in small talk about the size of the crowd and the expense of wax candles, and then he moved her into the next group.

She noticed each group contained not the debutants with their doting mamas with whom she had been associating, but dowagers with sons or nephews, or respectable nobles who seemed well acquainted with Delmore.

"You are trying to marry me off," she said under her breath, not sure whether to be outraged or amused.

"I'm trying to show you are not a murderous monster but an interesting young lady with an ability to converse with all and sundry. You shouldn't be pushed in a corner and left to manage Jonquil. That's your aunt's job. You should be meeting people your age and forming interesting associations."

"I'm not quite sure a noted rake is my best chaperone."

"Nor I." He offered her his devilish smile. In this mood, which she didn't understand at all, he was breathtakingly attractive. Her desire for him warmed her entire body. "I'll drop you off with a married couple I know. All through school, Huntsdale was my best friend. He gave up on me some years ago, but I have a mind to curry up to him now that I'm on my way to reforming my way of life."

Huntsdale happened to be the Duke of Huntsdale, newly wed to a delightful young woman, who didn't appear to know Delmore other than by name. When her husband introduced her to Delmore, she offered her hand and a pleased nod.

Using his formal smile, Delmore said, "And I would like to introduce Miss Anna Winters to you both. Anna is a neighbor from Danbury who knows few ladies here."

"Is this another of your tricks?" The duke, a well-built man with a careful smile, narrowed his eyes with suspicion.

Delmore turned to Anna. "A few years ago, I introduced a lady of the night into society. Huntsdale didn't discover who she was until he was dancing with her. Very respectable is Huntsdale. He took offence."

She took the hint, and a deep breath. "Oh, dear. And

now you are introducing me to him. Am I better or worse than a lady of the night? I'm Richard Winters' daughter, your grace. You may not wish to be seen talking to me, either."

"If your credit won't stand it, old fellow, I'll remove Miss Winters from your sight." Delmore's gaze hooded while he stared at his friend.

The tall, blonde duchess smiled at Anna. "Do you have treacherous leanings, Miss Winters?"

"I am sadly conventional, I'm afraid."

"If I can put up with your ancestors, you can put up with hers," the young duchess said to her husband.

The duke appeared to relax. "Delmore is rather inclined to lark around. Those days have passed for me. Cassia makes sure I don't cross the line."

"No more larks from me, either. I'm a reformed character now." Delmore's dashing smile appeared again, this time aimed at the duchess.

The duke still appeared disbelieving. "When did this come about?"

"A few weeks ago. Or I wouldn't have the temerity to drag a respectable young lady like Anna all around the ballroom. We have known each other for over ten years."

"That's not strictly true," Anna said to the newlywed couple. "He never took the slightest notice of me, being an older man. His brother Jeremy is a friend of mine. Lord Delmore took pity on me when he saw me trying to launch my younger sister into society."

"Anna had no launching herself, her situation being as it is. I have decided I won't allow her to be left as a wallflower."

The duchess nodded. "I won't either."

Nor did she. Before Anna could blink, she was introduced into exalted circles. Her father's name was bandied about freely, which initially made her wince, but Delmore's former and now possibly current friends had decided to befriend her, and that was that.

Before Delmore left her with the duchess and a selection of other men's wives, he told her he would call on her tomorrow and drive her around the park.

After being solicited to dance by three young lords, all polite, she moved back to her aunt's circle. "I don't think I have a dance left. Wasn't that kind of Lord Delmore? He surprised me."

"My dear, when he took you out that door, I thought I might have one or two conniptions. Ladies do not leave balls with gentlemen, and especially not Lord Delmore."

"He wanted to discuss his plan to introduce me to his friends. He could have done so in here, but he thought I might be offended."

"Why would you be offended by meeting the duke?"

Anna thought quickly. "He hasn't spoken to the duke in years. I may have been cut, for all he knew." That could, possibly, have been the truth. For whatever reason, Delmore had been inordinately generous. He had no reason to introduce a nobody into society when he himself saw the ton as irrelevant.

Mr. Fieldhouse arrived to partner Jonquil for the country-dance. When he deposited her back with Lady Prescott, Jonquil said the man was utterly charming.

"I'm glad you think so. Have you seen Jeremy tonight?"

"Rodney thinks he and John have other kittens to fry. I

suppose they are in some low gambling den." Jonquil tossed her head. "I don't care. I've been asked for every dance so far, which your aunt told me not to expect." She prattled on, but Anna turned off her hearing.

Her insides jittered. Tomorrow she would see Delmore again.

Chapter Thirteen

"Lord Delmore is waiting for you in the sitting room, Miss Winters." The maid bobbed a curtsey. "Could you inform my aunt, please, Beryl?" Anna asked in a low voice. Jonquil still slept, her palm under her pink cheek. Her nightcap sat awry. No one glancing at her this morning would suspect that she had charmingly flirted with each gentleman she had danced with. If she didn't receive an offer this season, Anna would be surprised.

"Her ladyship is still abed, Miss."

Anna stared distractedly at the brown bonnet she held. This year, the fashionable ladies wore higher pokes and brighter colors. "When she arises, tell her I am driving in the park with Lord Delmore."

The maid left after a nod. Anna carefully arranged the spinsterish hat on her head, tied the new blue ribbons into a bow under her ear, and struggled into her brown pelisse, which had been refurbished with ivory piping on the shoulders and in two stripes on the cuffs. She snatched up her cream gloves and reticule, not willing to leave Delmore's horses standing too long in the frosty air. His beautiful chestnuts enjoyed hearty exercise.

After taking a deep breath, she took the stairs. Delmore hadn't waited in the morning room. He stood in the hall, one shiny booted foot tapping an impatient tattoo on the faded Oriental rug. "Prompt as usual, Miss Winters." He moistened his lips while scrutinizing her, a strangely nervous move for a man so poised.

"Old habits are hard to break. I'm not vain enough to expect someone to stand around while I dress and prink a little."

"Nevertheless, without prinking you look very well." His gaze connected with hers.

Her heartbeat thumped and she drew a deep breath, not willing to let his compliment go to her head. He knew how to charm women. "As healthy as a spring chicken."

He laughed. Somehow, he looked younger today, his smile cautious rather than cynically amused. His greatcoat swathed him from head to toe and he wore his thick dark hair rakishly disheveled with the single lock that needed to be pushed back sitting on his forehead. As the footman opened the front door, Delmore planted his tall hat squarely onto his head.

She walked before him to his phaeton. Wilson held the horses. Delmore handed her up and crossed in front of her. As he sat beside her, Wilson took his regular place at the back. The horses pranced off into the early morning air, fresh and eager to go. The earl kept them to a sober trot through streets filled with noisy two-wheeled carts, barrow men, pie sellers, flower girls, and the scurrying shoppers hurrying off to the markets. Anna wrapped her gloved hands together. London chill seemed colder than Danbury chill.

"Although you look delightful, I would like to buy you a prettier hat." Delmore neatly maneuvered his horses around a brewer's wagon.

She blinked at him. "This as well as a sapphire necklace? Then, I am right to assume you have accepted my offer to be your mistress."

"No. I merely think you should have a prettier hat." His careful gaze flicked across her face.

"I spent an hour sprucing this one up for our city visit." Staring straight ahead, she squared her shoulders.

He made a sound of impatience. "Your sister has pretty hats. Why should you spruce up your old ones?"

"My sister has a father. I have no money other than his, and you can understand, surely, that he would rather spend his spare pennies on her debut than decorating me to accompany her. I'm fortunate that I was allowed to come, but possibly that was because my aunt offered to sponsor us. She has been marvelous."

"I'm glad to hear someone has been kind to you." He turned his horses into the street that led to Hyde Park and soon reached the entrance. "I had no idea that Beeby wasn't."

"He's not unkind. I'm the cross he had to bear if he wanted my mother as his loyal assistant. She is invaluable to him. I'm careful to be only valuable to my mother or I would never be able to escape waiting hand and foot on the dear vicar."

"You don't like him." He glanced at her.

"The poor man is an intolerable bore, and I am an impatient woman. There. I admit I am faulty."

"We all are, Anna. Some people's faults complement the faults of others. And when we find that person ..." His voice trailed off.

She closed her eyes momentarily, not wanting to know that he would eventually find that one person with whom he wanted to spend the rest of his life. Glancing at the tall trees that towered over the driving path, she heaved a breath. "Will anyone else be here at this time of the morning? I suspect most people are only just arising for a bite to eat."

"The people we hope to meet will be here, the people who like to be with others who prefer early morning exercise. If you rode, I would have escorted you here on horseback, but since you don't, we will have to be content with the phaeton. See? Jeremy is already here on his horse with a few of his friends."

"I didn't know you had it in you to keep your team to a slow walk."

"You would be amazed about the many things you don't know about me."

"I'm sure I wouldn't. Is that her grace over there on that gray?"

"Indeed, and Adam with her."

"Should I wave?"

"She has seen you and she is riding toward us." He lowered his voice. "This time last year no duchess would have done that. This time last year my passenger was La Gloriosa. You will be the making of me, socially." He offered her his wicked smile and a pair of raised eyebrows.

Her chest lightened. She tried for a prim expression. "I suspect it's the other way around."

"We make each other appear respectable, as I guessed. You will become indispensible to me, Anna, if I wish to redeem myself. Good morning, duchess."

"Good morning, my lord." The duchess wore a beautiful dark green riding habit with a green silk bonnet plastered with pink roses. "Or may I call you Calder as my husband does? You must call me Cassia. You too, Miss Winters."

"I would be delighted to be Anna to you, Cassia. It's fine morning for first names and friendly faces."

The duchess handed Anna a card. "You must call on us, Anna, and bring along Calder. Adam said last night, oh, there he is. I'll leave him to speak for himself."

The Duke of Huntsdale's gray ranged up beside his wife's. "I have no idea which cat she was about to let out of the bag, but my wife has decided I must become reacquainted with all my old friends so that she may have as many people as possible in her sitting room and become a great hostess."

Cassia smiled happily. "We had a belated honeymoon, and we've only recently moved back to the town house. I love hosting functions, and now that everyone is beginning to come back the city, I can begin socializing."

Anna fingered the pasteboard rectangle, not sure if she was important enough to be a friend of a duchess. While she participated in small talk about the ball last night, and explained about Jonquil's debut, the duke struck up a low-voiced conversation with Delmore. Anna concentrated on his young wife's words.

"Do bring your aunt and your sister to my afternoon party if you have a chance, today." The duchess offered a charming smile.

"I'm sure my aunt would be delighted. My younger sister will be overjoyed." Every contact her sister could make would help her to find a suitable husband. Last night she had not been pleased with Anna, who had left her group and joined Delmore's without taking Jonquil with her. Anna needed to remember that this sojourn in the city was not for her but for her sister. The duchess left with a smile and a wave, following her husband.

And Delmore sat by Anna's side, as large as life and twice as handsome. If she helped him find respectability that would be wonderful, even though she knew that if he did, she would have no chance at all to be with him. A respectable earl would have no need of a mistress.

A wise woman would do her best to seduce him and not mind if the whole of society scorned him forever more, but seeing him this morning so charmingly careful, so achingly handsome, had caused her heart to quiver inside her chest. Perhaps love wasn't selfish. Perhaps matters of the heart caused a person to want to make sacrifices for her loved one. She tucked her hand under his arm. "It's nice that they are so willing to take you back into their circle, despite all the dreadful things you did to make society wash their hands of you."

"They're nice people. I didn't want to be nice. I wanted to show my father ..." He shrugged.

She stared at him, well aware that even dead fathers needed to be shown. "Too late, though, because your father was dead."

He shrugged, his mouth wry. "And I had suddenly assumed responsibilities I was too young to handle. Drinking and carousing let me forget my duty as the Earl of Delmore. Perhaps I'm old enough now to do as I should always have done." He nodded at a waving man who drove past and then he turned back to her. "Perhaps it is fortunate that you wore that dowdy hat. No one is assuming you might be one of my inamoratas."

She lifted her chin, trying not to laugh. "I find that insulting."

"I told you before that your hat isn't good enough for you." He frowned.

"I mean that no one is assuming I might be an inamorato."

He took her hand and squeezed it. "You are far too wonderful to be anything so ordinary."

She sat completely still. Wonderful? She must have pleased him greatly by incidentally aiding him to appear respectable in front of his old friends. Perhaps this was worth the sacrifice of having to give up the idea of being his mistress, had she the choice, which she did not have. She basked in his mood, smiling at all and sundry.

The duke having given the example, other men Delmore knew raised their hats on passing, or called out a friendly greeting. Two came over to be introduced to Anna, or so they said. Jeremy finished flirting with chaperoned young ladies in barouches and drew his horse over to engage his brother in conversation. "What's this? You with Anna? Are you trying to steal a march on me, you dirty dog?"

"No such thing." Anna leaned forward. "He has decided to try for respectability and who better to use than the daughter of a traitor to the crown. Beside me, he looks positively harmless."

"There's that." Delmore gave her a strange glance. "But has it occurred to you that I might like having a charming lady in my phaeton?"

"Anna, what is this magic spell you have cast over my brother and Toddie? Even my mother mentioned this morning that your behavior is rather impressive—in relation to how you pass off your father's misdeed by behaving so well yourself. If you keep this up, she'll relent and call on you."

"I don't know whether to be offended or delighted if she does." Anna stared at Delmore. "What would be your advice?"

"Be tolerant of her faults. She tends to follow leads rather than find her own. Have you had enough respectability for today? Being on inspection tends to pall on a fellow after a time."

"It's not that it palls. You have me doubting my hat and I would like to go home to remove the orange roses."

"The problem with your hat is not the roses but the hat. You need something outrageous to suit your personality. You are not a little dab of a woman who would relish occupying the background, and that's what your hat says."

"My hat matches my pelisse."

Jeremy looked amused. "Calder, you are a brave man. I would never presume to advise a woman about a hat."

Anna frowned the reproof. "This from the man who has spent the past few years telling me that my hats are dowdy."

Delmore gathered his reins. "I wash my hands of the

subject of hats. Goodbye, Jeremy. I will see you later today, no doubt."

He drove Anna home, dropping her off at her aunt's front door. As he left, Mr. Fieldhouse drew up. Anna raced up the stairs to warn Jonquil. The front door opened as she reached the landing. Mr. Fieldhouse was duly admitted to the salon. Apparently, her aunt had arisen. The bedroom being empty meant that Jonquil was downstairs, receiving visitors too. Now in no hurry, Anna removed her pelisse and tidied her hair.

She had barely reached the top of the staircase on the way back, when she saw her sister, dressed in her blue pelisse and her matching hat with yellow roses on the side, leaving with Mr. Fieldhouse.

Lady Prescott sat alone in the drawing room, her embroidery on her lap. "There you are. Driving with Delmore so early. Surely that is unusual for him?"

"I think he likes early mornings, ma'am. When we were stranded at Jeremy's house, he was the first person to arise. This morning, we met the Huntsdales in the park and the duchess asked us to call on her today, if possible. She gave me her card."

Aunt Lucy's hand fluttered across her chest. "My. You are doing far better in town than my dear sister supposed you might. You may not be the only Danbury damsel to find a husband this year. Mr. Fieldhouse seems very pleased with Jonquil, too."

"I hope he isn't too old for her." Anna sat in a single armchair, glancing at the painting on the opposite wall of nymphs cavorting in a lush garden being spied on by a dark creature lurking in the background. Jonquil might be interested in the man's money and position, but a marriage based on affection would possibly make her happier.

"And with two children." Aunt shook her head. "She's not more than a child herself, for all her papa would like a good match for her."

"She's a sensible girl but her head has been turned by the attention she has received lately. It's no mean feat to attract a rich suitor in her first season."

"You seem to have captured an earl yourself, my dear. However, your birth is respectable despite your father's wretched affiliations. Jonquil is the daughter of a vicar."

"I'm afraid I haven't captured an earl, Aunt, not respectably or otherwise. He is simply behaving the way he should, being a gentleman like his younger brother."

Aunt's eyes widened. "And he has such a scandalous reputation, too. Not that I intend to discuss that with you, but my dear, do be careful."

"I'm in no danger from him. I believe he wants to redeem himself, which is the reason why he appears to have taken me up. Apparently, I'm seen as respectable despite my father's wretched affiliations. I'm simply not considered a suitable wife for anyone in the Hasting's family, or with royal affiliations."

Aunt stared at her hands and heaved a long sigh. "Someday you will meet a man worthy of you. And he will be a man with enough strength of character not to be concerned with the silliest of reasons not to marry a very capable and charming young woman."

Anna sighed. "That may be my dream, but dreams rarely come true."

~

Wilson took the phaeton to the stables while Delmore entered his house through the front door. He trailed from room to room and finally found his mother in the conservatory, cutting flowers. The glass roofed room, heated by a stove in the winter, dripped with moisture and smelled like rain on a warm day. Greenery reached out to brush against the shoulders of his coat.

The dowager raised her gaze and watched him approach, a faint smile on her face. "You were up early today, Calder. Apparently dancing with respectable ladies has enervated you."

"I would say not sitting up all night gambling has improved mornings for me. May I carry those for you?"

She surrendered a basket of long-stemmed flowers to him. "One of the maids will arrange those if you leave them in the flower room."

"Would you sit with me for a moment and take a cup of tea?"

She glanced at him warily. "I would be delighted if this is about Jeremy. I do worry about him. He is taking far too much interest in Anna Winters, and we need to discuss how to shake her off."

He held out his arm to her and walked her past the greenery whose existence had never impacted on him, while knowing this was the reason why he had strawberries in summer and flowers in the house all year long. "Although I hadn't thought to discuss this matter with you, I do have a plan."

Her head turned toward him, and her eyebrows lifted.

"We are agreed then. She is no match for him." She took the two steps up into the main house. "She would manage him, you know. She manages everyone. At times I feel sorry for her mother and at times I almost envy her." After a careful rearrangement of her dark red skirts, she sat in her usual chair near the fireplace. Possibly out of habit, she drew her embroidery stand toward her, frowning at her previous work. "Alice will be well cared for in her dotage, make no mistake." As if agreeing with herself, she nodded.

"So, you think Anna is a good daughter?" Delmore meshed his fingers together, concentrating on his crossed thumbs in front of him.

"The best." She searched in the basket of threads on her lap and withdrew a tangle of yellows. "She was born to be the spinster companion to her mother's later years. She can run a stillroom while organizing Horace Beeby's Sunday sermons."

"That would be a sad waste of a lovely woman, though, don't you think?"

"I will never approve of her marrying Jeremy. He needs a softer, sweeter woman. Anna is all ambition."

"Well, we certainly are agreed." He offered a rueful grin. "I plan to make her my wife. I need such a one as you describe and if anyone needs managing, I do."

"Calder! You wouldn't!" She stared at him, her eyes wide and her lips not entirely closed.

He gave a wry shrug. "I find I am most desperately in love with her. However, I can't ask her to be mine until I am sure I can maintain my new reformed way of life."

"In love with her?" Her embroidery silks lay disregarded

in her lap. "When did this happen? Not during that wretched time you were cut off by the snow?"

"Possibly even before that. It may have been when she told me she wished I would go away. That was the first time I really noticed her. I had accidentally caused her to fall into the stream. She was soaked and charmingly impatient with me. As you can imagine, few women express their feelings so honestly. And she laughs at my jokes. A woman like that is invaluable."

"And is she in love with you?" The dowager straightened, her fingers a tangle in her lap.

"I think so."

"I'm surprised you don't know." Her lips clamped.

He glanced at his hands. He was almost sure Anna returned his feelings, but being almost sure might not be enough. Before he had met her, he assumed that eventually he would marry a woman of his station with a good income of her own, but he had planned to put off that dull happening until he saw a need to breed. He would certainly have chosen a much younger woman he would leave in the country, as his father had, while he maintained his lifestyle of drinking, gambling, and keeping company with interesting women in the city. He raised his glance to his mother's. "Now, as to your plans after I marry."

"I suspect the next Lady Delmore would have plans for me, but what they may be, I have no idea." Her lips clamped. "I have never been more than tolerant of her. Perhaps she would like me locked up in the attic?"

He reached out and took her hands. "But then you wouldn't be able to dote on your grandchildren. I agree that two countesses in one house is one too many. I'm quite sure

Anna would run my houses efficiently. By all accounts she does exactly what you described—runs the vicarage while she writes Beeby's sermons."

"You think I should go to live with Jeremy at Drake House?" She blinked hard.

"I do not. I think you should have your own house. If you have gentleman callers, and you likely will because you are a very attractive woman, they would prefer not to be examined from head to toes by your sons." He drew a breath, maintaining eye contact with her. "After you left for here, I inspected the dower house."

"The dower house?" She examined his expression warily. "It's completely run down. We simply haven't had the money for the upkeep of all the Delmore properties." Her fingers picked at her silks, following a single thread, only to search for the next.

"I have a man and wife, formerly the butler and house-keeper from Packham Place, who would be pleased to take on the job of organizing a renewal of the house to your specifications. If you move in, they will take up the positions proposed, should they meet with your approval."

She swallowed. "The idea of ordering my own life is strangely appealing to me." Her voice sounded husky. "After so many years of seeing to your father's. However, I must tell you the sad truth is that my income won't allow me to make the necessary repairs."

"I have discovered new words for my vocabulary, words like budgets and savings." He took her hand and kissed the back. "I have found the money and as soon as you have inspected the plans, I will give the order to have the workers begin. When the roof is weather tight, you will tour the place and decide on new curtains and the furniture you would like from our other properties."

She toyed with his fingers. "How did you find the money?"

"I have been practicing economies. Until I started doing as I should, that is acting like a proper earl, I discovered that my father left you with no more than pin money."

"His own father started taking more from the land than he should, and your father merely continued along the same lines." She took a quick glance at him to gauge his reaction to the truth he had already discovered.

"And this is what I did, too. I wouldn't listen when my man of business hinted that my losses at the tables might be hard to pay. You were the one who paid for me, by keeping the staff here to a minimum, and doing the same at Hastings House, by managing with less and less each year. I only recently noticed that the houses and the lands had not been maintained in the same way they had been before my father died." He glanced at her with a question in his eyes.

She averted her gaze. "Your father lost money so fast that he made my head spin. We barely used this house. When he died, you moved into Packham Place. I thought the best thing to do was to run Hastings House as economically as I could so that when you decided to come to your senses, if you ever did, you would have something to inherit."

"And we both know if you had told me that, I would have taken no notice. I didn't always lose at the racetrack or the tables. I thought my luck would hold forever." He scratched his eyebrow, gentling his voice. "Never noticing what you did for me. It's my time to try to do something for you, and I hope I have. My grandmother Hastings' property wasn't included in the entail. It was costing a small fortune to keep it from falling down and would only have cost more with the repairs. I sold it last week to an up-and-coming merchant. We now have enough for you to live independently."

She squeezed his hand and let him go. "You are a good son. You always were. Your father set you a poor example, but I never gave up hope."

"Perhaps you should thank Anna Winters for the return of my sense. Without needing to show her that I wasn't the desperate rake she thought me, I may not have wanted to change my way of life."

"Then, I will thank her." She stared straight into his eyes and picked up her embroidery again. "If I become her mother-in-law."

"That will not happen until I have proposed. First, I have to impress her too, and let her see I have changed my way of life."

"Did she insist on that from you?" She concentrated on threading a needle.

He gave a rumble of laughter. "The opposite. When she showed me how she saw me, I saw myself at last."

"A duchess!" Jonquil's voice held the same high pitch as the vicarage kitchen mouse. "Oh, Anna. You are doing us proud, or should I say Lord Delmore is? Who would have thought that a rake would be friendly with such high sticklers?"

"He wasn't born a rake, Jonquil. The sort of reputation he has taken many years to accomplish."

"I know that, but a duchess! What should I call her?"

"Duchess or your grace. And you must curtsey to her."

Jonquil pursed her mouth. "Of course I would. I curtsey to everyone. Is she old?"

"She would be almost my age. Am I old?"

"I refuse to answer." Jonquil's eyes sparkled. She had returned a little contemplative after her drive with Mr. Fieldhouse. "Some people think I am very young and fresh."

"Most people do, because you are. When you are enthused you are quite adorable. Do wear your jockey hat with that gown. Here, let me help you." Anna rested a hand on Jonquil's shoulder, urging her to the chair in front of the dressing table. The dark blue hat boasted a tall brim lined with pink muslin that matched her gown. The outfit was simple enough to make a feature of Jonquil's prettiness. "Did you meet anyone interesting when you were driving with Mr. Fieldhouse?"

"Mainly married couples, which is to be expected. His fob has a diamond-studded case. Can you imagine spending so much money on an article that is barely seen?"

"When I am very wealthy, I will ask myself that question. While I have no money, I think that is a dreadful waste, but I don't imagine rich people think the same way as poor people."

"I don't plan to remain poor; you know." Jonquil examined her hat from every angle in the mirror and stood. "My face is my fortune. I don't think the life of a vicar's wife is for me. I would much rather dance the night away and eat cake every day."

"If you do, you will grow sadly fat," Anna said prosaically as she straightened the brim of her brown hat. Such a shame to be seen in the same headwear in the morning as in the afternoon but she only had time to remove the orange roses. At least she had changed into her cream gown. With a shawl, her brown spencer would keep her warm enough. She raised her gaze to the door when she heard a quick knock, which heralded her aunt's maid.

"My lady sent these for Miss Winters. She hopes at least one will suit."

Anna stood for a moment, mouth agape, and then she helped the maid dump an armload of hats on the bed. "I haven't seen more hats together even in a hat shop," she said, awed. Before her next breath, she raced out into the hallway and to her aunt's bedroom, knocked, and entered after hearing an invitation to enter. "Aunt, you are a life-saver. I haven't tried on a single one, but I know they are all lovely—the hats. I'm so thrilled." She kissed her smiling aunt and ran back to the bedroom.

"Twenty-three hats." Jonquil stood watching the load on the bed as if it might leap up and bite her. "Who has twenty-three hats?"

"I do at the moment. Quick, find one that will go with this cream gown. Won't Lord Delmore be surprised? That's if he is at the duke's town house too."

She finally chose a tall blue hat with a cream ostrich feather trim and blue ribbons. Then, the whole family, minus Sir Arthur who said he would love to be there, but he thought he might find a book to read instead. Lady

Prescott tapped him on the shoulder with her fan and laughed. "Old duffer," she said fondly.

The Duke of Huntsdale's town house stood in Berkley Square facing the park. Curricles and coaches stood lined up outside. This was, apparently, the place to be if you had social pretensions.

After paying her respects to the duchess with her nieces standing behind, Aunt quickly shunted herself off to the morning room where the chaperones were gossiping. The duchess greeted Anna and Jonquil with a friendly smile and held Anna's arm while a gushing matron interrupted a burgeoning conversation. Jonquil drifted off. Idly scanning the room, Anna noted Delmore on the far side, near the entrance. Unfortunately, his mother stood beside him. Anna sighed. Today had been so pleasant that she couldn't cope with being found wanting, yet again.

Finally, the duchess turned to her. "I do like entertaining, as you see. The duke is rather impressed to have met a respectable woman in Calder's company." She smiled with her eyes.

"I'm not quite respectable. I have no choice since my father wasn't."

"Nor was Calder's and he went the other way, entirely. How puzzling."

"But he is a man and being disreputable is more than likely so much more fun."

The duchess laughed. "I knew I would like you. One look at the hat of yours this morning, so interesting with those orange flowers, and I knew you could carry off anything. This afternoon's hat is also suitably interesting, and I very much approve of it. I have absolutely no taste. I need a friend who is otherwise."

Anna simply needed a friend, someone who enjoyed her deadly sense of humor. "I won't be much use to you. I'm no one."

"Oh, but you are about to become someone. Adam says anyone who can put that look of satisfaction on Delmore's face is a person to be admired. I can't get away to chat to you alone today, but we have luncheons planned, and a ball. You must come to everything. Promise me." She stared into Anna's eyes.

"I promise," Anna said in a dazed voice, not so much because of the offer of Cassia's friendship but because the duchess thought Delmore looked satisfied to be with her.

Chapter Fourteen

Anna knew that common courtesy would require her to speak to Lady Delmore. The fact that Delmore stood with his mother made the gesture more appealing. However, she had lost sight of her stepsister, who should also greet their neighbor. Scanning the room, she spotted the Honorable Jeremy chatting to the prettiest young ladies in the room, as usual. Although she hesitated to intrude, she needed his help. Normally her sister would remain in sight.

She sidled up to him. "Do excuse me," she said to the young lady who currently eyed him with adoration. "Jeremy, I have misplaced Jonquil. Have you seen her?"

"Over by the doors, flirting with Robert Fieldhouse." With an expression of quick impatience, he indicated the glass-paned doors leading to the patio outside, where neither Jonquil nor Mr. Fieldhouse stood. "Apparently not. Perhaps she is with your aunt." He frowned.

She hurried off, knowing she had allowed herself to become distracted. Yet again, she had been an inadequate companion. Aunt Lucy in the card room hadn't seen Jonquil either. Fortunately, she spotted John Temple and Rodney Toddington scanning the room as if for likely prospects. "Have either of you seen my sister?" she asked as soon as she reached the two men.

"I don't want to sound like a bleating sheep, Anna, but if I had seen Jonquil, I wouldn't be stuck in a corner with Toddie," John said, folding his arms across his manly chest.

Rodney grinned. "I'm the best he can do because I won't compete with him for her. If I should happen to see her, I will t-tell her you want her."

"I'll try the garden. She may have wandered outside for fresh air."

John drew down his eyebrows. "She'll freeze out there. I will fetch her back inside."

"I don't want her running off in the opposite direction." Anna marched through the French doors onto the stone patio. A scurry of wind whipped her skirts against her legs. Her cheeks stung with the cold. She lifted her collar higher, blessing her gloves. Surely even Jonquil wouldn't stroll around the garden in this uncalled-for weather.

The height of the patio allowed her to see only the tops of the shorter hedges. Finally, she noted a movement on the right. A dark blue hat and the glimpse of a kingfisher blue jacket, Mr. Fieldhouse's perpetual color choice, peeped through the privet. Then a glimpse of pink. She sighed. Mr. Fieldhouse surely knew better than to entice a young lady in her first season to a private spot. She bounded down the stairs and headed in their direction.

Voices lured her along the first path and then detoured her to the next. Under her feet, moisture seeped through the soles of her shoes. The leaves on the hedges brushed her pelisse, contributing to the prickles running down her spine.

"Yes, I do like pink roses." Jonquil's voice, with a silly laugh.

A deeper voice. "And your mouth looks particularly—"

"Is that you, Jonquil?" Anna called rhetorically, because by then she could see the couple standing far too close. Mr. Fieldhouse's hand sat on Jonquil's waist. "Dear me. Whatever would possess you to come outside on a day like this with only your shawl? Do go inside into the warmth, Jonquil." Anna shot her sister a stare of great disapproval.

Jonquil lowered her gaze, her mouth petulant. "I wanted to see the roses."

"The roses are mere buds. And I would like a word with Mr. Fieldhouse, alone, if you please."

At first Jonquil tried tilting up her chin and pouting her lower lip, but even she could see that a scene in front of Mr. Fieldhouse would do her no good. Her nose in the air, she pushed past Anna and disappeared.

"Best if you don't re-enter the room too soon after her, Mr. Fieldhouse. Lord knows how many people saw you leave together. It is really badly done of you, sir. This is not the way to behave with a young debutante. Any scandal would ruin her."

"You look rather wonderful when you are cross." He took his diamond-studded fob watch out of his pocket, clicked open the case door and checked the time.

"When I am cross, I look cross. How a cross woman could look wonderful is a puzzle to me."

"Good Lord. I pay you a compliment and you tear a

strip off me. I did no harm, after all. She asked me to go outside with her. What's a fellow to think when a young lady does that, eh?"

"He ought to think she is being foolish and leave the matter there."

He smirked. "Then again, I wanted to see what she would do when she was alone with me. And at the moment, Miss Winters, you are alone with me."

"And I will speak to you as courteously as I always have. I have no reputation to lose, sir, unlike my sister." She turned to walk back along the path. He followed. She stopped. "Would you like to escort me inside or would you prefer we enter one by one, which would look rather odd, to say the least."

After stepping up onto the patio, he opened one of the French doors and stood aside. "Better the older sister than none, eh?"

The offensive comment narrowed her eyes. Pressing her lips together, she lifted her chin and entered the room. The icy breeze whooshed in behind her, causing a slight flurry of her skirts. She marched through the room, her spine rigid, followed by Mr. Fieldhouse. Better the older sister than none.

If she had ever thought the man might make a good husband for Jonquil, she had changed her mind. Fieldhouse saw women as interchangeable, if not valueless. Unlike Delmore, who valued women and who even treated one he didn't plan to keep as carefully as if she might be his most precious possession.

Swallowing her annoyance, she turned to make her way to the card room, but Mr. Fieldhouse stopped her by standing in her path. Although she was tempted to thrust him away, she couldn't afford to make an enemy of a man who was considered to be a great catch. Instead, she managed to raise her eyebrows in query. Somehow, she held a civil tongue, though he wanted to discuss nothing more interesting than the masquerade ball tonight. He, vain man that he was, informed her that he intended to wear a cloak of his signature color, kingfisher blue, in case she failed to recognize him.

"I'm sure you won't recognize us," she informed him, hoping that a black cloak and mask would hide them in what she assumed would be a huge crowd.

"I would know you anywhere," he said with a smarmy smile. "Even if I don't, I will likely recognize your retinue. Your aunt tends to stand out in a crowd."

"I am about to join her in the card room, if you will excuse me," she said, hoping that, for once, her aunt would adopt a less colorful style.

Fortunately, he bowed and took his leave. She turned and saw Jeremy standing with his mother and Delmore. All three looked across at Anna. She instantly adopted a mysterious expression, adding a demure smile, as if she had been caught dallying with Mr. Fieldhouse. If any of them had seen him entering from the outside with her and thought the worst, her pride would never let her set them straight.

The countess smiled back, possibly because she did think the worst of Anna and hoped Jeremy had noticed who had entered from the garden, and with whom. Instead, her beloved younger son walked across to Anna and took her hand. "Well done," he said in a low voice. "She came back through the other doors, and I took her straight to your aunt." After a slight hesitation, he drew her into the group he had just left.

The dowager offered a smile that didn't reach her eyes. "Such a pretty hat, Anna. You do know the colors that suit you."

Anna accepted the compliment to Aunt Lucy's hat with a smile and glanced up at Delmore, whose eyes narrowed. "Surely the weather is too cold to be dallying outside?" he said in his arrogant earl voice.

Not knowing whether to be pleased that he clearly didn't approve of her being outside with Mr. Fieldhouse, or annoyed that he thought he had the right to comment, she dropped her gaze. "The shawl helped." She heightened her chin. "It's stuffy in here. I needed fresh air."

The dowager briefly touched Anna's hand. "Come to the fire with me, Anna, for I think your fresh air has chilled you a little. We'll leave these two to find us a small glass of sherry." Lady Delmore didn't quite take Anna's arm, but she stood close enough to guide her where she expected her to go. "You may not know," she said in a careful voice. "But Mr. Fieldhouse is hanging out for a mother for his children. All well and good, of course, but gossip says he didn't treat the first Mrs. Fieldhouse well. She rarely came to town with him."

"I'll keep that in mind."

"Anna." The older woman briefly touched Anna's arm before they had quite reached the crowded area around the massive fireplace. "Although it almost seems too late to hope for forgiveness, I will ask regardless." She lifted her aristocratic jaw in a way that expressed her pride rather than her attrition. "For many years I have tried to keep Jeremy away from you. Jeremy wouldn't be kept away. Countless times he told me you were quite wonderful if only I would give you a chance. I would not. Not because of your mother. Not even because of your wretched father." The countess finally met Anna's gaze, her tongue making a quick swipe over her bottom lip. "Because of what I did. I urged my husband to inform on your father."

Anna stiffened. For ten years, she had hoped for some sort of acknowledgement from this woman. After all, Anna had done nothing to offend her. Now she understood why Lady Delmore acted as if Anna only existed as a vague shadow. How could the lady do otherwise, knowing what she had done? Anna swallowed. "I didn't know my father, ma'am. By all accounts he was a foolish young man. I doubt you could blame yourself for his foolishness."

"Regardless, Anna, can you forgive me?"

Anna impulsively covered the Countess's hand with her own. "Do you honestly think, my lady, that you had so much influence over the late Lord Delmore that, despite his own wishes, he would have betrayed my father?"

The dowager made a wry face. "I doubt my late unlamented husband had quite so much respect for me, but my words would have backed up his thoughts."

"You can be easy. I thought it was sad that you so disapproved of me, but since it made no difference to my life, or I don't think it did, I'm willing to ignore the past. I'm only too glad to make a new acquaintance." She curtseyed to the older woman.

"That's exceedingly generous of you, Anna." The countess sounded a trifle humble. "You seem to be everything my son said you are. Let me introduce you and your sister too, of course, to those of my circle you have not yet met."

"By Jove," Jeremy said, overhearing as he arrived back at his mother's side. He handed her a small glass of wine. "You'll have poor Anna thinking you have lost your wits if you do so. They're a tedious coven of old witches."

"They have influence, Jeremy. Anna has been left with the task of being her stepsister's companion. She is too young for that task. I'm sure a little help would be welcome."

"You're right. Anna ought to be enjoying herself instead of chasing after that spoiled young miss."

"I thought you and she had called a truce," Anna said to him with surprise.

"The affairs of Jonquil Beeby are not quite as riveting ..." Delmore said, arriving and passing a glass of sweet wine to her. He stared straight into her eyes, his expression tight. "... as affairs with Robert Fieldhouse. Believe me." His gaze met his mother's.

A lump formed in Anna's throat as she noted the silent message that passed between the two. Lady Delmore had already warned her about Mr. Fieldhouse. Perhaps she and Delmore thought Anna had gone outside to meet the unspeakable cad. Delmore should know better ... but of course, he didn't. She'd participated in furtive behavior with him. He could only expand his suspicions when he knew his own experiences with her. She had been all too willing to misbehave with him. "I might not be quite as interested in society's approval as you may imagine. Do excuse me." She whirled around and left.

Blinking hard, she began to make her way to the

morning room, but her aunt appeared arm in arm with Jonquil who looked far from chastened after her escapade.

"Your Aunt Lucy owns more than fifty hats, Anna," Jonquil said in a gleeful voice. "Fifty hats! Papa would be shocked. He thinks anyone owning more than three is a disgraceful spendthrift."

"Sir Arthur agrees with him, my dear." Aunt patted Jonquil's hand. "He turns his eyes up in his head whenever I buy a new one. Therefore, I rely on you and Anna to relieve me of a few."

"I was perfectly thrilled to relieve you of this one." Anna willed away her incipient tears and touched the lovely confection on her head, all the time unable to forget the hard expression on Delmore's face.

"Sir Arthur will be delighted, my dearest niece. I can only hope you will accept at least another ten."

"You are too generous, Aunt." Anna's voice came out a little strained. She gave Lady Prescott a quick hug and a kiss on the cheek. "Do you mind if we leave now? We have a long night ahead of us."

"Indeed, and I'm sure I will need a nap this afternoon if I am to stay at the ball until the unmasking." Lady Prescott sandwiched herself between Anna and Jonquil to travel across half the room and bid farewell to her cronies. Civilities dispensed with, the party left.

On the way home, Anna's mind flittered around the Dowager Countess of Delmore's unexpected apology. Although a vicar's stepdaughter would never move in the countess's social circles, her apology about Anna's father had been generous. How the acknowledgment might affect her, she couldn't imagine because she had lived under her father's ominous shadow her whole life. As for Delmore, he had told her he didn't want her. She'd thought she might be able to change his mind, but he was already preparing to make a case about her and Mr. Fieldhouse.

She didn't participate in the steady stream of conversation in the carriage. Instead, she noted the apple blossom and realized spring had arrived. Back home, the stream would be running fresh and clear and the daffodils would be bursting out of the ground. Despite knowing this, the thought of going back to the draughty vicarage and sitting night after night sewing lowered her spirits even more. And yet sooner or later that would be her miserable fate.

She and Jonquil had barely reached the privacy of their bedroom, when Jonquil turned to face her. "You embarrassed me by coming outside to fetch me." Her bottom lip quivered.

"Please, Jonquil. I've had quite enough of listening to criticism today. If you behaved as you should, I shouldn't need to fetch you." Her voice and patience thin, Anna opened the door and began to untie her hat ribbons. "What on earth possessed you to ask Mr. Fieldhouse to take you into the garden?"

"The devil, I expect," Jonquil said flippantly, tossing her pelisse onto the bed. Her hat followed. In the vicarage she would at least put her own clothes away but here, with double the servants, she acted like a spoiled miss. "I thought I might let him kiss me. He wanted to."

"And did he?"

"Of course. He is a very nice kisser. Better than John Temple."

"John has kissed you too?"

"In Danbury. Not here. One kiss from him was enough for me."

"Well, John hasn't given up hope."

"I have far better prospects than the son of a squire, if I play my cards right, and I intend to do just that." Jonquil raised her chin, her expression smug.

"Although you might think being the wife of a rich man would be delightful, you would also be the mother of two small children before you even start to plan children of your own."

Jonquil laughed, prinking her hair. "Only if you assume I have Mr. Fieldhouse in my sights."

Anna took a deep breath. She would not argue all afternoon. Had Jonquil applied to be a rake's mistress as Anna had done, Anna would be shocked. She had no right to judge her silly sister when she was also a silly sister. "I'm not assuming anything. Perhaps we should have stayed in Danbury."

"And have Jeremy on his knees to you day after day?" Jonquil said as a parting shot as Anna left the room.

The reference lost on Anna, she went down to the library to find herself a book, in which she didn't see a word for the whole hour until the family assembled for a light meal.

After another change of clothes, she would be dragged along to the Marquess of Hamilton's annual masked ball.

Chapter Fifteen

Cursed by his smoldering jealousy, Delmore scanned the guests in the paneled reception area of Hamilton's town house. Although his height helped, he recognized enough groups to be able to quickly eliminate Anna. He pushed his way into the packed ballroom, greeted by the penetrating tones of at least a hundred persons. Had his mind not been completely focused, he would have given up before he started, hating these tedious formal functions as much as he did. However, the realization had hit him when Anna quietly had removed herself from Huntsdale House, that he needed to press his suit as soon as possible. Waiting until he was sure of his reformation was certain to be too late.

Fieldhouse must be rubbing his hands in glee to have so noticeably separated Anna from the duchess's crowded drawing room this afternoon. His smile had been incomparably smug when he glanced at her. Delmore had said to himself anyone but Fieldhouse, but he hadn't narrowed his target enough. What he really meant was she couldn't marry anyone but Delmore. What a blithering fool he had been to have criticized one of her suitors, which would, in a way, be a criticism of her. A woman who was accustomed to being a law unto herself would likely be sent in the opposite direction. Better a man who loved her than leaving the door open to one like Fieldhouse, who would ruin Anna simply to amuse himself.

In the past, Delmore had attended masquerades purely to drink with his equally irresponsible companions and to choose which pretty Cyprians would share his bed. Normally he wouldn't have considered attending a ball held among the respectable members of the ton. During the past few months, he had discovered that without alcohol to dull his mind, he had begun to enjoy events that would formerly have bored him. But not tonight. Tonight, he had a mission.

He pushed past guests whose disguises were so thin that he nodded and greeted them by name. Others had gone to great lengths to be mysterious. In a simple black mask and cloak himself, he expected to be easily spotted.

By the decree of the rigid host, the Marquess of Hamilton, masks would remain until midnight. Thereafter, having revealed their true identities, the more reliable members of the ton would disport themselves in their normal way. The less reliable would continue on until early morning and kick up their heels elsewhere, as he used to do.

After lurking between a set of marble columns for a few minutes, he noted his mother and his brother, each accompanied by their own circle of friends. However, he couldn't see Anna or her family. Once more, he circled the perimeter of the ballroom, picking up a glass of champagne on the way.

Tonight, he would redeem himself with Anna.

Jonquil had been fussing for over an hour. First, she didn't like the ruffles on the cap sleeves of her gown. They've been seen too often, she said. Anna carefully unpicked the stitches that she had so patiently sewn. Then Jonquil decided she would wear the white gown instead of the yellow. After she had redressed, she noticed that the curls in her knot drooped. Anna re-pinned them, beginning to wonder if Jonquil really didn't want to go out tonight. She had already detained the party for an hour.

A sharp knock, and the door opened. Lady Prescott marched into Anna's room behind her maid who carried an armload of cloaks and masks in various colors. "We really must leave soon my dears. Perhaps one of these will make you happy, Jonquil." She watched as Beryl arranged the articles for inspection. "I do so love masked balls. I would hate to miss this one."

Anna smiled at Aunt, relieved by the diversion. "There, Jonquil. Perfect for your white gown—a powder blue cloak."

"Powder blue," Jonquil said in a long drawn-out breath. "I must say that is quite perfect. The very idea of wearing black ... well, I'm glad I don't have to, now. Lady Prescott, you are the perfect aunt. I wish you were mine."

"I'm yours by default, my dear. The matching mask is

pretty too. See these paste diamonds? Anna, would you like one too?"

Anna glanced at the black cloak Mama had supplied and the plain black mask she had bought. "I adore the red, but would I be brave enough to wear red?"

Aunt pursed her mouth. "If you don't, I might, but I had decided on the purple for tonight. If I don't pull on the hood, I have the loveliest turban in yellow that would be just the thing with that shade."

Anna laughed softly. Few women could combine yellow with purple, but the combination would be expected of her aunt, whose appalling eye for color was accepted mainly because of her endearing nature. "In that case, I will be brave and take the red. I may never have another opportunity to be outrageous again."

Fashionably late and duly dressed in the colors of the rainbow, surrounded by black hooded cloaks and masks, the Prescott party entered the Marquess of Hamilton's packed ballroom. The guests were already dancing and had clearly been imbibing for some time. The place hummed with low voiced gossip, laughter, and shouts of merriment, all of which competed with the orchestra on the minstrel's gallery. A passing servant liveried in dark blue offered a tray of sparkling yellow champagne. Jonquil took one and Anna removed the glass from her hold, passing the drink to Lady Prescott, who looked surprised and sipped.

"Please don't keep trying my patience tonight," Anna said to her sister. "If you should, I'm likely to get a headache and insist on leaving right away."

Her sister turned her back. "Oh, there's Jeremy." She

lifted her arm to get the attention of a man in a hooded black cloak and mask like all the others.

Anna sighed. "What makes you think that is Jeremy?"

Jonquil's eyes blinked behind her pale blue mask. "That's how his outline looks, how he stands."

Anna concentrated, and the man waved, smiled and came over with another cloaked man. "Well, finally. I had almost given you up." Jeremy reached out and took Anna's hand. "We were looking for black cloaks, but your aunt's purple cloak and yellow turban gave you away."

Rodney Toddington lifted his mask, momentarily. "Would never have spotted you without spotting Lady Prescott, first." Rodney bowed and glanced up; his attention caught by a woman flitting past. "Isn't that—?" He stumbled slightly when Jeremy elbowed him in the ribs. "Pardon. I must have been mistaken."

"You were." Jeremy cleared his throat. "Everyone is waltzing. Would you honor me, Anna?"

"Not tonight. I'm taking my duties seriously. I'll watch Jonquil waltzing, instead."

Jeremy leaned his chin into his chest, his light blue eyes peering at her through his mask, clearly realizing he had yet again been maneuvered into looking after Jonquil. Without a demur, he sighed and took her hand. Having approved by the patronesses of Almack's, she almost ran him onto the floor.

Rodney tried with Anna, but she was adamant because she had noted a kingfisher blue cloak, which she instantly presumed was being worn by Mr. Fieldhouse. From the other side of the room, he bowed to her. Masked, she didn't expect to be recognized so easily, but he may have noticed the presence of Jeremy and Rodney and correctly identified the colorful trio nearby.

No more than two sets later, the kingfisher-blue masked man arrived at her side. The eyes behind the mask were dark in color. "Ah, a mysterious lady in red. You must have this waltz with me." The voice belonged to Mr. Fieldhouse.

"I would sir but—" Before she could finish her sentence, he swept her onto the floor. Unfortunately, she wouldn't make a spectacle of herself by leaving him partnerless, even though he'd had the discourtesy to snatch her up mid-sentence.

He returned her when the music ended and scooped up Jonquil for the next waltz. Anna didn't have a prayer of controlling the man. She stood watching, her foot tapping, and her arms crossed. Frowning, she practiced a harsh reprimand, muttering under her breath because she had also allowed herself to be grabbed up without a protest. As she was deciding between you may not and I will not allow a man in the regular black hooded cloak and mask took her hand.

She glanced up at him. The eyes behind the mask were a glittering shade of dark green, and the muscled height and broad shoulders belonged to Delmore. His warm, white-gloved hand enveloped hers. "Red cloak and mask," he said in a voice close enough for her to smell the alcohol on his breath. He led her onto the floor. "No wonder I couldn't see you. I hope your red disguise doesn't mean you intend to be a scarlet woman tonight." He moved her into the centre of the crowd on the floor.

"And how would that concern you?" she inquired with icy politeness.

His warm breath tickled her ear. "I offended you at the Huntsdale's and for that I am sorry. I didn't like to see you wandering off with Fieldhouse."

"I am as yet a single woman and I may choose my company." She turned her head as the dance dictated.

He murmured, "In that case, choose me."

She faced him. "I suspect that's the brandy speaking, because you know I tried, my lord, but you didn't want me." Her throat clogged. Nothing could be worse than admitting defeat. She had bluffed and bluffed and bluffed, but the time had come to give up. "A smart woman would cut her losses and that's what I intend to do."

A painful thickening formed in her throat. She jerked her hand from his grip, leaving him alone on the floor. Tonight, all her emotions had risen to the surface. Heeding the prickling of her eyes, she wound her way through the dancers, her throat closure growing even larger. She had loved and lost, and her world would never be the same again. Even for expedience, she couldn't imagine being with another man, in sin, or in marriage.

Swallowing her tears, she reached the sidelines of the ballroom, where she remained, trying to regain her poise. She should never have worn the red cloak. The bright color made her stand out. After much concentrated breathing, she withheld her watery moment. Raising her head, she wound toward the area where she had left her aunt. To let a woman pass, she turned sideways and from the corner of her eyes, she noted the flash of a kingfisher blue cloak. A powder blue cloak followed close behind toward the main doorway.

Her self pity instantly discarded; she squared her shoulders. Jonquil should not be leaving the ballroom. She must be returned to Aunt, not prancing off to places unknown with Mr. Fieldhouse. Tonight, had begun badly and no redemption had yet been offered at the masquerade.

For a couple of seconds her sister hesitated, turning back to scan the crowd. Mr. Fieldhouse appeared to be whispering into her ear. Then she gave a deliberate upward tilt of her chin, turned, and left with him.

Anna swiveled, trying to see what had put the rebellious spring to Jonquil's steps. Aunt's yellow turban stood out from the crowd, but she was gossiping with a crony who was staring open mouthed at the space where Jonquil had been. Aunt stopped talking when her crony pointed in that direction.

Expanding her chest with a huge breath, Anna put aside her maudlin thoughts. Her lips firmly pressed together; she pushed her through to the doorway. A gallery curved either side to the grand staircase. She took the left and ran to the stairs only to see two blue cloaks flittering down. As she chased, the figures hastened through the front entrance.

Horrified, she sped up. Surely Jonquil wouldn't leave the ball with Mr. Fieldhouse. Perhaps a duchess could behave that way, but not the daughter of a vicar. If anyone else had seen, she would be unmarriageable.

Coaches stood idle in the dark street outside. Other than a group of coachmen, sheltering from a night breeze against the outside wall, not even the flying edge of a blue cloak was visible. No errant sister and no Mr. Fieldhouse in the deserted street. Cold air swirled beneath Anna's cloak.

She started toward the men. If Jonquil had dashed by,

they surely would know. Footsteps echoed behind her. Her heart began a nervous beating as a large male presence loomed beside her. "If Cinderella is planning to leave the ball, may I offer transport?" said in a deep voice.

Recognizing Delmore, she slumped with relief. Although he was a disreputable cad, she could be sure he would help her, if only for the sake of the Vicar's daughter. "Jonquil has run away with Mr. Fieldhouse," she said in an undertone.

His eyes glittered behind his mask. "Your sister is respectably born and if Fieldhouse ruined her, he would have to marry her."

"I can't be sure that is not her plan." She rubbed her arms. "This is not the way her father would wish to have her marry. Not in disgrace."

One of the coachmen moved off the wall and stared at her. He made strange movements with his head. She glanced at him blankly.

"Speak up, man," Delmore said, visibly straightening.

The driver pressed a finger across his lips and indicated an idle black coach. Frowning, Delmore moved in front of Anna and stepped closer to the carriage. A muffled giggle, and the door of the carriage opened a crack. The coachman rushed forward to let down the steps. Jonquil emerged, her expression triumphant, followed by Mr. Fieldhouse.

She spotted Delmore and moved back, her face clearly astonished. "My lord. I wasn't expecting you."

"I'm sure you weren't, you selfish brat," he said in a rough voice. "You were expecting Anna to find Jeremy to help her. Unfortunately, he was otherwise occupied. He has his own interests, you know."

Anna's sagged with disappointment. Speaking to Jonquil that way was so unlike him, that she could only suspect he taken more than one glass of champagne. "I didn't have time, or I would have tried to find Jeremy."

"I am happy to serve in his place," Delmore said, folding his arms across his chest.

"Oh, go away and sober up. I can handle this," Anna said impatiently.

"Evening, Delmore." Mr. Fieldhouse's normal smug smile had deserted him. "Miss Beeby simply wanted to play a joke on her sister. She doesn't enjoy being so closely watched."

"I'm sure she doesn't. And I'm sure her sister has better ways to occupy her time than re-trieve her sister from men like you. You, sir, are no gennelman. Jonquil is barely eighteen and you are old enough to know you can't treat a young lady thish way. My friends will wade on yours." Delmore gave a stiff-necked nod. "I'm shoor my brother will act for me. Name your friends, if you please."

"I will not duel with you, Delmore, not when you are staggeringly drunk. Not over something as paltry as this silly little tease." Mr. Fieldhouse glanced with contempt at Jonquil.

"Are you crying craven?" Delmore stared, his expression a cross between disdainful and confused.

Mr. Fieldhouse's face turned surly. "Leave it go. She is anyone's. She has not the sense of a flea."

"I name you a spineless coward." Delmore lifted his perfect chin aloft.

Mr. Fieldhouse narrowed his eyes. A triumphant smile crossed his lips. With his fists raised, he took three hasty steps forward ... and tripped over Delmore's lazily extended foot. The villain sprawled onto the pavement. The coachmen, who had moved closer to watch, guffawed.

Frowning, Mr. Fieldhouse slowly rose to his feet, went into a stiff posture with his knuckles in front of his face, and tried for a punch. Delmore moved slightly to the side, reached out one long arm, and again Mr. Fieldhouse fell to the ground. "Had enough?" Delmore asked in a perfectly clear voice, examining the backs of his gloves.

The coachmen seemed to think they were attending a boxing match. One tried to urge Mr. Fieldhouse to his feet. Mr. Fieldhouse didn't attempt a further attack. He slowly arose, wiping at his bloodied nose, his mouth petulant. "She isn't worth fighting for."

"Apologize to Miss Beeby and leave, or you will be more than sorry."

Mr. Fieldhouse drew himself to his full height, and said, "Miss Beeby. I apologize for bringing you out here though this is what you asked of me. I shall not be such a gull in future."

"Are you satisfied with that?" Delmore asked Jonquil.

Her bottom lip protruded the way it did when she was asked to help in the kitchen at home. "How dare he say I'm a silly little tease. He's no gentleman."

"Whatever made you think he was?" Blinking, Delmore stared at her.

She tilted her chin up. "Your mother introduced us."

"I think you must learn to judge men by their behavior. Mr. Fieldhouse has misbehaved with you before, and Anna took the brunt of that. I think you owe her a rather eloquent apology."

Mr. Fieldhouse turned to one of the coachmen. "Find transport for me and you'll earn a guinea," he said in a reedy voice. The coachman began to walk up the dark street, and Mr. Fieldhouse followed, his cloak teased by a flurry of wind.

Anna's shoulders eased. "We shall speak about this later, Jonquil. Now we will return to the ballroom. You will need to think of a good explanation for leaving the ball with Mr. Fieldhouse, for Aunt and her friends all saw you go."

"She wasn't watching your aunt. She had her eyes on Jeremy." Delmore straightened his cloak over his shoulders. Blood seeped through the knuckles of his gloves.

"Did you hit Mr. Fieldhouse?" Anna asked in amazement.

Delmore glanced at his right hand. "I may have."

Her chest hurt. "I thought you had given up drinking."

He shrugged. "Although I considered taking a drink tonight, I stood with it until I was tired of watching the bubbles rise. Then I emptied my glass into the nearest fern."

For a few beats she held his gaze before she finally believed him. Relieved and slightly amused, for Fieldhouse might not have attempted taking a swing at him had he not thought he had the advantage, she nodded. "Then, what's to be done about Jonquil? I think she must exchange her cloak for mine and enter the ballroom with you, if you don't mind, my lord."

He straightened his mask. "I would rather escort you back. She has made her bed. Leave her to lie in it, for once."

Anna ignored his words. "And I will follow wearing the blue. You must dance with her and after you see me with

Aunt, bring her over. I will have told a torrent of lies by then and all should be well."

"And polite society will presume you left the ball with Mr. Fieldhouse? My dear, your reputation will be as shot as Jonquil's should have been. You've already been seen with him, and the gossips have taken note."

She frowned. "It doesn't matter in the least. I'm an elderly spinster. I have no marriage hopes to dash."

Jonquil slowly untied the knot of her cloak and changed with Anna. "And for what reason are we changing cloaks?" She used her pettish tone.

Delmore sighed. "So that Anna can accept the humiliation that rightly belongs to you."

Anna gave Delmore a quelling glance and turned back to Jonquil. "A whim, which can be yours. You wanted to look dashing in red rather than sweet in blue for a while. As well, everyone knew who you were in the blue. No one recognized you in the red, which was how you came to be waltzing with Delmore. That explanation is a trifle more ingenuous than you wanting Jeremy to rescue you from a wicked abductor." She removed her mask, holding the pasteboard out to Jonquil who slowly made the exchange.

"At least I won't be dancing with Jonquil for too long," Delmore watched the exchange. "It wants ten minutes until unmasking. And you, Miss Winters, are a very devious woman. I should waltz with Jonquil when I wasn't allowed to waltz with you? Do you plan to give me orders for the rest of your life?"

The rest of her life? If only.

~

Delmore made sure he and the red-cloaked Jonquil passed through the doorway among a crowd of people. What on earth had possessed him to think about drinking a glass of champagne? Since he had first started over-imbibing, he had known that alcohol cured nothing. Before he took the sullen Jonquil onto the ballroom floor, he noted Anna pushing through into the room. With the blue hood up and the mask over her face, she could be anyone. Only someone who loved her would note the hesitation and the nervous moistening of her lips, which would be caused by having to dissemble.

He mentally cursed self-centered Jonquil who assumed her stepsister would smooth out the trouble she had caused. He cursed himself for not remaining vigilant in case he was needed. Past experience should have taught him that Fieldhouse took whatever he wanted, in the belief that ten thousand a year gave him special rights.

"You said Jeremy has other interests. To what were you referring?" Jonquil asked in a challenging way as the music stopped.

"The usual for a young man his age."

"Meaning what?" She almost stamped her foot. She certainly moved with a thump of one.

Delmore sighed. "Do you imagine he doesn't have a lady friend in town?"

Jonquil stared at him, her mouth agape. Then she tossed her head, letting her hood expose her hair. Her eyes narrowed. "I thought only men like you took mistresses."

He let the insult pass, knowing what sort of man he was, and that he would have to try harder than he had to be another sort of man. Everywhere he looked, hoods were downed, and masks removed. The odd person laughed with surprise, but most appeared to have guessed their dancing partners by now. The powder blue cloak he had been watching for the past ten minutes drifted over to Lady Prescott, whose mouth opened when she saw Anna's face above.

The aunt hugged the niece and Delmore returned the recalcitrant sister to the folds of her temporary family. "How odd to find Jonquil in red," he said to Lady Prescott. "I thought I might have found a mysterious stranger, but no. Only young Jonquil. And Anna, my dear." He passed his love an overdone glance of lechery, which he might have done had he been drinking. No one would be surprised, given his reputation, which would be dealt with day by day. "You in powder blue. Very innocent, I must say. Perhaps now we each know who the other is, you could spare a waltz to me before supper?"

His love offered him a quelling glance in return.

"I'm so relieved to see you in the blue, Anna. When did you change?" Lady Prescott held her niece's hand.

"Some time ago." Anna smiled indulgently. "A masquerade should be a night of surprises, should it not?"

"It should be. Lady Rawlings told me Jonquil had left the ball with Mr. Fieldhouse. She was quite obnoxious about it, too. I must call your blue cloak to her attention." The flanges of Lady Prescott's impressive nose flared.

"I hope she doesn't mind if Mr. Fieldhouse escorted me to the gallery? I had a slight headache and needed a whiff of unused air. Then he decided the ball was a bore because I apparently wasn't the woman he supposed. He left."

Lady Prescott narrowed her eyes slightly. "I hope you

put him in his place, my dearest niece. The man is too free in his ways."

"I suspect he'll be more careful, now, Aunt. And yes, Lord Delmore. I would enjoy waltzing with you."

"And supper after." He held out his hand to her and led her onto the floor. Waltzing with her was doubly delightful since she not only took leads without a stumble, but she also created unusual warmth in his chest. Without a doubt, he wore a fatuous smile. He wanted to propose to her then and there, but being sober wouldn't allow him to take a rebuff quite as easily as when he numbed his mind. Knowing she trusted him, as she had proved tonight, and being almost sure she also loved him wasn't quite the same as being completely sure. After all, she would have asked Jeremy to help her with Jonquil had Jeremy not been chasing a light skirt all over a room that she would clearly have never been invited to grace.

With a deep bracing breath, he said close to her ear, "May I call on you tomorrow?"

"No need, my lord. You've made me respectable, and your job is now done." She glanced in the other direction as if bored.

His next breath was long and deep. "Not quite. I see I have one more task."

She flickered a strange glance at him and said nothing. After the music stopped, he delivered her back to her waiting aunt. "I will call on you tomorrow, Miss Winters, hoping that you will take a drive in the park with me."

She glanced at her aunt. "Are we free tomorrow afternoon?"

"Yes, my dear." Lady Prescott turned to Delmore and examined his expression.

He hoped she saw that he entertained no dubious intentions toward her niece. After bowing to her, he left the ball. Anna wouldn't allow him another waltz tonight, society's customs frowning on single ladies who let themselves to show a preference. Since he didn't plan to dance with anyone else, he saw no need to stay.

However, he had hopes of himself. Although he hadn't taken a drink that night, his denial of the urge in his moment of need had been more difficult than he imagined. A month ago, he had stopped considering even a whiff of a cork, having realized that a person could not drown his sorrows. A person could only try to make sure he exhausted all avenues before he gave up, and he meant to keep that in mind.

He would never give up. Tomorrow would be a nerve-wracking day and he needed to be entirely himself if he meant to have Anna.

Chapter Sixteen

nna made sure of her grooming for her last meeting with Delmore. A final inspection in the mirror showed not a single displaced curl in her hair. Her brown pelisse sat squarely across her shoulders.

The dearest aunt in the whole world had provided the perfect bonnet of dark brown taffeta, lined with pale green silk. Surrounding her face, the delicate color set off her hair and brightened the murky blue of her eyes, somehow adding elegance to her facial structure. The man would surely regret rejecting the most enthusiastic mistress he could have had.

Unfortunately, Delmore arrived with not a single touch of the disreputable rake about him, no irresponsible smile, and no errant curl needing to be pushed back from his forehead. His coat was perfection itself, black with lapels of bronze wool. He showed no sign of the inebriety of last night, not even a hint of puffiness around his thick lashed eyes.

She offered him a serene smile, hoping he would never

know how much she wanted him and how hard her final goodbye would be. This would be the last time they would see each other as people with wants and needs rather than distant neighbors. "Yet again we are lucky with the weather, my lord."

"The rain has most considerately held off, Miss Winters. Good afternoon, Lady Prescott. Have you recovered from the excess of gossip last night?"

"Barely. Fortunately, I have nerves of iron and took little notice of Lady Rawling's suspicion that Jonquil was misbehaving with Mr. Fieldhouse. Of course she wasn't. And dear Anna would always be the lady her mother taught her to be. No one would think of accusing her of dallying with Mr. Fieldhouse." Her smile aimed at Anna didn't waver.

Anna nodded circumspectly. "Mr. Fieldhouse is only willing to try his seduction techniques on younger women, Aunt. I suspect that anyone older than eighteen would see him as too obvious."

"I'm sure you are right, my dear. Now off you go." Aunt gave Delmore a roguish smile. "Mind you take good care of my favorite niece."

He smiled politely. "It will be my pleasure, Lady Prescott." He bowed to Aunt Lucy and, using his hat, he indicated that Anna should precede him through the doorway of the formal sitting room. He followed Anna through the hall and outside to his smart phaeton.

Wilson held the horses while Delmore handed her up and sat on the front seat beside her. He moved the team into a smart trot and skillfully negotiated his vehicle between wagons, market carts, and town carriages. Once into the avenue of trees near St. James Park, he pulled up his team. He swiveled to face behind. "Wilson, meet me at the front entrance, if you will."

The phaeton arose by a mere hair's depth when Wilson stepped off the back. "We are not to be chaperoned, my lord?" Anna asked with surprise as Wilson departed.

"I don't need Wilson's supervision while I propose to you." He paused and took a long breath, staring right into her eyes. "Anna Winters, will you take me for your husband?"

For a moment she couldn't speak. Of all the words she had expected from him, these had been the last. "Of course I won't." Her back stiffened. He had no right to make a game of her. "If you brought me here to discuss absurdities, you may take me back right now."

"Anna, my dear one. You have made a man of me using only the barest ingredients a drunk and a fool has to spare." He paused, watching her face, his expression tender. "Now I have expectations that I can be a better man, and with you by my side, I shall have all the incentive I need."

She stared back at him, her mind spinning, her hopes deadening, as they must. "If your plan is to be seen as reformed, I am the last woman who should be by your side. What would society say if you married the daughter of a traitor, a woman of whom your mother disapproves?"

"Ah, yet again we are back to the sins of the fathers. Your father died because of my father. He may as well have pushed your father out of that window for all the effect it had. Can we not be the children who forgive?"

She dragged in a deep breath, willing the prickling at the back of her throat not to result in ridiculous tears. "I can forgive, Delmore, but society can't forget. You will remember that I applied for the job of your mistress. If you want me, you should give me that role. I have not applied for any other."

He sat with his hands hanging loosely between his knees, gazing downward. "You want me to ruin you, but I want to be a better man than my father."

"Then you may as well drive me home." She held her breath, thinking he might protest and try again, but even if he did, her answer would be the same. His mother disapproved of her, society on the whole disapproved of her, and she would not join his current effort to earn society's approval. She would rather be a hermit than try to please people who judged her, not by her careful behavior, but by her father's immaturity.

He sat up straight, offered her a crooked smile, and picked up his reins. "I want you, Anna. If the only way I can have you is as my mistress, then, as you so advise, I will take you as my mistress instead."

She stared at him, her mind whirling, relief not her foremost emotion. Instead, panic shortened her breath. "I don't think I can start right now. Jonquil has to finish her season," she said in a weak voice.

"Of course she does, and we have contracts to sign first. We will be making a business deal. We both need to agree on the terms." When he reached the first turning circle, he eased one horse and the carriage nicely clipped back onto the original path again.

"I haven't read the book of rules for mistresses but I'm sure you know best." She stared straight ahead, struck by the reality that, if she needed to sign a contract, being a mistress possibly might not be quite as romantic as she had supposed. Perhaps she merely wanted to be his lover.

"My man of business will meet with you and have your terms recorded. I was about to sell off Packham Place but perhaps I should show you over the house first. It is conveniently situated near Delmore House. You may wish to live there rather than wait for me to find a more convenient set of rooms to lease for you."

She stared at the bushes on her side of the carriageway. "Do I have to make a decision right now?"

"Of course not, but I would like a decision on the house today. Let me take you there first before I return you to Lady Prescott."

Her chest hollowed and she noticed her hands were tightly clasping each other. The enormity of the hole she had dug for herself made her head hurt. "You want me to live in town?"

"Earls don't have country mistresses, my dear. The country house is for wives and children, for when earls want to relax and stroll around their acreages telling their tenants how to improve their yields."

"So, that's what earls do."

"Indeed. Earls travel to the city for their entertainments. Mistresses need to be available at all hours. I might like to drop in after a late night sitting of parliament with my more respectable friends, for I mean to be respectable now, or I may be interested in dallying during the day. While you are still a new acquisition, I am sure to be."

A new acquisition? She wouldn't be special; she wouldn't be his love; she would be a mere hireling. Her hands began to twist together. "This is beginning to sound rather too businesslike. It seemed so romantic while we were in Danbury."

"At the time I thought you might have been glossing over a few of the practicalities," he remarked in a dry voice.

"I certainly hadn't thought this through. What on earth will I say to my aunt? Or my mother? And don't mistresses need to take other names, like La Gloriosa, so that their families remain in ignorance of their doings?"

"My dear, it is unlikely that your family will remain in ignorance even should you rename yourself Mrs. Blank."

"Then what about Jonquil? Life might be rather awkward for her if she wishes to make an advantageous marriage."

"I don't think we should worry about Jonquil's prospects. She was quite prepared last night to throw your reputation into the wind."

"And you. You plan to be respectable, but do respectable earls take mistresses?"

"I had planned to take a wife but if my only choice is to have you as my mistress, I will take you as my mistress."

"You know very well why I can't marry you," she said in her crossest voice.

He drew a long breath and smiled sadly. "I had hoped my children would be legitimate, but these days it may not be so important as in the old days. After all, I have Jeremy to take the title when I'm dead and he may have legitimate children." His shoulders lifted with a weary shrug.

She frowned at his over-acting. He couldn't manage solemnity even in a matter of such importance. Surely, he didn't love her enough to be ostracized by the Prince of Wales and all his friends? Of course not. Squaring her shoulders, she said, "Oh, dear. That is such a sad thought."

"I'm pleased to know I have your sympathy. Wilson will be most disappointed in me. He thought I would never take another mistress." He pulled up the phaeton where Wilson stood leaning against the gates. "You didn't like my former mistresses, did you, Wilson?"

"No, my lord. Pack of grasping harpies, they was." Wilson swung himself up behind.

"A gentleman should never disappoint his groom. Wilson, Miss Winters says she will not marry me."

"She never," Wilson said in a scandalized voice. "We want her, me and Pickering. She makes you laugh, gov. You'll 'ave to change her mind."

"In the meantime, I'm taking her to see Packham Place." Delmore gave her a quick sideways glance.

Wilson grinned but remained silent as he settled back into his place.

Wary, she said, "You really ought to take me straight back home. My head is in a whirl."

"And I will. But first, indulge me, my dear one."

Having backed herself into a corner after refusing a proper marriage proposal, she had choice other than to do so. Totally appalled by the realities of being a mistress, she couldn't see the point of looking at likely premises in which to do her mistress-ing. Her mind began to turn over and over. She watched the road ahead, only half focusing on the traffic, which Delmore wove through. Finally, in one of the side streets, he stopped outside a tall narrow building constructed from gray stone. Only a small amount of paving fronted the house behind the spear-railed front fence and gate. While Wilson held the horses, Delmore walked her to the heavily paneled front door. Ignoring the lion's-head knocker, he used a large key found on the head jamb.

"When you see inside, you must understand that I hoped you would say yes to my marriage proposal," Delmore said to her as he pushed the door open. "I hoped to bring you here to celebrate."

She stepped into a hall tiled in black and white, holding a single table overpowered by an enormous vase filled with red roses. The heady scent reminded her of summer in Danbury. The romantic gesture touched her. "Where does a person find roses in winter?"

"I had them sent up to town from Hastings House."

She smiled as if men decorated houses with red roses for her every day of the week, while every beat of her heart reminded her that her greatest hopes must forever remain unfulfilled.

His expression bland, he indicated the way into a sparsely furnished sitting room where the walls had been papered with bright peacocks sitting among branches of stylized roses and butterflies. A lit fire warmed the air. Pulled up in front of an alabaster fireplace, a long red couch held cushions in colors that echoed those in the wallpaper, most a darker green. Two single, buttoned chairs in gold stood close by. A side table contained heavily cut crystal glasses, a wine bottle, and a set of Meissen plates painted with flowers and birds.

"I have begun moving out, as you can see. The house is no longer fully furnished but I wanted a place for us where we wouldn't be disturbed. First let me ring for a cup of hot chocolate. It would have been champagne had you accepted me, but I can't very well celebrate being refused."

"If you want champagne, you could celebrate being well rid of me." She drew a deep breath.

He smiled suddenly, and his usual devil-may-care expression appeared as he pulled the bell rope near the door. A young maid appeared. "Bring the refreshments, if you will."

She bobbed a curtsey. "Yes, milord."

Apparently, everything had been prepared beforehand. Far too impressed, Anna removed her bonnet and perched on the couch. Before she could summon up the fortitude to meet his gaze, an enormous silver tray arrived bearing dishes of fresh strawberries, tiny macaroons, éclairs, and tartlets. Delmore popped a champagne cork and filled one and a half glasses. He took the small one for himself and breathed in the aroma.

She gulped hers. He had hoped to have his proposal of marriage accepted. Despite his bluff, she doubted he would take her as his mistress instead. And, of course, she wouldn't accept the position now that she had faced reality. Being Calder's mistress would not only comprise making love with him. She would also distress her family, help to make Jonquil unmarriageable, and only see Calder when he chose. However, if she married him, could he bear having a wife who would not be received by members of the upper ten thousand, the ton? He might be trapped in the throes of passion now, but he would soon tire of society's scorn.

She swirled her champagne, glancing at the orange macaroons. "I must admit that I like the way you indulge a woman."

"I'm afraid I am still trying to get you to see sense. But that's for you to see, and for me to hope you do."

"By bribery?" She decided no matter how delicious; she couldn't eat a thing. Instead, took another gulp of her wine, savoring the warmth that flowed through her veins, completely understanding why he had delighted in drinking to excess.

"Not only that." He put his untasted drink on the side table, took up a long thin bundle, and got down on one knee in front of her. "Would you accept this as a token of my love?"

She should have said no because she shouldn't accept tokens of his love, but curiosity forced her to unwrap ... a purple umbrella. Not any purple umbrella but the one she had been wishing for when she had met him in the haberdashery shop in Danbury. Stupidly, she burst into tears. These past few days had been too much, and now this.

He stood, took her glass, placed her almost finished drink on the mantle, and urged her into his arms. "The color is putrid, but you seemed to want it. I'll buy you any color you desire, my love, only don't cry."

"I love the color. Who has a purple umbrella? No one. Everyone has black. Thank you, Calder, and thank you for offering your love. I don't want to be your mistress." She tried not to wet his coat with her tears, but a few escaped regardless.

"Then, will you be my wife instead?" he asked tenderly. "I would much prefer that."

She buried her face into the warmth of his chest. "If I married you, would you be able to bear people cutting you when they discover who I am?"

"I'm an earl, Anna. Who would cut me? The prince? Despite his former friendship with my father, I don't think he can afford to cut earls with impunity because they fall in love. He has fallen in love a number of times and none too wisely, himself."

She offered him a watery smile, her fingers threading through the hair on the back of his head. His body stood warm and steady against hers. "Your argument is specious and unconvincing, but I love you and the purple umbrella, oh, the purple umbrella ..." Her voice cracked and she turned her head so that he couldn't see her face.

"You love me and the purple umbrella," he repeated in a patient voice.

She leaned back and stared at the tender expression on his face. "The purple umbrella convinced me that you love me." The closure in her throat made her voice sound uneven. "You noticed how much I wanted it and you remembered."

"May I ask the purple umbrella to let me show how much I love you?" He settled his hands on her waist. His gaze held hers and he smiled as he lowered his mouth. One kiss, two kisses, and his lips stayed soft against hers.

She slowly relaxed. This was where she wished to be, safe in Delmore's arms. Calder's arms. In the arms of the man she had loved since he had caught her on his hook and kissed her.

She slid her arms around his neck. The full length of his body rested against hers and his rising began to press against her belly. "Calder," she said, her skin beginning to heat. "Surely not here?"

"Not if you don't wish it." His breath warmed her ear.

"What about the servants?"

"I only have the maid indoors and she would not come unless called."

"Wilson," she said weakly, being moved until the couch touched the back of her knees. "He is waiting outside."

"That's his job. My job is to show you how much I love you." He leaned down and scooped her up in his arms, only to settle her full length on the couch.

She wriggled a cushion from beneath the small of her back and tossed it behind her and held out her arms to him. He sat beside her, folding her into his embrace again. His kisses grew hot but never urgent, never frantic. Instead, hers did, and she dragged him down on top of her. After lots of wriggling on her part to get his part rubbing on hers, she lifted her knees on either side of his hips. He bore that for quite a while, with scattered kisses on her face and her neck, and long, deep kisses on her mouth.

He shifted his hands to beneath her behind and her skirts were scooped up, but the buttons of her pelisse pressed too hard on her sternum. His jacket seemed to confine him also. Almost abruptly, he sat up. "I want at least your pelisse off, if you don't mind," he said in a deep, breathy voice.

"Good idea. I want at least your shoes off." She laughed and sat up.

He removed his jacket and his shoes and helped her with her pelisse. She kicked off her shoes and resumed her former position on the couch. "I hope we are going to do this properly." A certain shyness affected the heat of her cheeks.

"It depends on what you mean by properly."

"I don't want you to only satisfy me. I want you sated too."

"We can do that two ways."

"I'm sure you know at least three ways."

He grinned. "I don't like to suggest the third way which involves your virginity."

"Please. Let's involve my virginity."

"I don't want to hurt you before we are married."

"Implying you don't mind hurting me after marriage."

"Not at all. Implying I don't want you to change your mind before I marry you."

"And you a rake," she said in a scandalized voice. "You should be seducing me, not trying to put me off for another day."

"Anna, Anna, Anna. I love you. Because I used to be a very careless man, this time I want to be careful. I don't want you changing your mind about our wedding."

"If I am not completely compromised, I might perhaps cry off." She tried to look guileless.

"Then you will be completely and thoroughly compromised, make no mistake." He leaned over her, and she lay back, her arms around his neck, taking the kiss he offered.

While he continued the kiss, he did the same as he had the last time, using his fingers to take her to the heights and forcing one long racking convulsion of pleasure from her. This time she undid his trouser flap and gave him pleasure too. But in the midst, he shifted her hand aside and used his rising instead of his fingers on her. She wanted him inside her. The blunt tip of him began to stretch her.

"You might bleed. Should I stop now?" he said in a deep whisper.

"In case I make a mess of the couch?"

"In case we make a mess of you. You are so tight, my love."

She wriggled onto him. Although his body tensed, he stared deep into her eyes before lowering his mouth to hers and beginning a careful entry. She accepted the pain, which he eased somewhat by withdrawing and re-entering several times. Then he was completely inside her, expanding her, and she didn't care about anything other than the thrilling stretch and rhythm of his hard, deep strokes. He finally finished, dealt with himself into his handkerchief, which was perhaps wise, for she thought she might burst with pleasure again, with all this wondrous lovemaking.

In the aftermath, he lay atop her, his lips against her throat. A languor such as she had never experienced before overcame her and she wanted to sleep. Perhaps she did for a moment, but he kissed her and began to mop at her with a table napkin.

"Did I bleed?"

"No, fortunately, but keep the napkin there in case you do." He sat her up and pressed a kiss on her forehead. "I love you, Anna. I never thought I would love anyone, and you came along and now my life has changed."

"I love you, too, Calder. I never thought I would love anyone, and you came along, and my life has changed."

He stared at her. "You love me?"

"Was that a question or a statement?"

"Both, I suppose. You haven't said you love me before, but I was quite sure you did."

"Your huge ego would surely tell you that."

He laughed, buttoned his falls, and stood. "Would you like another glass of champagne before I take you home?"

"Now the deed is done, you are in a hurry, my lord?" She stepped into her shoes.

"Not at all. But we have taken far longer than you led your aunt to expect. Although you look delightful, you also look like a woman who has been thoroughly loved. But she will excuse you when I tell her we plan to marry. And we have to know, because that was an inadequate bout of loving on my part."

Her mind raced as she watched him tidy himself. Never would she love him so little as to ruin his life when he had only recently taken the right track. She forced a smile as she donned her pelisse. "We can't make an announcement yet, Calder. This is Jonquil's season, not mine. It wouldn't be kind to take the attention from her."

"To hell with Jonquil."

She managed not to blink while she shook her head. "I am her companion. My first duty is to her." Her fingers trembling, she tucked her hair back into her bonnet, unable to meet the gaze of the most precious man in the world.

He reached out, took her upper arms gently, and kissed her on her forehead. "Then I shall have to help you find a husband for her."

Her breath ached through her chest. "Last night gave me the idea that she had plans for Jeremy." She picked up her reticule and turned toward the door.

"I doubt he is quite ready to take on an eighteen-year-old."

"I thought it would be rather splendid, but he does seem more interested in Miss Goodings."

"He is more interested in sewing his wild oats."

"You, at least, have done that."

"I have done with that, my dear one. Now I have only you." He opened the door for her, and she walked past him to the waiting phaeton.

The butler opened the door to Lady Prescott's house. Delmore waited for Anna to walk inside. The butler took Delmore's hat. In the morning parlor, he bowed to Lady Prescott whose smile seemed forced.

"Out in the air for so long, Lord Delmore! You must be desirous of a quick nip of sherry and a slice of cake."

"Indeed, Lady Prescott. But perhaps I should apologize for keeping Anna so long. I needed her advice on a house I plan to sell."

Lady Prescott stared at him. "Anna's advice?"

"She is a lady of excellent taste, as I'm sure you have found. She advised me to sell the place, for now I won't need it." He squared his shoulders, glancing at Anna.

"No doubt that is a wise decision, Delmore. Now, Anna, here we have a roomful of suitors awaiting you. You turned a few heads last night. I knew that red would be right for you." Lady Prescott took Anna's arm, clearly trying to usher her away from Delmore.

Anna smiled. "Ah, but Jonquil wore red too. She has the suitors, not I." She very wisely didn't look at Delmore who was still unsure of her game.

He didn't want to believe that she had tricked him into making love to her by promising to marry him, though she had certainly had her way with him without marriage. No reformed rake could live with that. "You must accept that men admire you, Anna." He tried an indulgent tone. If any admired her too much, he would grab them by their collars and the seats of their breeches and hasten their journey out of the room.

Except that the suitors numbered four, his brother Jeremy, not a starter in the race, John Temple, Rodney Toddington, and young Lord Aires, all pups and too well mannered to be competition. Jonquil sat with a face of thunder. She could barely smile when she saw Anna. In a group, the gentlemen rose to their feet, all greeting her at once, but Anna sat beside her sister.

Delmore moved toward Jeremy and engaged him in conversation until he could leave without causing offence. He had a long trip to take this afternoon and wanted to be back early in the morning.

Chapter Seventeen

Delmore arrived in Danbury late in the afternoon. Shrouded in eerie darkness, he rapped on the door of the vicarage. Morag, the elderly maid answered through a small opening. "You," she said, tersely. Her candle flame wavered, highlighting her witchlike features.

"I have come to call on Mrs. Beeby, the lady of the house." He doffed his hat.

She stared at him, her white-rimmed eyes blinking rapidly. "If anything has happened to Miss Anna ..."

"You have no cause to worry."

She widened the opening, and he stepped into the lamp-lit hallway. When Anna married him, he would make sure she would never have to bear another dark winter in a cold house. He walked into the sitting room where Mrs. Beeby sat sewing in front of a meager fire, a single lamp burning and a lap blanket covering her knees. She glanced up when the door opened, an anxious expression on her elegant face. "My lord. You came from London?"

"Indeed. In quite a rush, I am afraid. I haven't yet been to Hastings House to change. Please excuse my travel dirt."

"Has something happened to my girls?" She clutched at the woolen shawl covering her upper body, her expression apprehensive.

"Safe, and as far as I can tell, happy. I must inform you that I have asked your lovely daughter, Anna, to be my wife."

Her eyes widened and her jaw loosened. She swallowed before she spoke. "And you are now worried about the reception you will have from your family. Your mother will be most unhappy to be allied with the Winters' name." She stretched her mouth in a travesty of a rueful smile.

"My family very much approves, but Anna has the idea that she will ruin me if she marries me. I need your help to convince her otherwise." He smiled at her. "May I explain my plan?"

She looked defensive. "Perhaps Mr. Beeby should be present."

"First, tell me you would be happy to accept me as a son-in-law."

Her mouth curled up on one side. "Does Anna love you?"

"She said she does."

"If Anna loves you, I must love you too." She rang the handbell at her side and Morag entered so fast that she must have been listening outside the door.

"Yes, ma'am." The maid used her eyebrows to silently query Mrs. Beeby.

"Could you fetch Mr. Beeby, Morag? Anna has received a proposal of marriage from Lord Delmore."

"Not before time," Morag said in a belligerent voice, straightening and facing Delmore. "Mooning away, she was, for a month or more." Chin up, wrinkled face stern, she marched off.

"I had no idea, my lord." Wetting her lips, Mrs. Beeby anxiously watched the door.

Her husband arrived within a minute, standing in the doorway with a fatuous smile while he caught his breath. "I'm to be your father-in-law, I hear, Delmore. How fortuitous." He shook Delmore's hand until Delmore's shoulder ached. "I shall officiate at the ceremony, of course."

Delmore nodded politely. "If Anna wishes you to do so. However, I am here to set Mrs. Beeby's mind at rest about the bad blood between our families. I have a plan for reconciliation." He lifted his coat and sat on the edge of a sagging chair, prepared to discuss what must be done.

In the morning as the sun rose, he drove back to the vicarage and collected Mrs. Beeby and her trunk. On the way to London, she clung to the seat, possibly as nervous about his high sprung phaeton as she was about her reception at Delmore House.

However, his mother, prepared for her visitor, greeted her with two hands and a kiss on either cheek. Mrs. Beeby was given the best bedroom and left to freshen up. The two women would settle their differences over a cup of tea while Delmore went to Jackson's salon to find Jeremy.

Making love to Anna night after night would not be possible without marriage and he wanted Anna in his bed every night, beginning as soon as possible.

~

Anna sat in the morning parlor with a still slightly chastened Jonquil, a fidgety Lady Prescott, John, Rodney, Miss Goodings and her mother, and Jeremy. Sir Arthur had gone to his club to read the newspapers in peace.

She heard the various conversations without listening. As if by rote, she passed cups of tea and refilled the sugar bowl. Whenever carriage wheels sounded close, she casually wandered over to the window and flicked the lace open, in case Calder should be outside. Not seeing him for twenty-four hours seemed like a month to her. And when he discovered she had no marriage plans, she would probably never see him again. She wished that day would never dawn.

Her father's parents had slowly died after the shame loaded on them by her father. She herself had learned to ignore the sly glances and nudges when her name was recognized. Better to be oblivious than embarrassed. Calder would not be subjected to the same because of her.

At exactly two o'clock, the best time for morning calls to end, the Goodings ladies left. Jeremy rose to his feet, buttoning his coat and indicating that John and Rodney should go too.

"Your fault we must leave, Temple," Rodney said to his friend, rising to his feet. "You were not wise to remind Anna that your horse used to try to take a nip out of her. To be diplomatic, you should have mentioned instead that your horse loved the taste of her when she was fourteen." He nodded portentously. "Courting is a m-matter of learning how to twist your words."

Despite her aching heart, Anna smiled. "Women are not smart enough to notice, do you think, Rodney?"

"Women are exceedingly clever. They never try to catch out a chap. They let us think we have them confused."

"With that attitude, you are likely to be married within a twelvemonth." Anna stared at gorgeous Rodney. No wonder Jonquil had the sulks. He had ignored her and made a fuss of Anna yet again.

"I doubt women want to be lied to, Toddie," John said, assuming a saintly demeanor as he buttoned his jacket. "But we shouldn't let them think that because they turn into beauties at a certain age that they may behave as badly as they wish."

"You are talking about me now." Jonquil's mouth tightened. "I have never been a saint like Anna, and you shouldn't expect me to change simply because I am now in London."

"She's right, you know," John said to Rodney. "We ought to be expecting her to be tattling about everyone to everyone else, the way she used to."

"I am not a tattletale." Jonquil folded her arms across her chest. "I didn't say a word about Anna being unchaperoned with Lord Delmore for over two hours yesterday."

Frowning, John glanced at his two friends. "And no one said a word about you changing cloaks with Anna at the ball so that it would appear she had been outside with Robert Fieldhouse and not you."

Jonquil made a sound of outrage. "And what if I did? Anna—"

"No more." Lady Prescott rose to her feet. "You had a lucky escape because of Anna, and that is the end of the matter."

Anna stared at everyone. "I seemed to have missed the

moment when everyone decided that Jonquil and I changed cloaks for nefarious reasons. Have you all been discussing this without me?"

"The subject came up yesterday when Temple mentioned Jonquil, dressed in blue, left the ball with Fieldhouse, who disappeared."

"Then I saw Anna in her red cloak come inside with Delmore." Rodney shrugged. "Except, perhaps it was Jonquil."

"But if it was Anna, she was outside with Lord Delmore. Isn't that just as compromising as me being with Mr. Fieldhouse?" Jonquil crossed her arms. "Or was I with Lord Delmore and she with Mr. Fieldhouse?"

"You hit the nail on the head," Jeremy said bitterly. "But if you mess with Delmore's arrangements you will have me to deal with." He gave Jonquil one last dark stare and then he ushered his friends through the doorway.

Anna stood staring after them, her heartbeat frantic. She had no intention of marrying Delmore, despite the fact that she loved him. But she had believed he loved her. Instead, he had proposed marriage mistakenly assuming that he had compromised her. He hadn't. The confusion with the cloaks had already been tittered about last night and accepted as nothing more than a harmless game so easily played at masked balls. Aching with disappointment, she perched on the most uncomfortable chair in the room when the door opened again.

Not only did Calder arrive during the very worst moment in her life, but he also brought her mother. Shocked silent, Anna rose to her feet, glancing between the two.

"My darling daughter. How I have missed you." Her mother wrapped Anna into a warm hug.

"I have missed you, too, Mama." She averted her gaze from Calder. "Is something wrong at home?"

Her mother leaned back, smiling. "Not a thing. Mr. Beeby sends his regards to both his daughters and hopes you have been behaving yourselves."

Lady Prescott moved across to kiss her sister. "Your girls are quite wonderful. I have so enjoyed having them here to stay. I hope you haven't come to take them back."

"Not at all. But I'll leave Lord Delmore to speak. He brought me here to stay with his mother."

"No, not Lady Delmore, mama," Anna said, aghast. "Surely not?"

"I thought it best, Anna." Calder offered her a winsome smile. "By the way Lady Prescott, yesterday I asked Anna to marry me."

Lady Prescott almost fell back into her chair, and she slapped her hand over her heart as if doing the beating herself. "Not a thing did she say to me. Not a thing. Anna, you wicked girl. You had me terrified, waiting for someone to mention your re-entry at the ball with Lord Delmore, when it wasn't you at all."

"I did think Anna was being optimistic imagining that she would not be discussed, even though it wasn't her." Calder's mouth lifted on one side.

"Since it wasn't me, I didn't mind." Anna blinked at him.

"You are all speaking in riddles. If it wasn't you, who was it?" her mother asked. "Or if it wasn't you, does it matter who it was?"

Aunt said, "Of course it doesn't matter," while Jonquil said, "No," and Calder said, "We should be speaking of more important subjects."

Mama stared at Anna. "Does it matter?"

"No. Lord Delmore had no need to propose."

Mama sat on the couch beside her sister. "Lord Delmore thought I should stay with Lady Delmore if we are to have a wedding between him and Anna. If we can show society that we have forgiven each other, the rest of the world will need to accept that. It was so long ago and, well, we each want our children to be happy in marriage."

Lady Prescott crossed her arms and jutted out her jaw. "You did nothing other than marry Richard Winters. She has nothing to forgive you, Elizabeth."

"As I have nothing to forgive her. Our husbands caused the rift and now their widows need to end it. In the meantime, despite the fact that I had no time to pack, I'm staying with her for a week. Lord Delmore wanted me here today."

Anna and Jonquil both stared at Lady Prescott, who rose beautifully to the occasion. "If you had no time to pack, you must raid my wardrobe, Elizabeth."

"I hoped you would say that." Elizabeth Beeby clutched her sister's hand and gave her a swift kiss on the cheek. "You are the most wonderful sister a woman could have."

"And the most wonderful aunt." Anna glanced at Calder, who appeared to have aimed a doting expression toward her.

"Raiding we should go," Aunt said, taking mama by the hand. "Finding appropriate clothing for you would be our priority, bearing in mind the functions you will need to attend while you are here. Oh, and Delmore." She glanced at the noblest man in the room. "I must kiss you for being so wonderful. I knew you had it in you to take responsibility for your actions." Two steps and she had presented Calder with a kiss on each cheek.

The two ladies left arm in arm, leaving Calder with Jonquil and Anna. Anna could scarcely look at him. For so short a time she had basked in the thought that he loved her as she loved him. Now, she and the rest of her family knew he was merely doing his duty by asking her to marry him.

She hardened her face, hoping her heart would copy the notion. "How far should we go with this, my lord?" she said in a voice that sounded dull and stupid. "Do we let my mother meet society knowing she is now welcome because you have kindly offered for my hand? Do we break our engagement as soon as she leaves, or do we keep up the pretence until the end of the season? And who calls the wedding off? You or I?"

He frowned at her and then aimed an even more ferocious frown at Jonquil. "What on earth have I missed?"

Jonquil squared her shoulders. "I said you compromised whoever wore the red cloak at the ball."

He blinked. "Does your silliness never end? Even had I compromised you, I wouldn't marry you."

"Anna thinks you would. She thinks you are good and kind and clever, and she loves you. You think she is wonderful, and you love her. I think I should leave the room." With that, Jonquil marched out.

"Anna." He softened his voice. "I think you are wonderful, and I love you." He held out one hand to her.

"You learn your lines well, my lord."

"I am not good and kind, and I'm clearly not clever. I

have let you think I am not madly in love with you. How could that be? You are my life, Anna. You are every beat of my heart. You are my inspiration. Not an hour goes by when I don't think of you. Yesterday I could barely let you go but I had to do the right thing and not run off with you straight away because you are very precious to me, and I must live up to you. Please honor our betrothal and please don't call the wedding off."

"Very pretty words, my lord."

"Very true words, my only love." He stepped into her and rested his hands on her waist, staring deep into her eyes. "I bless the day I went fishing and caught you on my line." His breath whispered across her face as he said the last words.

Her vision misted. He put a finger under her chin and lifted her face, leaning down to touch his lips on hers. "My only love," he said again. "If I didn't love you, I wouldn't have sat for two hours with Beeby trying to convince him to stay in Danbury while I brought your mother to you."

"Calder," she said with reverence, her gaze meeting his. "Two hours." She circled her arms around him, hugging him, loving him. His heart thundered against her, and he tightened his hold, resting his cheek against her forehead. She lifted her face, and her lips met his, once, twice. Leaning back, she absorbed his hopeful expression, and the very dear hint of mischief in his eyes. "Nothing you have done could have done more to convince me. Such a sacrifice and with the knowledge that you will have to do so many more times."

"Not two hours again, Anna. One hour at the most."

He kissed her until she wanted to be naked with him

and while she tried to discuss how this could be managed, he laughed. "Nothing else for it, my darling. We shall have to elope."

"Not until mama has had her week in London." She kissed him again. "Did I tell you I love you?"

"Not yet."

"I love every small thing about you and at least one large thing."

He snuggled her close and held her for a very long time.

Two weeks later, Delmore obtained a special license and married Anna in his town house.

Both mothers were present, a sister, a brother, two aunts and uncles, and with Mr. Beeby officiating.

Delmore's mother was proud of him, possibly for the first time in more than ten years, for choosing not only the woman he loved, but for finding the woman who should be the best reason to end the long running guilt and resentment of his father's treatment of another man's foolishness.

He couldn't have done better for himself, and he blessed the day he went fishing and caught Anna Winters. If he could have afforded to take her to Italy for a month instead, he would have, but Hastings House and the tenants needed him to continue to make the changes needed.

"Is it normal for a new bride to be more interested in the garden than the bedroom?" he asked as she began braiding her hair before she slid into his bed. He liked her hair loose because of some sort of visual he had in his mind, that of being twisted into the coils and never being free of the adorable woman he had married. He mentioned this.

"Don't be fanciful, Calder. I would never have to tie you. I've never known a man so willing to be seduced."

And again, he let his love seduce him.

~

Read Forever Amused

Book 2 in The Spring of Love series

Desperate to enter society before someone else snatches up the rake she loves, messy Daisy Gerard doesn't plan on being left with the elegant mother of her country neighbour, the reclusive Lord Ashford. She hadn't planned on falling in love with the annoying Ash either, but who could help adoring a man who understands . . . every unwanted word she says.

Being the guardian of a pair of two orphaned little girls, Ash has enough on his plate without having the precocious Daisy interfering in his life. However, she seems to know how to share the absurdities in life, and problem-solving seemed to be her forte – for everyone except herself.

More from Serenade Publishing

**Brigadier Station Series
By Sarah Williams:**

The Brothers of Brigadier Station

The Sky over Brigadier Station

The Legacies of Brigadier Station

Christmas at Brigadier Station (An Outback Christmas Novella)

The Outback Governess (A Sweet Outback Novella)

**Heart of the Hinterland Series
By Sarah Williams:**

The Dairy Farmer's Daughter

Their Perfect Blend

Beyond the Barre

A New Page

by Aimee MacRae

It Happened in Paris

By Michelle Beesley

Middle Women

By Jack Garrety

Mim and Wiggy's Grand Adventure

By Jay McKenzie

A Dying Second Sun

by Peter A. Dowse

Winner Winner Chicken Dinner

by Sarah Jackson

Resurrection

M H Austin

For more information visit:

www.serenadepublishing.com

About the Author

After training at the South Australian School of Art, Virginia accepted a job at an advertising agency. With a more interesting working life in mind, she retrained as a nurse, and then a midwife. By then, she met the man of her dreams, married, had two children, worked part time, and began writing romance.